# THE ANTONOV PROJECT

# The Antonov Project

ANTONY TREW

ST. MARTIN'S PRESS
NEW YORK

**Library of Congress Cataloging in Publication Data**

Trew, Antony, 1906-
    The Antonov project.

    I.   Title.
PZ4.T817An  1979     [PR9369.3.T7]     823      79-3113
ISBN 0-312-04518-2

All of the characters and incidents in
this book are fictitious, and any
resemblance to actual persons, living
or dead, is purely coincidental.

*Excerpts from a report in The Times, 10 June 1978,
of a debate in the House of Commons on the Soviet
threat to Western shipping.*

Most Soviet merchant ships were equipped
with advanced naval equipment and with
interchangeable crews. The Soviets had
devoted vast resources to the creation of a
large ocean-going fleet with considerable
military potential.

*Mr David Hunt, for the Opposition (The Wirral, C)*

The long term strategic value of all these
developments to the Soviet Union could not
be dismissed – the auxiliary support for the
Soviet Navy on a global scale and the wider
support of Soviet political ambitions.

*Mr Clinton Davis, Under-Secretary for Trade
(Hackney Central, Lab)*

# 1

Patches of mist left by the evening thunderstorm swirled about Trafalgar Square, dismembering the National Gallery, which glistened ghostlike above the lines of moving traffic. To the South, Nelson's column poked into the darkening sky, the bronze lions at its base, still wet from the storm, strangely animated by changing patterns of reflected light.

The hurrying raincoated figure looked up as he passed the column, but mist and a jutting plinth hid the statue. The bronze plaques at the base depicting the moments of death and victory at Trafalgar evoked in him that emotional response common to men of the sea. He thought of Rowse's '. . . *such genius, such courage, so transcendent a fate.*' That triggered other thoughts: his final year at Annapolis; the passing out parade and the ball afterwards; Rosie's tears; the fight with Vachell. Why did he have to think of that? So long ago, such a faded memory.

He reached the kerb and stopped, his thoughts swept away by the problem of crossing, the subdued roar of traffic, the squelch of countless tyres, the never-ending stream of lights. A break came and he made for Admiralty Arch. Under its shelter he waited again, a long wait this time; but he crossed at last and made for the old Admiralty building which housed the naval component of the Ministry of Defence. He ran up the steps, checked through security and hurried along to the conference room. As he reached the door and rang the bell the chimes of Big Ben sounded in the distance. Seven o'clock. He was late.

It was a high-ceilinged room, large and gloomy, the leather-topped table a good deal too big for the scatter of men around it. At the head sat a small man with a worried, frowning face; Oliver Rathouse, Commodore (Intelligence). To his left was Martin Briggs, a lieutenant-commander, his assistant; on his right Freddie Lewis, a group captain of RAF Intelligence. Next to him Paul Kitson, a naval captain, representing the C-in-C Fleet, Northwood; beyond him a pale balding man with a bulbous forehead, Gordon Slingsby, an Admiralty research scientist, was carrying on a subdued conversation with a small ferret-like man whose eyes blinked nervously through gold-rimmed spectacles – Reginald Ayott was his name and he too was an Admiralty research scientist. Opposite the Commodore, at the far end of the table, a dark-jowled, large-bellied man overflowed a chair a good deal too small for him. He leant back, smoking a pipe, the waistcoat of his suit wrinkled, straining at the buttons. On his right a cadaverous man with dark pouches under his eyes stared gloomily at the ceiling; starchily dressed, dark suit, old Etonian tie, Fothergill's imprint was distinctly Foreign Office; in fact he represented the Secret Intelligence Service. He gave no indication of having heard when the door opened and the raincoated man came in and made his apologies – hadn't been able to find a taxi, the thunderstorm he supposed.

'I daresay,' the Commodore looked mildly disbelieving. The latecomer hung his coat on the antlered stand, glanced briefly at the gilt framed portrait over the fireplace: Drake, Raleigh, Effingham, Frobisher . . . ? The Brits had so many, who could say? There was a faint background noise in the conference room. He identified it as the pulsing of an electronic baffler. Good, he thought. They counter-bug too. He sat down next to a lean man with crew-cut hair and a fawn suit. 'Hi, Jack,' he whispered. 'Long time, huh?'

'Five years I guess.'

Jack looks a hell of a lot older, he thought. Expect he's thinking the same of me. Jack Rossiter had been a year ahead of him at Annapolis. Later they'd served together as lieutenants in a carrier.

He whispered again. 'Party started yet?'

'Nope. Just chat.'

'The late arrival,' the Commodore addressed the fat man, 'is Commander David O'Dowd. Like Rossiter he's in USN Intelligence.'

The fat man nodded acknowledgement, smiled briefly with his teeth. 'You from Grosvenor Square?'

'No, sir. Pentagon. Flew in this afternoon.'

'Thank you.' It was said with about as much warmth as a commuter accepting a cup of British Rail tea. He looked at the Commodore, bared tobacco-stained teeth once more. 'Perhaps we might *now* begin.'

The Commodore didn't much like that. He wasn't the sort of man who took kindly to prompting, but Maltby of the Cabinet Office was a rather special person; *éminence grise* of the Intelligence Co-ordinating Committee in Whitehall, his presence at the meeting was an indication of its importance.

So the Commodore did no more than frown at the sheet of paper in front of him and turn to Briggs. 'Let me have the *Antonov* file.'

The Commodore opened the file and leafed through it, while the group captain leant across the empty chair which separated him from the Americans to ask O'Dowd about an old USN friend. Predictably O'Dowd had never heard of him. Maltby, breathing heavily between pipe-puffs, sank further into his seat.

The Commodore found what he wanted, the report prepared by Briggs, glanced at the first page, then at the ceiling, and those who knew him braced themselves for the staccato bursts with which he would convey the essential information. Briggs's report was a lengthy, conscientiously compiled document; he had done the Greenwich staff course but he was, as the Commodore often reminded him, long-winded. Leave something to the imagination, my dear boy. Don't fog the issue with all that bloody detail. It was Briggs, the Commodore once remarked, who Ludendorf must have had in mind when he declared that the stupid but industrious staff officer was the greatest threat to the German army.

Rathouse looked up, frowning under bushy eyebrows. 'I believe you know the background . . .'

'Don't really think I do,' said Maltby. 'At least I need reminding. Lot of hay on my fork. Nobody gave me any of this on paper.'

'The security classification did not permit that.' The Commodore smiled coldly. 'Now then, let me see.' He did a sharp rat-a-tat with his fingers. 'Six *Simeonovs* in service, eighteen building. Completing and commissioning at the rate of two a month. The twenty-four ships planned should be operational within a year.'

'Where are they being built?' Maltby puffed away, eyes half closed.

'In various yards with commercial shipbuilding capacity . . . Baltic, Black Sea, North Russia. Well spread: for example the Nikolayev and Oktyabrskoye yards in the Black Sea, the Vyborg and Kaliningrad yards in the Baltic. The ships are of uniform design. Small for modern bulk carriers. Twenty thousand gross, thirty-two thousand deadweight. Suitable for ore, coal, grain and other dry cargoes.'

Maltby stirred. 'Photos?'

The Commodore performed a two finger exercise on the table. 'I was coming to that.' He glared at the inoffensive Briggs. 'Let us have them.'

Freddie Lewis exchanged covert smiles with Kitson.

The lieutenant-commander produced a briefcase from the floor, took out the photos, handed them round.

'All are of the *Sokolov* or *Antonov*,' explained the Commodore. 'Taken in the Channel this summer and autumn. Not much to learn from them other than the aerial configuration. Some taken by Skyfotos, others by our people.'

'That is to say *ours*,' said Freddie Lewis getting in his plug for the RAF.

The Commodore ignored him. 'Seven holds, steel hatches electrically operated. The foremost hold – number one – rather smaller than the others. Nothing unusual about that. Normal bulk carrier design. Two self-tracking cranes for on board cargo handling.'

'That normal?' Freddie Lewis squinted at a geodetic pattern he'd sketched on the notepad in front of him.

'Yes. Typical of many built nowadays.' The Commodore turned a page. 'Now if I may get on with the *Simeonovs'* specification : twin screw, single deck, diesel engined motor ships. Machinery and accommodation aft. Speed, seventeen knots : endurance, fifteen thousand miles nominal. Could be considerably extended by using ballast tanks for fuel. Nothing unusual.'

Maltby took out his pipe, pouted full red lips under a bushy moustache. 'Let's get to the nub of this. What is unusual?'

'You asked for the background; I'd have preferred to skip it.'

The fat man was contrite. 'Sorry, Ratters. Good point. But I've got the pace now. Let's get on to the inside track.'

Rathouse found Maltby's rare moments of humility confusing : they came so unexpectedly, were so out of character, but they usually succeeded in lowering the temperature. He forgot his irritation.

'Quite a lot we don't like,' he said. 'First – on completion all six so far built were taken to the Zhdanov Naval Yard in Leningrad by naval steaming parties. Why? In some cases it meant journeys from the Black Sea . . . thousands of miles. For what purpose? In each case time in the Zhdanov Yard seems to have been about three months. What were they up to there? All in all we don't like that much. Then there are the rigorous on board security precautions which I'll come to later, and the question of number one hold. I'd like now, however, to get on to something else. The antennae configuration. It's out of character, even for Soviet merchant ships. Suggests they have some purpose over and beyond their principal employment of carrying cargo. I'll ask Slingsby to enlarge on this.' The Commodore nodded to the pale man who squinted at him through pebble-lens glasses. 'Keep it brief, Slingsby. We're not boffins. And have pity on the uninitiated.' He shot meaningful glances at Maltby and Fothergill.

Slingsby ran his tongue over his lips, directed a credential-checking stare at the faces round the table. 'Where they are known,' he began, 'I will use the NATO designations. First – communications. These ships are fitted with VEE CONE antennae for long distance radio transmitting and receiving: standard equipment in a number of Soviet warships, scientific ships and auxiliaries. For navigation radar they have DON 2. Again standard equipment in many Soviet warships and naval auxiliaries. Another *Simeonov* antenna we have identified from photographs is SIDE GLOBE. It's for ECM radar.' He winced at the Commodore's frown before hastily turning to Maltby and Fothergill. 'Electronic counter measures. Basically used for jamming enemy radar signals. Nowadays, however, there are highly sophisticated applications. Microwave valves, backward-wave oscillators and voltage-tuned magnetrons make possible . . .'

Rathouse held up a commanding hand. 'For Heaven's sake, Slingsby. This is not an electronics course. Keep it simple.'

Slingsby frowned uncertainly. 'Sorry. I thought I had.' He paused as if to recall where he'd erred. 'Now let me see. What's left? Ah, yes. The IFF antennae. Those in the *Simeonovs* are known to NATO as HIGH POLE. We believe . . .'

'What *is* IFF?' growled Maltby.

'Identification Friend or Foe.' With a slight shake of his head Slingsby managed to convey disbelief at such ignorance.

The Commodore shuffled his papers. 'Any more, Slingsby?'

'No. I think that completes the antennae picture.'

'Thank you. Any questions?' The Commodore's frowning stare swept the table.

'Yes,' said Maltby. 'Tell me, Slingsby, how reliable is this stuff?'

'This stuff, as you choose to call it,' interrupted Rathouse, 'is highly reliable. The antennae data Slingsby's just given comes from Admiralty research establishments. Much of the rest is from CLEMATIS in Leningrad. You may recall his reports on the *Zhukov*. That Marshall class ballistic missile submarine which went aground on Vrakoy. You were sceptical at the time, if I remember rightly.'

Briggs looked pleased with the ace his boss had served into the big man's court but Maltby, busy refilling his pipe, appeared not to have noticed it. 'May I ask,' he said, fixing a critical eye on Slingsby, 'what conclusions you people have drawn from the antennae picture?'

'Quite simply that the *Simeonovs* are intended for use as naval auxiliaries should the need arise.'

The Commodore looked at Ayott, the weapons man. 'Is there in your opinion any possibility that these ships could be firing platforms for missiles of some sort?'

'Most unlikely I would say. There would have to be aerials for m-missile command or guidance systems, fire control and radar tracking. Slingsby will confirm that they don't have such aerials.'

'What then is your view as a weapons expert?'

'M-Much the same as Slingsby's. They probably have a role as naval auxiliaries.'

'Nothing extraordinary about that I take it,' said Maltby. Ignoring the fat man's remark the Commodore addressed the scientists. 'Thank you, gentlemen. That was very helpful. I don't think we need detain you any longer.' Slingsby and Ayott took the hint, gathered their papers and left the conference room.

# 2

The Commodore, a stickler for protocol, questions through the chair, avoidance of interruptions, a curse on all irrelevancies, addressed Maltby with studied coolness. 'Now that the boffins have gone – and *if* you've finished – perhaps I might continue.'

'But of course, my dear chap. Forgive my keenness. Never meant to outpace you.' Briggs appeared to enjoy that. Maltby, unbelievably, had got an athletics Blue at Cambridge. The semantics of the track had coloured his language in much the same way that too much beer had distended his stomach.

'Our people abroad,' said the Commodore, 'report that ships of the *Simeonov* class have never been seen to work number one hold. Two – their crews never go ashore. Three – gangway and on board security is of an unusually high order. Access to the ships is limited to agents, stevedores, port officials, and others who have legitimate and important business on board. And even then few are permitted on the main deck forward of the accommodation tower. Four – despite charter enquiries we've had put out, here and abroad, the answer's always the same : *regret these ships are not yet available for charter.* We believe *yet* means *never.* And this I can assure you, is most unusual.[1]

'Surely our people, *and* yours,' Maltby jabbed his pipe in the general direction of the Americans, 'could've got on board by now. I mean . . . six *Simeonovs* flitting around the world for months.'

'Four,' corrected the Commodore. 'The last two have just gone into service.'

'All the same, Ratters, I'd have thought we'd have got something on them by now.' Maltby's chair creaked as he re-arranged close on twenty stone.

'We have. In Rio and Luanda recently our people made discreet enquiries about number one hold in chats with ships' officers and shipping agents. The general drift of the replies was the same. It is reserved for refrigerated goods, but it's never available if requested. Always full. Loaded at a previous port of call.'

Kitson, a grave man with a mournful face and jutting ears, made one of his rare contributions. 'Could that not be the fact, sir?'

'Improbable. Why has number one hold never been seen to be used, the hatch never to have been lifted? Our people and yours,' the Commodore flicked a hand towards the Americans, 'have had these ships under observation in more than twenty ports around the world. The foremost hatch has never been lifted. Add to that the Zhdanov Yard business, the other points we've discussed and . . .' he hesitated, looked across the table at Rossiter, 'recent and most important information on which I'll ask Rossiter to report since its origin is USN. I think you'll then understand why we're worried.'

Rossiter looked up, ran a hand over his chin. 'First, I'd like to say there has for some months now been very close collaboration on this between RN and USN Naval Intelligence. Until recently we had no more information than you've heard about tonight. A few days ago, however, something came in from . . .' he hesitated as if unsure how far he should go, 'that is from our CIA station in Leningrad. Nothing definite. Classified as rumour, no more. But the Pentagon felt it required immediate action and well – ah, I guess that's why we're here.' He smiled apologetically. 'An agent, a Russian working in the Zhdanov Yard, picked up a hint from another artisan in the

Yard who'd heard it from a fitter who'd worked on a *Simeonov* ship – a hint that they had a nuclear capability.'

'Of what sort?' Maltby asked.

'The agent said his informant knew no more that that – that they had a nuclear capability.'

'If you've finished perhaps Rossiter might continue,' suggested the Commodore icily.

Maltby nodded. 'Of course.'

'Until then,' said Rossiter, 'we'd taken the view that the *Simeonovs* were earmarked for auxiliary duties in the event of war – units of a fleet train to act as store and ammunition carriers, to provide logistic support for squadrons operating far afield. In the Indian, Southern and Pacific Oceans for example. This could call for special fittings and equipment. Maybe number one hold was a sophisticated workshop for maintenance of fleet electronics, high technology weaponry – that area.'

'Your people must surely have *some* ideas about the sort of nuclear capability? Ideas,' repeated Maltby, 'if nothing more.'

'We certainly have,' continued Rossiter. 'Most likely, we reckon, they could have a missile replenishment function. Number one hold might be equipped to carry missiles for transfer to submarines or surface vessels at sea. The dimensions of that hold, the lifting capacity of the self-tracking cranes, make this a feasible proposition.'

'The Soviet Navy already has missile cargo ships,' pointed out Kitson. 'Six ships of the *Lama* class.'

Rossiter overrode the point. 'Sure. That's right. But they are naval ships with the sole function of carrying nuclear missiles for transfer to strategic submarines at sea. We figure that when the building programme is completed, twenty-four ships of the *Simeonov* class – most of them at sea around the world – able to act as missile replenishers, could give the Soviet Navy a substantial strategic advantage.'

'Until they've been sunk,' Freddie Lewis grinned.

'Could be too late then.' Rossiter was not amused. 'Other possibilities we envisaged were that the *Simeonovs* might them-

18

selves have a launching capability for surface-to-surface missiles. We had in mind improved versions of the Soviet Navy's SHADDOCK missile. Something with a range of about five hundred miles – capable of carrying nuclear or conventional warheads.'

Maltby said, 'What about the absence of the essential aerials?'

'Our scientists figure that masts and aerials for the command and guidance system could be concealed. Maybe in the funnel casing or some place else high in the superstructure. Kept housed and out of sight but capable of extension when needed.'

'Any other alternatives?'

'Not really. Those seem to be the most likely.'

The Commodore frowned deeply. 'It is always wise to assume the worst. The *Simeonovs* may be able to launch missiles with nuclear warheads. I need hardly stress the strategic implications of a dozen or so *Simeonovs* at sea or in Western harbours on or shortly before the commencement of hostilities.'

Maltby leant back in his chair, patted his stomach. 'What would you do with a *Simeonov* lying in harbour able to destroy not only the harbour but the city around it?'

Freddie Lewis returned to the fray. 'Including itself presumably.'

'The blackmail angle in that situation,' said Rossiter ignoring him, 'something like a *Simeonov* in say New York, Sydney, Cape Town – any big port for that matter – is currently one of the Pentagon's headaches.'

There was an uneasy, self-conscious silence in the conference room as if those around the big table were reluctant to comment on what they'd heard. It was broken by Maltby. 'I must say I have my doubts. The Soviets would be running enormous risks if they indulged in that sort of thing.'

'I'd like to make it clear,' said Rossiter, 'that the CIA has stressed the report is rumour, no more. Their agent got it third hand. But the Pentagon has to give it a hard look.'

'I still have substantial doubts,' said Maltby doggedly. 'Nevertheless I require no convincing that we must do everything possible to check the report, even if it has rumour and improbability stamped all over it.'

'How splendid that you should feel like that,' said the Commodore. It was not clear whether this was sarcasm or an expression of relief. Whatever it was, it seemed not to worry Maltby. The Commodore looked at Briggs. 'Let me have that Luanda report.'

Briggs flipped through the contents of a file and found the wanted paper. The Commodore glanced at it, no more. He had a photographic memory. 'This came in from Lisbon yesterday. I'll give you the gist of it. The *Antonov* will shortly complete loading chrome ore and copper in Luanda and sail for Leningrad to discharge. She has waited in Luanda for a berth for eight days. Been alongside now for three.

'DAEDALUS,' the Commodore used the agent's cryptonym, 'asked the chief officer in a casual way about number one hold. Wondered if the ship could provide refrigerated space for a fruit consignment from up country if it arrived in time. The chief officer said no – number one hold already full. Fruit, he explained, loaded at a previous port of call. DAEDALUS reported that there were three previous ports of call : Beira, Durban and Cape Town. Fothergill's people then checked. In none of these ports did the ship load fruit of any kind. Nor was the hatch to number one hold lifted.'

Maltby's eyes narrowed. 'Who is DAEDALUS?'

'Care to answer that, Fothergill? He's your man,' said the Commodore.

Fothergill sat bolt upright, wriggled his neck in its high starched collar. 'He works for Luanda shipping agents who handle Soviet ships. Half-caste. Born in Portugal. Long time in Angola. We acquired him years before the troubles.'

'How does he report?' Maltby leant forward, waistcoat buttons straining.

'Through his linkman in Lisbon. Brother Luis, a *retornado*.

Cleared out when the MPLA took over.'

'Reliable. Both of them?'

'Absolutely,' said Fothergill. 'Blood enemies of the Marxists. Undiluted hate relationship with the MPLA. Luis is an FNLA man. An old political opponent. DAEDALUS always liked money. *Our* money. On top of that he lost a wife and child in the troubles. They just disappeared. He blames the Marxists.'

Maltby relit his pipe, puffed at it noisily, leant back, grunted. 'I see. Daresay it's all right.'

The Commodore looked at the Americans. 'Anything you people would like to add . . . Rossiter?'

'Subject to what I've already said about the CIA report, your information in general matches ours. First time I've heard that Luanda story. Interesting. Fits the picture.'

'You, O'Dowd?'

'I guess that until somebody gets down into number one hold there'll be no mileage on what goes on in the *Simeonov* class.'

'Quite. The sooner the better.' The Commodore looked round the table. 'And that brings us to the project. Which is what this meeting was called for.'

Maltby put a hand in front of his mouth and yawned. 'Good. I was hoping we'd come to that.'

'We would have some time ago if you'd been familiar with the background.' This remark seemed to please Briggs who smiled approvingly at Kitson.

'Sorry about that, Ratters. But your summary was fascinating. Had me on the edge of my seat.' Maltby rubbed his hands together with the relish of a man who's aware he's scored a winning point. 'Now we're in the finishing straight let's move ahead. What *is* the project?'

The Commodore was turning the pages of the *Antonov* file. 'What's that?' he said, looking up, knowing the calculated inattention would irritate Maltby.

'I said WHAT . . . IS . . . THE . . . PROJECT?'

'Ah, yes. Of course. It is to place two operatives on board

*Antonov* in an acceptable role during the course of her return voyage to Leningrad.'

As discussion on the project moved into the late hours Maltby became more sleepy and the Commodore more irritable.

When what was thought to be the last detail had been settled he said, 'Well that seems about all. I think we might now – as a final task – run over the allocations of responsibility.'

'Must we really, Ratters?' Maltby's noisy yawn exposed rows of uneven teeth.

'If you'd care to leave now, Sir James, I think we might just about manage.' The Commodore had become very chilly and formal.

The irony was lost on Maltby. He consulted his watch. 'Think I *must* go. We've cleared the worst hurdles and the water-jump. Rather good that.' He exploded with sudden laughter, looked round apologetically. 'Can't do anything about the finishing straight. That's up to you people. Fothergill will keep me in the picture.' He gathered his great bulk, pulled himself upright, struggled out of the creaking chair, stretched his arms, tugged at the wrinkled waistcoat, took hat, raincoat and umbrella from the stand and made for the door. Once there he turned. 'We require evidence. Hard, explicit evidence. Urgently. While I remain sceptical, I accept that there may be something in the *Simeonovs* which could be relevant to détente and the current SALT talks.' Maltby licked his lips, blinked at them in silence for a few moments, nodded his head in a knowing way and said, 'Good night to you, gentlemen.'

'One moment, Sir James.' The Commodore raised a peremptory hand. 'May we confirm that you will clear the project with the ICC and the Cabinet?'

'But of course. Isn't that why I was invited?' He grinned sardonically. 'Good night, my dear Rathouse.'

When he'd gone the Commodore said, 'Strange man. Surprisingly effective. Now let's get on.' He consulted a notepad. 'Rossiter, you've undertaken to clear the operation with the

Pentagon and the CIA.' He looked up. 'And to get them to provide the man.'

'That's right, sir. I'd just like to confirm that C-in-C, USN, Europe is *not* officially in the picture, though I have to keep him privately informed.'

'That is correct. *And* we keep it off NATO's plate. Too much of a leaky sieve there for this sort of thing. Kitson, you will liase with Rossiter and C-in-C Fleet's staff at Norwood. Arrange with them the planning and operational requirements for the first phase – and the requisition through private channels of the units for the second. You're also responsible for the operational briefing of the naval units involved in phase one – *and* all units in two, should we reach it. I've had general clearance from the Vice Chief of Naval Staff on this so you shouldn't meet with any opposition. Just as well – you've a pretty full load. Happy about it?'

'Yes, sir. Quite, thank you.' In spite of this assurance Kitson looked a shade more mournful than usual.

'Briggs,' the Commodore shot a sideways glance at his assistant. 'You are generalissimo communications. Agree necessary details with Northwood, Kitson, Rossiter and O'Dowd. Channels, frequencies, cyphers, codes – that sort of thing.'

'Yes, sir.'

'Better let me see your notes – hand written, Briggs, no typing – before you go to Northwood. By the way, what signal have you in mind for the execution of the second phase should the operatives decide it's necessary?'

The lieutenant-commander hesitated, seemed lost in thought, then came up with, 'Lima Charlie Charlie, sir.' He managed to look both hopeful and embarrassed at the same time.

'Good God, Briggs. Where did you dig that up?'

'LCC. Acronym for Land Cod Catch, sir.'

'Confusing, Briggs, confusing. All that LCC stuff. Alert half the local authorities in Britain. And why cod? They may be in waters where there aren't any. But I like *land catch*. Not at all bad. Soviet monitors will think it's a trawler.'

Briggs looked pleased. 'You mean use Land Catch?'

'Yes. I thought I'd just said so. Incidentally if some emergency arises – if they're in trouble, serious trouble – I suggest they add the name of a trawler base : Yarmouth for example.' That having been agreed the Commodore pressed on. 'Now let me see.' He consulted his notes. 'O'Dowd.'

'Sir?'

'Your job is to look after the Bullock people, the Baron and the Paris briefing. Quite clear on that?'

'Yes, sir. No problems there, I guess.'

'I trust not. You, Fothergill, will keep Sir James, me and your SIS bosses informed throughout the piece – *and* provide the lady.'

Fothergill nodded gloomily.

'Good. Now, Freddie. Last but by no means least on my list. You will arrange flight schedules for the Baron and liase with O'Dowd on all flight aspects throughout the operation. Right?'

The group captain worked away at the maze he was constructing on his notepad. 'Yes. I've got that, Ratters.' He looked up. 'One final point. In the event of an abort . . . bad weather . . . failure to intercept, whatever . . . we've agreed the Baron is to proceed to Il da Sal and wait there for further orders. In that event what communication channel do we use?'

'Good question.' The Commodore gave the matter thought, his fingers drumming an accompaniment to an inaudible melody. 'Look – *Aries* will be in operational control down there. She can transmit whatever's necessary to Northwood through the RN station at Lossiemouth. Northwood will then instruct the Baron by *private* telex through the Il da Sal airport authorities, via the Bullock people in Paris. Briggs to arrange a suitable plain language code for that. Something authentically commercial. Once the Baron is airborne and clear of Il da Sal, *Aries* will take over again. But I trust an abort won't be necessary. Got that, Briggs?'

'Yes, sir. I'll see to that.'

'Right. If there's nothing else I suppose we now pack up.' He looked at the tired faces round the table. Not surprisingly no one had anything else to say. It had been a long haul. He got up, handed his papers to Briggs. 'Collect *all* the notes, Briggs. See to their shredding personally. Do it now.'

'Aye, aye, sir.' Briggs levered himself out of his chair. A tall man with a good-natured face, he towered above Rathouse as they made for the door. Once there the Commodore stopped, glared at those still in the room. 'We'll meet again tomorrow at the same time. Good night, gentlemen.'

There were murmured good nights as the small determined figure strode from the conference room.

# 3

From its eminence on Cap Vert the Ngor Hotel looks out towards the Atlantic over a small bay fringed with the bungalows of Dakar's socialites and the thatched huts and beached pirogues of Lebou fishermen. To the north Ngor Island, lying across the mouth of the bay, protects it from the big seas which sweep in from the west at certain times of the year. To the south the ragged Points des Almedies, the westernmost reach of the Cap Vert peninsula, and therefore of Africa, faces the South American continent.

The night was dark and humid, the view from the lounge one of black sky and brilliant stars. Beneath it there was more darkness relieved by the lights of Ngor Island, of passing ships far out at sea and, nearer at hand, those from the fishermen's huts and the bungalows of the well-to-do who lived in and around the big city twenty kilometres down the coast – still Paris Noire to the French, as it had been in colonial days.

The hotel lounge, protected by air conditioning, was insulated from the sub-tropical heat outside; a heat itself tempered by the remnants of the north-east trades. The dissonant hum of voices in the lounge, the strains of music in the background, combined in a soothing texture of sound, broken at times by the muffled roar of jets coming into and out of Yoff. Dakar was the principle staging post for air traffic between Europe and South America and what had been French West and Equatorial Africa.

A tall loose-limbed man with weathered face, greying hair and horn-rimmed spectacles crossed to a settee near the windows and sat down next to a woman whose good looks caused men who passed that way to find an excuse to do so again. Women in the lounge discussed her critically as women do when they sense competition, speculated as to who and what she was, wondered about her relationship with the tall man – wife or girl-friend, dear? – then forsook her for other small talk.

'It was the Paris call.' The tall man spoke quietly; a deep voice with a North American accent.

The woman regarded him gravely. 'Price still the same?'

'Advanced thirty.'

'That makes it?'

He cleared his throat. 'Nine-three-five. Dave'll call me first thing in the morning if there's any change.'

'I see.'

'Have that again?' He pointed to her glass.

'Please. Less gin this time.'

A Senegalese waiter came over in response to the American's signal; a signal quickly seen because the African's eyes had been on the woman. The American ordered the drinks in faultless French and with equal fluency the woman added a friendly warning about the gin. The waiter knew they were English-speaking, and the quality of their French surprised him. When he'd gone the American said, 'We'd better make a late night of it. You won't get much sleep. Too much to think about.'

'I can always sleep, Ben. But yes – I don't mind a late night. We've had two fabulous days lounging in the sun. Bathing in that warm sea. Absolute heaven.'

'Needed a rest after Paris and Lisbon. Lived it up a bit didn't we, Judy?' His expression was uncertain, as if he awaited approval.

'Yes.' She looked at him with calm, unsmiling eyes. 'It's been marvellous.'

'Mean that?'

'I do.'

'Strange scenario.' There was something slightly self-conscious in his laugh. 'Feel I've known you for a long time.'

'A long time? Four days.' She smiled and he thought how attractive she was.

A long silence followed. Afterwards he said, 'What are you thinking?'

'All sorts of things.' She turned dark eyes towards him.

'Tomorrow?' he asked.

'Of course.'

'Are you . . . afraid?'

'Yes. I'd have to be pretty insensitive . . . pretty thick . . . not to be. You?'

'I suppose so. I always try to kid myself I'm not. But sure. It's there. Not that it makes any difference. I wouldn't miss this. Wouldn't be in it otherwise. Nor you. We ask for trouble. We get it.'

She nodded slowly, several times, her face serious, evidently weighing what he said. 'Why do we do it?'

'Difficult to say. Lots of reasons. I suppose basically because we're made that way. Need a sharper edge to life.'

'I wonder. Sometimes I think it's just one big ego trip. I'm not sure.'

'Could be. I don't like to think that. Maybe we can't resist the urge to prove ourselves to ourselves. Maybe it's . . .'

A man wearing sunglasses came up to them. He wore the uniform of a PanAm pilot and carried a briefcase under his arm. 'Excuse me. Ben Gallagher isn't it? Remember me? Ross Churchill. *Saratoga*?'

Gallagher stared at the newcomer, stood up, laughed and shook his hand. 'Ross Churchill it certainly is. Hi, Ross. How could I forget?' He turned to the woman. 'Judith, meet Ross. We were flying shipmates in the *Saratoga*. Years ago. Used to share a cabin. And clothes. Ross, this is Judy. She's from England.'

'Hi, Judy. Nice to know you.' He bent, extended a hand. She took it, looked up at him with serious, questioning eyes.

'Won't you sit down?'

'Glad to.' He turned uncertainly to Gallagher. 'All right? Not intruding?'

'No more than you used to.'

'That's my Ben. Always a rude bastard. Don't worry, I can't stay long. Bus'll be along shortly to take us out to Yoff. We're bound for Paris.'

'What is it? Jumbo?'

'That's right.'

Gallagher signalled the waiter, ordered the drinks. Judy pointed to her still full glass. 'Not for me, Ben. I'm still on this.'

There were the usual exchanges about mutual friends, *Saratoga* days, Vietnam flying. Churchill wanted to know when Gallagher had taken to wearing spectacles. Gallagher told him. The common ground exhausted there came the inevitable pause, the problem of how to keep the conversation going when old acquaintances meet again after many years.

Churchill broke the silence. 'Still flying, Ben, or gone respectable?'

Gallagher cleared his throat. 'Still flying. Maybe a little respectable. Combined with business these days.'

The waiter came back, set down the drinks. Gallagher signed the slip.

'What's your outfit, Ben. You on your own?'

'No. I work for Bullock Development Corporation, St Louis.'

'BDC, huh. Big people. What brings you here? Business? Holiday?' His smile to Judy suggested she might be the holiday.

'Business. We flew in from Paris couple of days ago. Off to Sao Paulo tomorrow.'

'Sao Paulo. What are you flying?'

'Beechcraft Baron.'

Churchill looked surprised. 'You can make Sao Paulo in that?'

'Yeh. It's a Fifty-Eight. Refuel at Port Natal.'

'That's a long hop over water for a little one.'

Gallagher held his glass to the light, squinted at the golden liquid. 'Sixteen hundred and fifty nautical miles. The Baron can make close to fifteen hundred on normal tankage. This job has an additional tank in the fuselage. Gives us all we need.'

'Long time since I flew small. How long in the air to Port Natal?'

'Nine hours at normal cruising. Maybe less if we get a touch of north-east trades.'

'Nine hours,' marvelled Churchill. 'Oh, boy. Under two hundred airspeed. Not for me. No way.' He laughed, switched to Judy. 'I figure the Jumbo's six hundred is too slow. Can't wait for PanAm to go supersonic. Give me Concorde. Sooner the journey's done the better. Especially over water. That's flying for me.'

'Couldn't agree more.' Judy's faint smile hid an involuntary shudder at the prospect of the day still to come.

'There are compensations, Ross.' Gallagher eyed him quizzically. 'The passengers I get. The stop-overs.'

Churchill looked from one to the other, not quite sure what to make of that. 'You going along then, Judy?'

The dark eyes considered him gravely over the rim of a tumbler. 'Yes.'

He fumbled for a moment, searching his memory. 'You're not . . . ?' He looked confused, turned towards Gallagher, then back to her, 'I mean . . . *are* you Mrs Gallagher?'

'No. I'm Judy Paddon. I'm a friend of Bud Allerton's. It's at his request Ben's giving me a lift.'

Gallagher cut in. 'The Baron belongs to the Bullock Corporation. Bud is executive vice-president.'

Churchill held up a defensive hand. 'Sorry. Wasn't checking you out. I . . . I wasn't sure if you'd re-married?'

Gallagher shook his head. 'No. Still on my own.'

There was an embarrassed silence, rescued by a PanAm stewardess who seemed to appear from nowhere. 'Excuse me, Ross . . . Captain Churchill,' she corrected herself, 'the bus is waiting.'

' 'Kay, Sue. Coming.' The American drained his glass, stood up, collected cap and briefcase from beside the settee. 'Guess that's it,' he said. 'Remember me to Sao Paulo.'

Gallagher rose to his feet, shook his hand. "Bye, Ross. Happy landings.'

Churchill said. 'Great to see you again, Ben.' He smiled at Judy. 'Glad to have met you, Judy. See you some time I hope.'

When Churchill had gone she raised an interrogative eyebrow. 'All right?'

'Sure. Ross is okay. Bit loquacious. Curious about you of course. Who wouldn't be?'

It irritated him that her long cool stare, the silence full of unspoken questions, should make him feel uneasy. At length he said, 'What's the trouble?'

'Nothing. Just that . . . I didn't know about your marriage.'

'It ended years ago.' He was on the defensive. 'Divorce. My fault I guess.'

'Funny. Somehow I assumed you weren't.'

'And I'm not.' He laughed dryly. 'Maybe O'Dowd should have included that in the briefing. Not really relevant in our line of business, is it? That's why I didn't ask you. It's not that important.'

She looked out into the darkness beyond the lounge windows. 'Isn't it?'

He sensed the rebuke. 'Right.' He cleared his throat. 'Are you married?'

'I was.'

'What happened?'

'He disappeared.'

'Cleared out?'

She shook her head, still peering into the darkness as if there were something there she could focus on. 'No. Just disappeared. In Beirut. Shot in the back in some dark alley, I imagine.'

'I'm sorry, Judy.' There was a pause. Once again the distant music was muted by the roar of a jet passing over.

'What was his job?'

'Same as ours,' she said.

'With the Brits. Your people, I mean?'

'Yes. SIS.'

'You two in it together?'

'No. They recruited me after he'd gone. When I was full of hate. Five years ago.'

'Hate for what?'

'The other side. Who else?'

'Were they involved?'

'Theory was the KGB arranged the dark alley scenario.'

'Why should they do that?'

'He was in Moscow for years. Deep cover. British press correspondent. Infiltrated the KGB in a Kim Philby act. Got a last minute tip-off that his cover was blown and cleared out. After that he knew he was on their liquidation list. It was only a matter of time before they caught up with him.'

Gallagher took her hand, very gently. 'Come on. Let's dance.'

# 4

He woke next morning to the ringing of the bed-side telephone. It was six-thirty. He was down for a call at six-forty-five. He lifted the handset. 'What is it?'

'Paris wants you, sir.'

' 'Kay. I'll take it.'

There was a click on the line followed by O'Dowd's, 'Morning, Ben.'

'Morning, Dave. What's new?'

'The Sao Paulo contract I phoned you about last night. I've had their reply. Price now nine-four-two for E-seven grades. Negotiate on that basis will you?'

'Okay, Dave. NINE-FOUR-TWO for E-SEVEN GRADES.' He said it very slowly, very distinctly.

'That's right. Nine-four-two for E-sevens. How's the weather out there? Good for swimming?'

'Looks okay through the window. Blue sky, blue water. Hot day coming, I guess. How's it in Paris?'

'Cold, wet and grey. You can imagine. 'Bye now, Ben. And good luck. We need that contract.'

' 'Bye, Dave. We need the good luck.' Gallagher put the phone down, lifted it again and dialled Judy's room number.

They managed a grapefruit and cornflake breakfast before getting into the taxi which took them out to Yoff. Gallagher called in at the Met. office, checked on the latest meteorological forecast, went on to air traffic, filed his flight plan, collected Judy and checked out through customs and immigration. An airport Jeep took them across to the apron where the Baron was parked. 'Isn't she beautiful,' said Judy.

Gallagher looked at the Baron with new interest; the gleaming white fuselage and engine nacelles trimmed in black and gold, the metallic prop spinners glistening in the bright sunlight of tropical morning, the outspread wings. He knew the aircraft's aerodynamic efficiency owed much to its classical lines; it was, he thought, much the same with the woman beside him. The light blue shirt and slacks of Sea Island cotton, the flimsy red scarf – the simple clothes emphasized her classical good looks. 'Yes,' he said. 'She is a beauty. And so are you, ma'am.'

'Oh, Ben,' she reproved. 'So early in the morning.'

Gallagher chatted to the African who'd overseered the refuelling of the wing tanks and checked the aircraft for flight. Having signed invoices on behalf of the Bullock Development Corporation, he helped the Jeep driver put their luggage into the after baggage compartment. That done he and Judy climbed into the Baron with their overnight bags and a briefcase, he started the engines and completed the check list.

The airport was already busy as they taxied out to the holding point on the north-south runway behind an Air France Boeing. They waited in silence as the Boeing began its take-off. Gallagher glanced at the tense face beside him, saw the tightly clenched fists, the white knuckles, and patted her knee. 'Okay?' he said.

She nodded, smiled unconvincingly; the wistful smile he'd got to know. He exchanged horn-rimmed glasses for sunglasses, adjusted the boom-mike on the headset and called the control tower for take-off clearance.

At the far end of the runway the Air France Boeing was climbing into the cloudless sky as the flight controller's French accented English came through on the cabin speaker, granting clearance for take-off on a left turnout.

Gallagher acknowledged, said, 'Right, Judy. Let's go,' and

pushed the throttles wide open. The Baron surged forward, accelerating rapidly, until runway markers and lamps blurred into continuous lines. When the airspeed needle touched 95, he lifted the aircraft off the ground, retracted the undercarriage and flaps and put it into a steep climb. They were soon out over the sea.

He set the chronograph to record elapsed time and began a slow climbing turn to port; when the altimeter showed 10,000 feet he eased back the throttles, levelled out, put the Baron on a heading of 223°, and engaged the auto-pilot. 'We're on course for Port Natal, Brazil, Judy. Would you believe it?'

'No I wouldn't, funnily enough.'

'Anyway. Lie back and relax.'

'Not a chance.' She grimaced. 'When do they take over?'

'In about forty minutes. By then we should be a hundred and forty miles south-west of Dakar. Now, let's have a look at O'Dowd's chart.' He opened the briefcase, put on the horn-rimmed glasses, took out a blown-up section of Admiralty chart on which a grid had been superimposed and attached it to a clipboard.

He studied the chart intently before passing it to her.

'There,' he pointed with a pencil. 'Grid E7. The 0942 ETA for Romeo Victor is based on that position. Slap on course for Port Natal. These are one mile grids, so there's likely to be a change. We'll know when they take over.'

'I see.' She nodded, looked away from the clipboard and down at the sea below. 'I suppose we should be grateful we've got this weather. Practically no wind.'

'Yeh. I guess that's why they chose the place. Latitude twelve north. In the equatorial trough. The Doldrums.'

'You sound like Conrad.' She laughed.

First time she's done that today, he thought. She's sorting herself out. Like a fighter in the ring. Worried, anxious, afraid before it starts, but once the bell sounds and he's committed everything goes. He turned to her, deliberately made himself sound matter of fact, masked his own fears. 'We'd better run through the drill again. Fill in the time. Help make sure, I guess.'

'Yes, I'd like that.' She gave him the clipboard. He put it in the map-pocket beside the seat.

They went through the drill painstakingly, discussed the imponderables, the things that might go wrong and what to do if they did. When they'd finished he looked at the chronograph. 'Another eighteen minutes before we call them. Sit back now and take it easy, Judy. Make your mind a blank. It's great therapy.'

'They used to say that to the Christians in the Forum, Ben. While they were waiting for the lions.' But she leaned back in the co-pilot's seat, stretched her legs, closed her eyes and tried consciously to relax limbs, fingers and toes. It didn't work.

It had all begun seven days ago but it seemed much longer. She'd been in Dervaig on the Isle of Mull, staying with her sister in the stone cottage on the hillside at Quinish above Loch Cuin, enjoying a badly needed rest after an assignment in Teheran from which she'd returned mentally and physically exhausted. The cottage was near the house where she'd spent most of her childhood. No other place gave her the same sense of security, of belonging, of being part of a solitary landscape, totally isolated from the bustle of the world in which she normally moved. So it was always to Quinish that she went when resting from her forays abroad, or from dull periods of waiting in London; periods of briefing and debriefing, of attending 'school' in the remote country house in Wiltshire where mock operations were played out as 'games' and the distilled know-how, the blunders – sometimes fatal – of operatives of long standing were considered and discussed under the watchful eyes of case officers.

She had been resting in the afternoon when her sister woke her. 'Phone, Judy. A man. Sounds nice.'

'Blast him' she said. 'Say I'm coming.'

When she heard the long drawn, 'Ju-u-d-ee, how a-rr-re you, my dear?' she felt cold shivers of apprehension. It was

Roger Beamish, her case officer, phoning from a call-box in Tobermory.

'How *are* you, my *dear* Judy,' he repeated.

'Bloody tired,' she said abruptly. 'What is it, Roger?'

'I happened to be passing through. Staying with a friend at Salen. Thought it would be nice to see you, Judy.'

Liar, she thought. If that story *were* true he wouldn't be phoning. 'When?' she asked.

'Now. I'll come across right away.' He sounded boyishly enthusiastic. 'Marvellous afternoon. Perhaps we might go for a walk. Along that road above Loch Cuin. So peaceful.'

'It was until you came.' Oh God, she was thinking, I know what all this means. Why now, dear Lord?

'I'll be with you in half an hour,' he said.

'D'you really think it's a good idea?'

'I do, Judy. Absolutely, my dear.' He'd said it with that heavy-footed finality she knew so well, and put the phone down. It was, she reflected, an order, not an invitation – and they both knew it.

The track they were following towards the headland led through gorse and heather, dried bracken and brushwood from which rose the trunks of oaks, sycamores, beeches, silver birches, pines and larches growing in wild profusion amid a tangle of vines and creepers, moss clad rocks and old dead trees. At times the loch showed through breaks in the foliage, cold and grey, its shore line brown with rotting kelp.

At the start of the walk Beamish had launched into his usual social chit-chat – how well she looked, so relaxed; what an extraordinary change in such a short time, more beautiful than ever, he thought; lovely to see her in that gorgeous environment, so much her ambience. (How like him to use that word.) Of course he hated bothering her, most positively hated it, but there were no alternatives, positively none; no one else remotely fitted the bill.

'Oh, Roger,' she'd protested. 'For God's sake cut out the bull. Get to the point. What is it that's so dreadfully urgent that it's brought you all the way to Mull to ruin my holiday?'

They had come out of the trees on the side of a creek from which they could look across to the headland, and beyond it to Coll and Tiree, the islands dark against the setting sun like great whales basking in a copper sea.

She was glad that Beamish had chosen to be silent at that moment when everything seemed to stand still, the only sounds the calls of oyster-catchers and plovers, the cries of seagulls and the lap of water in the creek. Over it all there hung like an unseen mist the heady, pervasive smell of sage and seaweed. It was intensely evocative of her childhood.

Beamish broke the spell. 'Very lovely, isn't it?' Then, after a pause, 'Well, to come to the point, Judy, it's an assignment. Frightfully important, frightfully urgent. I mean it's been sprung on us. Things, events, just don't seem to wait for suitable moments, do they?'

'What is it?' she said flatly.

'Extraordinarily interesting – exciting, I daresay. Nothing you've been on so far quite like it.'

'That doesn't attract me in the least, Roger. It simply terrifies me.' She looked at him with a worried frown, knowing that he would believe her to be joking. She shivered because she wasn't.

'As I was saying. It's frightfully urgent, I'm afraid. Means leaving for Paris tomorrow.' He watched her nervously, like a doctor conveying bad news to a patient.

'Tomorrow,' she echoed. 'Oh, no. I've only been here for five days. I'm worn out, Roger. I can't. I really can't. Get someone else. Maria. Yes, Maria.'

'I know.' He was sympathetic, touched her shoulder, his eyes entreating but his mouth setting in a hard line. 'I really *do* know, and I'm most frightfully sorry. I tried awfully hard to dissuade Father . . .'

'That's a lie for a start. I know you too well, Roger. Your nostrils are twitching.'

He ignored the interruption, ' . . . this project has Cabinet backing, Judy. It's as important as that. Not official of course.

But they know and they've approved. And that's most unusual because they are, well – a pretty pussyfoot lot, aren't they? What's more, MOD and the Pentagon are jointly involved . . . it's a liason operation . . . RN and USN . . . SIS and CIA. That's pretty rare. At any rate on this scale. I can't recall a clandestine operation with such fantastic support. Financial and *matériel*. Quite, quite unusual support, I may say.'

She stopped, turned and faced him. 'Please, Roger, leave me out of it. I'm tired. Teheran was awful for me. Don't you understand?'

They walked on. He took her hand. She snatched it away.

'You know I'd do anything I could to please you, Judy. It's just that – well, on this one it's impossible.'

'You're a damned liar, Roger Beamish. You wouldn't do anything to please me if it frustrated your precious plans. And it may occur to you that you haven't told me a thing. Just waffled on like a randy rooster. What is this madly important, madly urgent assignment? *Tell me.* For God's sake.'

Beamish looked away from the sullen, challenging eyes. 'I can't, simply daren't, give you any details now, Judy. You'll be one of two operatives. The other is a man.' He hesitated, watching her very closely. 'A fieldman from Langley. A quite outstanding man I'm told.'

'Langley: CIA!' Her voice rose. 'Bloody hell. Why not SIS? Why can't I work with my own people?'

He shook his head, looked at her in sad bewilderment as if her vehemence shocked him. 'Judy, my dear. Be rational. The Americans are our gilt-edged allies, our blood cousins. The people at Langley are very close to us . . . *and* extremely efficient.'

'Bunch of corrupt assassins.' She spat the words at him.

'Judy, my dear, don't tell me you've fallen for the junk pedalled by the media rodents. The Langley people operate the most effective secret service in the West. *After ours,*' he added thoughtfully and by way of correction. 'You've never worked with one of them before, but I can assure you many of us have – and with excellent results. And of course they have resources far larger than ours.'

'I hate the idea,' she said defiantly. 'I'm English to the core. Who is this man?'

He disregarded the question. 'You arrive in Paris tomorrow evening. Go to the Hôtel de Seine, at 52 Rue de Seine. That's on the left bank in Saint Germain des Prés. Book in, be downstairs in the lounge at eight o'clock that night. There you'll be contacted by David O'Dowd. Here's his photo.' He took it from his wallet, showed it to her, put it back 'I'll give it to you when we return to the cottage. He has one of you. Doesn't do you justice of course. But how could a mere camera.' He smiled ingratiatingly. 'O'Dowd is USN Intelligence. Charming. He'll introduce you to the Langley man. And he – that is O'Dowd – will be responsible for the briefing. A very full, very thorough briefing, I may say.'

'I'm sure it will be. Does a personal accident policy come with it?'

'Judy. Please. Don't be flippant, dear. It's a tremendous feather in your cap getting this assignment. Father thinks a great deal of you. So, of course, do we all.'

She stopped again, confronted him. 'Balls to Father and the feather in my cap. I don't want it. Tell him what he can do with it. Why does it have to be me?'

'Really, Judy. For a beautiful woman your language is at times astonishing. As to why you've been chosen, my dear, well – your talents made any other choice unthinkable. Fluent Russian, fluent French, sound nerves, athletic prowess.'

'Watch it, Roger. I won't be insulted.'

'You know perfectly well what I'm referring to. We have your curriculum vitae. Where was I . . . your physique . . .'

'Thank you, Roger, you're too kind.'

He ignored the sarcasm, closed his eyes, smiled like a curate at a christening. '*And* you are a very beautiful woman.'

'Which means, Roger, that once again I'm to be the bait. I bloody well knew it the moment you began your silly spiel.' She gave him a furious look, quickened her pace.

'No, no. Not at all. A lot of women believe that Mohamed

40

Ali is beautiful. That's not what made him world champion. Same with you, Judy.'

'Oh, rubbish. What a silly analogy.' She thought of something. 'How d'you know I can get a room at the Hôtel de Seine, or flights to London and Paris tomorrow?' Her voice, her eyes, were full of suspicion.

'Don't worry, my dear. The reservations have been made, including the Islander flight to Glasgow tomorrow morning. Visas arranged, travel cheques, the lot. *All* the detail has been seen to.'

'I thought as much. Which visas?'

'Senegal and Brazil.'

That had done something to mollify her. She'd been in neither country. They sounded attractive. She loved travel. It was one of the spin-offs. 'For how long? What clothes do I take?'

Beamish laughed happily. 'Good. That sounds like the Judy I know. Travel light, my dear. Anything you feel you may need *after* the briefing you can buy in Paris – at our expense. Father's idea.'

'Oh. That's really rather nice of Father.' With heavy irony she added, 'this *must* be important.'

'Don't overdo it, Judy. Our budget hasn't all that stretch, you know.'

# 5

The Hôtel de Seine turned out to be an unassuming but comfortable three-star establishment. It was altogether suitable for the assignation. She'd arrived in the evening, unpacked, bathed and changed before going down to the lounge. O'Dowd arrived at eight o'clock and she'd had no difficulty in recognizing him as the man in the photograph Beamish had given her : sandy hair, freckled rather careworn face; not unlike Jimmy Carter's she decided as she watched him come across the lounge.

She smiled, held up a hand. 'Hullo, David.'

'Hi, Judy. Good journey?'

'Not really. Those long waits. Transits to and fro. All for less than an hour's flight.'

'Yes. That's what bugs flying.' He looked at her with unconcealed admiration. 'The camera didn't lie, I guess.'

Her shrug suggested it was a compliment which had become commonplace. 'Let's sit down.'

They found a corner. After a casual chat about Paris, the weather and the day's news stories, he got down to business. He would pick her up in the morning. Take her to the Bullock Development Corporation's offices to meet René Champlon, BDC's top man in France. CIA orientated, O'Dowd had hinted, and she wondered exactly what that meant since it was not a word used in the Craft. He sketched briefly the purpose of the visit to Champlon, filled in the background with which she should be familiar before meeting him, who the Allertons were and how they fitted into the scenario. 'Won't stay long after you've met René. He'll introduce you to Gallagher once I've gone.'

'Who's Gallagher?'

'The Langley man.' O'Dowd said it casually as if it were of little importance. 'We're having dinner at René's place in the Bois tomorrow night.'

'Who's we?' She was watching him with calm eyes in an unflinching stare he'd already found embarrassing.

'Ben Gallagher, you, me and René. René's a bachelor at the moment. His wife's over in California. Visiting her family. He'll lend us his study after dinner. That's where we'll do the briefing. Okay?'

They're leading me up to this gently, she thought. Not showing the horse the difficult jumps until he has to leap them. Should be 'mare' and 'she'. She smiled whimsically. Man's world.

'You smiling, Judy? Something I should know?'

'Was I? I wasn't aware of it.'

The Bullock Development Corporation's offices were in a modern, characterless block off Rue Balard. A secretary had taken them up to the sixth floor, shown them into an executive suite where the good taste of French interior decorators had triumphed over the limitless funds of a multi-national corporation. O'Dowd was greeted by a dapper moustachioed man who came forward briskly with outstretched hand. He spoke North American English with a French accent, smelt of after-shave lotion and displayed too much starched cuff. For a moment, before O'Dowd had done the introductions, she thought this must be some sort of corporation lackey; but no . . . it was René Champlon himself.

They sat down, a severe-looking woman with a built-in look of disapproval brought coffee, and they chatted non-committally until O'Dowd, with fulsome apologies, got up and left. An appointment at the Chase Bank, urgent, unamenable to delay.

When O'Dowd had gone, Champlon discussed her forth-coming visit to Sao Paulo. 'Understand you'll be staying with old friends, Bob and Pauline Allerton.' He turned the silver-framed coloured photograph on his desk towards her. 'Taken last summer. In Paris,' he explained.

'Awfully good likeness,' she said, never having seen the Allertons before and wondering if it were mandatory for BDC regional bosses to have the photo on their desks.

He looked at her enquiringly and she wondered how much he knew. Not that it mattered. She was sticking to the line laid down by O'Dowd.

'Bob was on the phone yesterday.' The small man teased the underside of his moustache with a little finger. 'Told me you'd be in today. Asked me to fix the San Paulo flight.'

'Very kind of him. Bob's a sweetie.'

'There are no problems. It's a small aircraft. Six seats, but it'll be just you and the pilot on this trip. He'll be one of our sales executives. There'll be overnight stops in Lisbon and Dakar. He has Corporation business in both places. I'd like you to meet him.' Champlon spoke into the desk phone. Soon afterwards the door opened and a tall, lean man with weathered face, greying hair and horn-rimmed spectacles came in.

'Judy Paddon, this is Ben Gallagher,' said Champlon. She and the newcomer acknowledged the introduction with serious unsmiling eyes; she sensed that he was uncomfortable, a little self-conscious. Champlon explained that she was a close friend of the Allertons. At their request she'd be his passenger on the flight to Sao Paulo. 'Handle her with care.' His cautionary smile revealed neat white teeth beneath the immaculately trimmed moustache. 'She's a guest of our Executive Vice-President.' Champlon had said the E.V-P bit with the reverence the pulpit reserves for the Almighty. He and Gallagher then discussed the business to be done in Lisbon and Dakar. While they talked she watched the American closely, trying to sum him up. He wore a hearing-aid, the inconspicuous sort with microphones and batteries concealed in the arms of the horn-rimmed spectacles. She'd been prepared to dislike the man; Roger Beamish's enthusiastic recommendation had been enough for that. But her prejudice was short lived. The newcomer was quiet and modest. In spite of a certain hesitation there was something reassuring about the deep voice, the slow Southern drawl. He'd not given her that 'I can't wait to lay you' look which she'd sometimes experienced when meeting for the first time a man with whom she had to work, and for this too she liked him. Indeed there was little about him she could fault other, perhaps, than a slightly irritating habit of clearing his throat before speaking.

Before the American left, Champlon gave him a letter typed on BDC letterhead authorizing Mrs Judy Paddon's flight to Sao Paulo in the Corporation's Beechcraft. She was, the letter recorded, the guest of the Executive Vice-President, Mr Robert Allerton, and would be staying with the Allertons while in Brazil.

The dinner at Champlon's that night had been a pleasant affair; the food and wine good, the conversation interesting for they had all lived lives very different to those of ordinary mortals. Though much that each would like to have known about the others could not be said, what came through was worth listening to. At ten o'clock Champlon led the way to his study and left them there. 'I have to get a letter off to my wife,' he'd explained. O'Dowd spent the next two hours on the briefing. He'd done it without notes and she was impressed, though her first reaction to the project had been one of pure unadulterated terror. She'd put forward objections which were neither brushed aside nor accepted, but at least she'd been allowed to have her say. As the briefing developed and she became aware of the thoroughness of the planning, her professional interest grew. That and Gallagher's self-assurance, his confidence in their ability to accomplish the task, did much to reassure her. Gradually the worst of the fear had gone and she'd been able to think rationally about what was involved.

\*

Fear had returned in the early hours of morning when she awoke from deep sleep to the reality of the immediate future : but it was muted later by the congenial task of shopping in and around Rue St. Honoré for clothes she could never herself have afforded.

'You have to shop here for whatever you think you'll need in Brazil,' O'Dowd had said with a quizzical you're-going-to-enjoy-this smile. 'But keep it light. The way a woman travelling by air would. Southern hemisphere, sub-tropical summer. It must look right to customs officials and hotel servants.' She'd taken him at his word. What she bought didn't weigh much but it had cost a lot.

The shopping was followed by lunch with Gallagher at Fouquet in the Champs Élysées. This had been a happy affair and it too had helped allay her fears. It was at that lunch that he'd said in a diffident, apologetic way, 'You don't have to raise your voice, Judy. My hearing's okay.'

'Oh, I'm sorry. I didn't know I had.'

'It's natural. People do that when they see a hearing-aid. Mine's a phoney. I hear better than average.'

'Of course. You wear it because . . .'

'Good cover,' he interrupted, clearing his throat. 'If people think you're deaf they're not so afraid of their asides being overheard. That often helps. But this outfit,' he tapped the spectacles with a forefinger and lowered his voice, 'has another purpose. You'll see what it is in time. No point in telling you now.'

She laughed gently, touched his arm. 'Ben. You're sweet. You didn't let me finish. I know what they're for.'

'You do?' He sounded genuinely surprised.

'Yes. Dave O'Dowd mentioned it at the briefing.'

'My memory.' Gallagher shook his head. 'It's a shambles. Old age you know.'

She said, 'I'm sure it is,' and they both laughed.

There'd been more shopping in the afternoon. That night he'd taken her to the Lido, afterwards they'd gone on to a night club in Montmartre and danced until she confessed to tiredness. He seemed inexhaustible. There'd been a few hours' sleep before a taxi took them out to Orly where she'd seen for the first time the Beechcraft Baron which was to play such an important part in their lives over the next few days. They'd flown to Lisbon that day; a flight during which, for much of the time, she'd slept. The night was spent at Cascais in the comfortable luxury of the Estoril Sol. There had been another gourmet dinner and more dancing, something he did unusually well. He'd spent the next morning attending to BDC business in Lisbon, leaving her to her own devices until he returned. On the morning of the second day they'd taken a taxi out to the airport and flown on to Dakar, via Las Palmas where they'd refuelled. They'd spent two days in Dakar waiting for the 'go' signal. During that time he'd done some business in the town, taken her sightseeing one day and swum and sun-bathed with her for most of the next.

She was too intelligent not to realize that their programme had been designed, among other things, to keep her busy and amused. There was little time to brood on what lay ahead.

As the days passed she'd found herself liking the American more and more. He was a considerate man, courteous in a quaintly old-fashioned way; quiet and reserved for much of the time, entertaining at others. He was, she knew, at pains to encourage and reassure her. If she *had* to do something difficult and dangerous she couldn't think of anyone she'd rather be with than Gallagher. She supposed that was why she would have tumbled quite happily into bed with him on that last night in Ngor had he asked her to. But he hadn't. And she liked him for that, too.

She was awakened by his voice. 'Very soon, now,' he was saying as he switched on the aircraft's VHF, took the code-card from the briefcase and clipped it on to the board which held the gridded chart. 'I call them in another two minutes.' He passed her the clipboard. 'We're about there.' He indicated the position with a ball-point. 'Approaching Papa One-Five.'

'I see.' She put a hand to her mouth to hide a yawn.

'Have a good sleep?'

She looked mildly embarrassed. 'Yes. Sorry.'

'No, ma'am. It's what I wanted for you. Great therapy.'

With his eyes on the chronograph he put up a warning hand, pressed the transmission switch, cleared his throat and spoke into the mike. 'Foxtrot Seven-Nine – this is Five-Three-Seven.' The Southern drawl had gone. The accent now was Irish. Like many good linguists, Gallagher was an excellent mimic.

A disembodied voice at once replied. 'Go ahead, Five-Three-Seven.'

It was a hot summer day under a cloudless sky, the surface of the sea faintly ruffled by a breeze from the north-east. The *Leander* class frigate rolled gently to the long swell, a comfortable, sleepy rhythm, dampened by her stabilizers, enough movement to evoke squeaks and groans from straining metal and plastics. Seabirds wheeled and dived astern and an occasional flying fish broke the surface of an otherwise placid sea.

'Not exactly a busy stretch of ocean, Pilot,' said the bearded man who sat hunched in the Captain's chair on the bridge of HMS *Aries*.

The navigating officer, sensing a trap, looked round the horizon, then into the hood of the radar display. There were only four ships in sight; two tankers well down on the eastern horizon, the trawler they'd overtaken still astern, and eight miles away on the port beam *Jupiter*, the frigate exercising in company with *Aries*. Two Wasp helicopters from the frigates were airborne, carrying out an anti-submarine sweep fifty miles to the north-east. For the purpose of the exercise they were under the orders of *Jupiter*'s helicopter control officer.

'No, sir,' said the navigating officer. 'I imagine we're too far to the west for the main traffic stream. But of course there's a lot more on radar than we have in sight. Mostly to the east.'

'You imagine right, Pilot,' said the Captain. 'We *are* too far to the west. But not by accident I would remind you.'

'Yes, sir.'

'The dubious miracle of radar,' sighed the Captain. 'What fun it must have been in the days of sail. No engines, no radio, no radar, no sonar, no satellites, no electronic navigators, no signals from MOD, no choppers. Had to depend on your eyes, your wits, a seaman's instinct and God's mercy. Really were men, those square-rigged boys.'

Unaware of this contradiction the bearded man rambled happily on. The navigating officer busy at the chart table at the back of the bridge winked at the officer-of-the-watch. Familiar with the Captain's philosophical sorties they did no more than express polite agreement at suitable intervals.

Later the Captain said, 'Shouldn't be long now.'

As if in response to this remark a buzzer sounded and a light flickered on the bridge console. The officer-of-the-watch picked up the phone. 'Bridge-Ops Room,' he said. There was a pause, after which he continued. 'I'll repeat that. Contact made with Five-Three-Seven now at Papa One-Five.' He put down the phone, repeated the message to the Captain.

'Good.' The Captain eased himself out of the swivel chair, looked at the bridge clock. 'Three minutes ahead of ETA. Must have had a tail wind. Tell the operations room I'm coming down. You'd better come, Pilot. Nothing to be seen up here.'

He made for the stairway. 'Haslett, maintain ASW search diagram Delta Five-Nine. And see that *Jupiter* behaves herself and isn't beastly to our Wasp.'

The officer-of-the-watch said, 'Aye, aye, sir.'

The Captain went below followed by the navigating officer.

# 6

Deep in the bowels of the ship, the frigate's operations room had about it something of the atmosphere of *Tomorrow's World*. Dark but for muted lights and the green glow of radar and data displays, of weapons systems controls, plotting tables, computers and other electronic hardware . . . silent but for the hum and click of these systems, the subdued scratch of tracking styluses, the scarcely audible hiss of air-conditioning and the low murmur of human voices.

The Captain disregarded the command chair he normally used when the operations room was fully manned, and went instead to a display where the helicopter control officer was talking into a microphone. The Captain had given orders that apart from himself and the navigating officer, the only men permitted in the operations room on this occasion were the communications officer and the helicopter control officer. Normally, when fully manned for action stations, there would have been many more officers and men on duty. The Captain stood behind the HCO, touched him on the shoulder. 'What's the situation, Blades?'

'Five-Three-Seven's here, sir.' The HCO indicated a position marker at the end of a red track drawn on the glass surface with a grease pencil. 'Zero-six-two degrees, thirty-three miles from Romeo Victor. *Danbuoy's* ETA now 0940.' Blades shifted his pencil to a blue course line and position marker. 'Here is *Danbuoy's* position, sir. One-five-five degrees, three-point-four miles from Romeo Victor. Reported by *Narwhal* less than two minutes ago.'

'Good,' said the Captain. 'Got either on radar or sonar?'

'The aircraft on radar, sir. *Danbuoy* and *Narwhal* are still too far east.'

'Five-Three-Seven's height?'

'Eight thousand feet, sir.'

The Captain moved over to the communications officer. 'Everything all right, Wilson?'

'Yes, sir. *Narwhal* has been reporting *Danbuoy*'s position at ten minute intervals over the last half hour. We pass these out to Five-Three-Seven together with his own position, using the coded grid reference for both. It's working smoothly.'

'Five-Three-Seven made a sighting?'

'Not yet. Should do so within the next five minutes.'

'Have we broadcast a weather report?'

'Yes, sir. He'll know it's a calm sea with a long swell from the west.'

'Good. Let's have the loudspeaker on. Not much time left. I'd like to hear the end-game.'

'Aye, aye, sir.' The communications officer pressed a button and a loudspeaker came to life. There was the familiar click of a transmission switch-on, followed by Blades's voice. 'Five-Three-Seven . . . *Danbuoy* on Golf Five. Maintain present course and speed.'

'Will do . . . Foxtrot Seven-Nine.' The man spoke with a rich Irish brogue.

The Captain looked at the time – 0932 – then at the plot; the converging tracks of 537 and *Danbuoy* – due to intersect at Romeo Victor at 0940 – conjured up for him a mental picture of what was happening in the air and on the sea ninety miles to the east of the frigate. The call sign 537 used by the aircraft was not its own. It happened to be that of *Aries*'s helicopter which was – for two hours of that day only – observing radio silence while conforming to *Jupiter*'s orders to her own Wasp. Radio surveillance stations, ships, airports, hearing the exchanges would believe them to be signals between two frigates carrying out an exercise with their respective helicopters – an exercise evidently involving a danbuoy dropped by one of the frigates; presumably a target marker. The Captain had in his mind's eye aircraft 537 and the ship – code named *Danbuoy* – proceeding from very different directions at very different speeds to Romeo Victor, the rendezvous fixed by C-in-C Fleet forty-eight hours earlier; 537 aware of every detail of the secret operation. *Danbuoy* aware of none.

The picture in the Captain's mind included the US Navy's submerged nuclear submarine *Narwhal* shadowing *Danbuoy* by sonar from a position miles astern – a task she'd undertaken for the last forty-eight hours – and reporting the shadowed ship's position to *Aries* at intervals which though long at first had grown steadily shorter.

It was an unusual operation, he reflected, and the high security classification accorded it by C-in-C Fleet was a measure of its importance. The Captain had told those concerned what he'd been instructed to tell them – that it was a highly secret interception exercise being carried out by a US Navy submarine and a long-range reconnaisance aircraft. *Aries*'s only concern was to act as a communications link in terms of C-in-C Fleet's orders. The Captain had warned that under no circumstances should the operation be discussed, that any breach of that instruction would have the most dire consequences. Since only six members of his crew were concerned – each either an officer or chief petty officer – he had no fears.

His thoughts were interrupted by the voice of the communications officer who was answering an internal phone. Still holding it he turned to the Captain. 'The radio supervisor has just picked up a MAYDAY, sir. The pilot of a US private aircraft, November Zezo-Four-Nine-Three Charlie, reports fire in the starboard engine. Says he's preparing to ditch.'

'Poor devil. What's his position?'

'He was about to give it, sir, when the transmission failed.'

'Typical,' said the Captain. 'Now the whole bloody equatorial trough will have to be searched at the taxpayer's ex-

pense. Well, I'm afraid there's nothing we can do but keep a
sharp lookout. Let the bridge know.'

'Aye, aye, sir.'

The message had no sooner been passed to the bridge than
the loudspeaker crackled into life again. 'Foxtrot Seven-Nine
. . . this is Five-Three-Seven.' It was the Irish voice again.

'Go ahead, Five-Three-Seven.'

'Have sighted *Danbuoy*.'

'Bravo Zulu,' replied the communications officer.

'Good,' said the Captain. 'Up the Irish. We were rather
hoping for that.'

The time was 0937.

'I've brought her down to eight thousand,' Gallagher was
saying. 'Jettisoned all but forty minutes' fuel. Twelve minutes
to go now. Should make a sighting before long.' He sounded
very calm and matter of fact. As if they were going into
Kennedy or Heathrow.

'You *have* been busy while I slept.' She brushed a strand of
hair from her forehead, frowned at him. 'Life-jackets?'

'Yes. We'll put them on now.' He engaged the auto-pilot,
helped her into an orange life-jacket, tied the tapes, reminded
her of the inflation drill, patted her arm affectionately. 'You
look great,' he said, struggling into his.

'I'm frightened,' she said.

He cleared his throat. 'Of course. All intelligent people
are. That's what bravery's about.' His weathered face relaxed in a half-smile. 'Don't worry, Judy. I've done this twice
before. And I'm still around. With the undercart retracted the
Baron's bottom's like a boat. She'll ditch nicely.' He wished
he could be certain of that. It depended very much on how the
touch-down went in the westerly swell.

He thought of the first time he'd ditched. A half gale in the
Pacific off San Diego, not long after he'd completed his flying
training at Pensacola. It had nearly been tickets then. Head
injuries, broken leg and arm, half-drowned. Would have been
tickets but for quick thinking and good seamanship by a de-

53

stroyer captain. The next time was years later. In the China Sea, returning to *Saratoga* from a bombing mission over Hanoi. That hadn't been too bad. Calm sea, and they'd got rid of most of the fuel before ditching. Only fifteen minutes in the water before one of *Saratoga*'s choppers fished them out.

He was okay now. Scared as hell and all pent up of course, but he knew what ditching was like. The girl didn't and he was sorry for her. He took a sideways glance, tried to make out what was going on behind the calm face. He said, 'Better move in back now, Judy.'

'Okay.' She held up a small zip-topped vanity bag. 'My face things. Can I put them in the briefcase?'

'Sure. Go ahead. Put this in too.' He passed her the pocket calculator he'd taken from his denim jacket.

She put the vanity bag and calculator in the briefcase, moved into the seat behind and fastened the safety harness.

'When I give you the word,' he was saying, 'get your head down between your knees and against that cushion. Shoes off, I'll bring her in parallel with the westerly swell. Normal landing speed. The lighter the touch down the better. There's plenty of flotation. Tanks almost empty, I've jettisoned most of the fuel. Lakenheath's flotation bag in the nose luggage compartment inflates on impact. She'll come to a stop soon after we strike the water. That's when I throw the life-raft out. You'll have plenty of time to open that door and get out. The raft self-inflates. Go straight to it, grab hold and swim away from the aircraft. I'll be right there with you. When we're clear we'll climb in.' He watched her closely to see how she was reacting.

'Remember, when we ditch you won't have time to worry.' He sounded full of confidence. 'Too much to do.'

'I'll do my best.'

'Bet your life you will.' He smiled sympathetically. 'One day you'll be dining out on this. Laughing about it . . .' The sentence trailed away as he held up a hand for silence. The voice of the frigate's flight controller came through on the earphones.

54

'Five-Three-Seven . . . this is Foxtrot Seven-Nine. *Danbuoy* on Golf Five. Maintain present course and speed.'

'Everything all right?' asked Judy from the seat behind him.

'Yes, great. Foxtrot reporting *Danbuoy* on Golf Five. We should make a sighting in the next few minutes. Ahead to port . . . left hand side,' he added by way of explanation. 'We'll begin losing height now.' He throttled back the engines, put the nose down, adjusted the tail-trim for a gradual descent. He leant forward, his eyes straining as he searched the sea to port. It was a hot day and there was a heat haze over the water. But the sun was astern on the port quarter and that helped. A few minutes later he saw the ship. Suddenly, closer than he'd expected, a tiny elongated shape at the head of what looked like a thin strand of white cotton – the wake which had first caught his eye.

'There!' He pointed, then with binoculars checked the detail comparing it with the aerial photograph O'Dowd had produced at the Paris briefing. Bridge and accommodation tower aft; seven hatches; two cranes. Seen from that height and distance it was a minute scale model.

'That's her all right,' he said and felt a surge of excitement. It had happened at last. All that planning, the meticulous preparation, careful briefing; so many factors, so much detail, and here she was . . . at the right time and place, with more or less the right weather. His excitement hid no illusions. The crunch had still to come; the biggest imponderable of all. Would they be able to make it the way they'd planned? Or any way? He could have done without the westerly swell. He cut short his thoughts. There was little time left.

'Let's go,' he called to Judy over his shoulder as he disengaged the auto-pilot and closed down the starboard engine. Next he shut the red starboard switch which released a chemical extinguisher in the starboard engine nacelle; a modification made by USAAF at Lakenheath in the previous week – one of a number important to the Baron's mission. It caused that switch also to trigger a smoke-bomb in the nacelle. Thick black smoke began to stream from the starboard engine.

Gallagher switched the VHF frequency back to the civilian channel, spoke into mike. 'MAYDAY . . . MAYDAY . . . MAYDAY,' he called, a note of urgency in the Southern drawl. 'Fire in starboard engine. November Zero-Four-Nine-Three Charlie. Preparing to ditch. My position is . . .' He paused, allowed ten seconds to pass, then switched the frequency back to the naval channel. 'Foxtrot Seven-Nine,' he called in the Irish brogue he reserved for that channel. 'This is Five-Three-Seven.'

The response was immediate. 'Go ahead, Five-Three-Seven.'

'Have sighted *Danbuoy* . . . repeat, have sighted *Danbuoy.*'

'Bravo Zulu,' came back from *Aries*. Gallagher smiled. Bravo Zulu . . BZ – the Royal Navy's signal for *Well done.*

Unconsciously his grip on the control column tightened as he concentrated on the difficult task ahead. Smoke was still streaming from the starboard engine. The altimeter showed 2800. He checked airspeed, rate of descent, relative position of the ship below before putting the Baron into a slow descending turn.

From behind came Judy's anxious enquiry. 'The destruct charges, Ben. Okay?'

'Yeh. Okay. When you're out the last thing I do is shut the fuse-switch. The smoke-bomb in the fuselage will ignite right away, the self-destructs a few minutes later. That's plenty of time to get clear.'

'I see,' she said doubtfully. 'Let's hope the charges don't feel as churned up as I do. Go off too soon.'

'They won't, Judy. Nor will you.' Jesus, he thought, must she talk right now? I have to concentrate.

'It seems wicked to destroy our beautiful Baron,' she said sadly. 'And my lovely new clothes. How bloody unfair.'

'That's right.' He spoke without conviction, suddenly adding, 'Give me a break will you, Judy. No time for chat right now.'

'Sorry.' She sounded hurt, contrite, and he felt brutal. It was tough for her just sitting there, watching and waiting.

The chat was her personal safety valve. But not his. There was too much to do. He slipped off his shoes, took off the sunglasses, put them in the pocket of his denim jacket, slid the pilot's window open just enough to push out the clipboard with the gridded chart and code-card and saw the airstream snatch them away. Then he shut the window.

# 7

At a console in the radio office of the Soviet bulk carrier *Antonov* a thin man with a pock-marked face switched off the transmitter, pushed aside his headset, lifted a phone and dialled a number.

'What is it?' came the deep voice of Sergei Yenev.

'Grotskov here, Captain. We've just picked up a MAYDAY from a US aircraft, November Zero-Four-Nine-Three Charlie. Fire in the starboard engine. Pilot said he was preparing to ditch. Strong signal, bearing north-east.'

'What position did he give?'

'The transmission ceased before he could give it. I acknowledged, asked for a position. So did other ships and shore stations . . . Freetown, Conakry, Dakar, Bathurst. A few minutes later Yoff airport reported that the aircraft was a private one with two people on board. It was on a flight from Dakar to Port Natal, Brazil. Took off from Yoff less than an hour ago.'

There was a pause before the Captain replied. 'If it's come down north-east of us, it's in a busy shipping lane. They may be lucky. There is nothing we can do, Grotskov. Inform the officer-of-the-watch; listen for further signals. Let me know if anything develops.'

Yenev had no doubt the senior communications officer would do that. Little though the Captain cared for this Cassius-like man, he had to admit he was fiercely efficient, obsessively zealous. While the incident lasted he and his assistants would be monitoring the ether like bloodhounds casting for scent.

A dark-haired, dark-eyed man with Mongolian features went from the chartroom to the wheelhouse. He spoke to the quartermaster who, relieved of the wheel because the ship was on auto-pilot, was cleaning brightwork. 'Leonid Grotskov has picked up a MAYDAY signal. Aircraft on fire. Pilot says he's ditching to the north-east of us. Not far away.'

The quartermaster stopped polishing, straightened his back. 'Rather him than me. It's hot enough in the tropics without a fire to warm you.'

'Don't envy him. Even if the plane gets down safely it may not be found.'

The quartermaster grunted agreement. 'It's a big ocean, Comrade Grigor Ivanovitch.'

'At least it's calm today,' said Ivanovitch. 'But it's like looking for a needle in a haystack. No position given.' He took binoculars from the rack, went out of the starboard door and made for the bridge-wing. Less than half way there he stopped suddenly, looked with disbelief at the object in the sky which gleamed so brightly in reflected sunlight. It was an aeroplane with a dark trail of smoke streaming from one wing as it lost height. He made a quick estimate of height and distance, ran back to the wheelhouse, snatched a phone from the console and dialled the Captain's number.

Gallagher brought the Baron down in a slow sinking turn until he was flying parallel to the westerly swell and slightly across wind. With wheels still retracted, flaps down, he began the final approach.

The sea reflecting the brilliance of the sun, the surface of the water rising and falling with the passage of the swell, made his task of judging the height above water immensely difficult as he reduced to threshold speed and waited for the touch down. He began to wonder where the sea had got to when the Baron shivered suddenly. Slamming shut the throttle on the port engine he shouted, 'Now.' Almost immediately afterwards came the impact, more severe than he'd expected. Violent deceleration threw him forward against the safety harness as a great sheet of water struck the windscreen. He experienced sudden shock, an unaccountable numbness that made him shake his head several times before his vision cleared and he realized that the Baron was floundering on the surface, listing to port. He released the seat harness, moved back to where Judy sat slumped in her seat, a trickle of blood on her face. She made no attempt to move. He shook her, shouted, 'Come on, Judy. Get going!' There was no response. He manhandled her body in order to release the seat harness, slapped her face several times and was conscious of the warm stickiness of her blood on his hand. For anguished seconds he thought she was dead, that he would have to leave her. Quite suddenly she sat up. 'All right,' she gasped. 'I'm all right.' He got her clear of the seat, helped her to the door, forced it open against the slap of the sea and pushed her out. The water in the cabin was knee deep and there was a persistent hiss of escaping air. He grabbed the briefcase, shut the fuse-switch and threw out the tightly packed life-raft. With the canvas strap he'd fitted to the briefcase round his waist, he put his weight against the starboard door once more, got it open and fell into the sea. The water was warm. He went under briefly, surfaced, saw where Judy was and swam towards her. Only when he reached her did he inflate his life-jacket.

He urged her along towards the small orange life-raft which had by now inflated itself. When he'd got one of her hands on to the rope cringle which ran around it, he tugged loose the lanyard attaching the raft to the Baron and grabbed the cringle next to her. 'Right. Let's go,' he said. With kicking and one-handed paddling they worked the raft away from the aeroplane.

They'd not gone far when from behind came the sound of a double explosion. Debris splashed into the water and an acrid odour from the Lakenheath charges drifted down to where they were. Gallagher turned in time to see the shattered remains of the Baron begin to slide beneath the surface. There was soon nothing to be seen but a few pieces of floating wreckage and a cloud of dark smoke which climbed lazily into the sky.

On reaching the wheelhouse Sergei Yenev at once stopped engines. Having told the quartermaster to let the engineroom know what was happening, he hurried out on to the bridge followed by Ivanovitch, the third officer.

The aircraft was about a mile away, broad on the port bow now, within a few hundred feet of the water. Smoke from its starboard engine had left a dark trail which marked the spiral passage of its descent. As he watched the engine sound faded, the plane straightened out, began to sink towards the surface of the sea. Yenev realized that it was landing slightly across wind but parallel with the long westerly swell. The pilot must have decided that was the lesser of two evils.

Without taking his eyes from the binoculars he said, 'Tell the second officer to make the skimmer ready for launching. He's to stand by it with the bosun and steward Trutin and a seaman.'

Ivanovitch hurried away. Yenev called after him, 'Put both engines half astern.'

The words were scarcely out of his mouth when he saw the end of the distant drama as if in slow motion: the plane gliding towards the water then, as it seemed about to touch down, disappearing from view behind the crest of a swell and a great cloud of spray leaping from the sea. Though it could only have been a matter of seconds, the spray seemed to hang in the air for some time before it drifted away. After that, each time the swell lifted, Yenev could see the white fuselage and outspread wings lying on the water like some stricken seabird. He shivered involuntarily as a column of smoke rose from it. Poor devils, he thought, what chance for them now?

The ship was still carrying its way, the astern movement of the engines causing the bridge structure to vibrate harshly. Yenev went into the wheelhouse, ordered Ivanovitch to stop both engines and put on port wheel. 'Keep the plane fine on the port bow,' he said. 'I want to stay to windward of it.'

The quartermaster repeated the order, applied port wheel and soon afterwards the bow began to pay off.

Only a minute or so had elapsed between Ivanovitch's sighting report and the ditching of the plane but already the *Antonov* was humming with activity. The chief officer appeared on the bridge clad only in shorts; close on his heels, puffing and blowing, sweating profusely, came the ample figure of Boris Milovych in vest and underpants. Milovych, the staff captain, was a man for whom Yenev had little time. He was the ship's commissar but he was no seaman however efficient he may have been in his political role. All in all, Yenev found him a detestable fellow.

A group of seamen gathered on the port side were animatedly discussing the distant drama which, brief though it was, relieved the monotony of a long sea voyage.

Milovych ran up to the Captain. 'Why are we going astern, Comrade Yenev?' The shrill, high-pitched voice, suggested emasculation.

Damn his 'comrade', thought Yenev. Why doesn't the man forget these party affectations and call me 'Captain'? Without dropping the binoculars he pointed with a free hand. 'An aircraft has gone into the sea. It's on fire. We must try to save lives.'

Milovych challenged the wisdom of this decision in a querulous whine.

'I will deal with your point later,' interrupted Yenev. 'In the meantime we respect the traditions of the sea.' As he moved away from the Commissar he saw something which made him sigh with relief. Because he was a good seaman and a compassionate man nothing pleased him more than the sight of the small object which came clear of the ditched plane. It was an orange life-raft and it was moving away slowly from the broken white shape on the water.

Gallagher pulled the life-raft round until the canopy opening faced them, then pushed and shoved as she clawed her way in. He followed and she did her best to help. Drenched, gasping for breath, they sat on the sagging floor looking at each other in silence. Gallagher broke it with a forced laugh. 'Guess we look like a couple of drowned rats.'

She pulled at the long wet strands of her hair. 'I'm sure I do.' A tiny scarlet stream ran snakelike down her forehead. 'Let me look at that.' He dabbed at the blood with a wet handkerchief, sighed with relief. 'It's superficial. A cut. Not to worry. Use this.' He gave her the handkerchief. 'Stretch your limbs. Check if they're okay.' He set an example and she followed.

'My knees hurt,' she complained.

'Mine too. Okay as long as the legs move. It's just bruising.' He found the emergency pack, took out a smoke flare, pulled the ignition strip and threw out the flare. A column of white smoke rose into the air.

With a half-smile she said, 'Ben, you do look funny. You've got a black eye.'

He felt his eyes – the left was tender to the touch. For the first time he saw his hands were cut, badly grazed. He looked at them in dismay. 'Don't know how that happened.' He wriggled over to the canopy opening, paddled the raft round until it lifted on a swell and he saw the ship to the south. 'That's great,' he said. 'We're less than a mile ahead of her. They can't have missed the ditching – or the smoke flare – unless there's no one on the bridge.'

'Oh, Heavens! If they don't pick us up. All this for nothing.'

'Yeh. But I reckon they will.' He paused, waiting for the lift of the next swell. 'If they don't, Narwhal will. Guess she's at periscope depth right now. Watching the play.' He took a plastic pill container and an unopened pack of Polo Mints from a polythene bag in the briefcase, put them in an inside pocket of his jacket, snapped shut the lid and threw away the bag. He looked at his Rolex wristwatch and saw with relief that the second-hand was moving round the dial. 'Really is shock and waterproof,' he muttered.

'What's that?' she asked.

'Nothing. I was just thinking that advertising isn't always bull.'

'I don't know what you're talking about.'

'Forget it,' he said.

Back at the canopy opening he again manoeuvered the life-raft by paddling. As it sank into the trough of a swell he turned to her with a wide grin. 'Know what, Judy? They've put down a skimmer. It's on the way. Make yourself beautiful. Won't be long now.' He put an arm round her shoulders, kissed her in a spontaneous gesture and felt the salty taste of her blood on his mouth. He took the first-aid box from the emergency pack. 'Sorry. Should have done this long ago.'

The Captain of HMS *Aries* was settling down to paper-work at his desk when there was a knock on the door. 'Come in,' he called.

The door opened. It was the communications officer. 'From *Narwhal*, sir.' He handed over a message sheet. Because of its highly secret classification he had himself decrypted it.

*Aircraft November 0493 Charlie ditched 0941. Exploded and sank few minutes later. Two survivors in life-raft thereafter picked up by Soviet bulk-carrier ANTONOV. Not possible ascertain survivors physical condition but they appeared active. Surveillance continues.*

'Good for the Soviets.' The Captain handed the signal back to the communications officer. 'Pass that to Northwood right away, Tom. It'll relieve their twitch.'

# 8

The business of picking up the November Charlie survivors had occupied less than twenty minutes. The Russians pulled them on board the skimmer, took the life-raft in too – despite Gallagher's suggestion that it be deflated and abandoned – and headed back towards the ship.

During the journey Trutin, an outward-giving young man whose English had evidently gained him a place in the skimmer's crew, began to question the survivors. Gallagher touched an ear, explained that he was deaf. He opened the briefcase, took from it the horn-rimmed spectacles and put them on. 'Okay,' he said; the Russian nodded, returned to his questions.

Once alongside the deeply-laden vessel they climbed pilot ladders, the skimmer and life-raft were hoisted on board, and the *Antonov* trembled as her propellers turned and she gathered way.

Trutin led the survivors to the sick-bay, handed them over to the ship's doctor, then hurried up to the Captain's suite to make his report. He took with him Gallagher's briefcase. The American had been reluctant to part with it. 'It's water-tight,' he'd said. 'Doesn't need drying out.' But Trutin with smiling charm had insisted. 'You get it back when I make him dry.'

Boris Milovych, who'd done the mandatory interrogation and surveillance course at Kiev, was with the Captain when Trutin arrived. The Commissar's first action was to switch on a tape-recorder. That sort of thing always irritated Yenev. It was in his view something more appropriate to Lubianka Prison than a ship at sea. He knew that Milovych sometimes bugged officers' and seamen's cabins and messrooms for what he chose to call 'security and anti-subversion purposes'. He suspected that criticism of Milovych – he was much disliked in the ship – was about the only 'subversion' he was likely to find. Yenev had long suspected that his own quarters might have received attention and from time to time he'd looked for a transceiver but never found one.

Trutin launched into a straightforwarded account of what he'd learnt from the survivors during the journey back to the ship. Their names, nationalities, the type of aircraft, the flight on which it was engaged, to whom it belonged, the reasons for ditching and so forth. Both survivors spoke English and French, he said, but not Russian. When he'd finished and Milovych and Yenev had exhausted their questions he was excused.

Milovych then examined carefully everything in the briefcase. The passports, logbooks, the aircraft's registration and licence papers, Gallagher's flying licence, the letter from the Bullock Development Corporation authorizing Mrs Judy Paddon's flight to Sao Paulo, business papers relating to the Lisbon and Dakar visits, customs and immigration documents, vouchers and receipts for airport and fuel and other items. Milovych was also interested in the pocket calculator, the contents of Judy's vanity bag and Gallagher's plastic toilet bag. He laid out everything with meticulous care, minutely examining each article before returning it to its bag : among them were Gallagher's battery shaver, pack of spare batteries, toothbrush, toothpaste and nailbrush.

'Everything seems to be in order,' he admitted grudgingly. 'I never expected it to be otherwise.'

Milovych managed a mirthless smile. 'Security precaution, Comrade Sergei Yenev. Made necessary by your decision to pick up these people. Their presence on board is an embarrassment, to say the least.'

'Seamen do not abandon those in distress at sea, Boris Milovych.'

The Commissar winced at the use of his name unadorned. The Captain rarely called him 'comrade' and when he did the stress laid on the word suggested irony.

'They will not be with us for long,' continued Yenev. 'We can land them at St Vincent, Cape Verde, in twenty-four hours if we are prepared to accept the delay which the detour and landing will involve. Or at Tenerife in forty-eight hours. That is directly on our course, they have helicopter facilities there and we would not be delayed.'

Milovych arranged his face in a humourless smile. Yenev knew that the expression had little to do with humour. It most likely signalled indulgence in some secret knowledge. The Commissar could smile like that when talking to a man he intended reporting to the Party for a political misdemeanour, real or imaginary.

'You decided to pick up these people,' he said. 'I expressed my doubts. However it was a maritime matter and I accepted your decision.' Milovych paused, examined his fingernails, his porcine eyes avoiding the Captain's. 'The decision to land them is a political one. That will be my responsibility. I shall not exercise it until we have completed their interrogation. In the meantime we must inform Leningrad that we have them on board. Tell them that we will send a further message after the interrogation.'

Smug bastard, thought Yenev. Loves to parade his political authority. And why use the word 'interrogation'? Poor devils. Hadn't they been through enough without having to endure that? But all he said was, 'Very well, Milovych. As you wish.'

'I suggest then, Comrade Yenev, that we ask the sick-bay if these people are now ready for interrogation.'

The Captain picked up a phone and dialled. A woman answered. It was Olga Katutin, the ship's doctor.

'How are the survivors?' asked Yenev. '*We* should like to have a word with them as soon as possible.' She would understand the stressed *we*. Katutin had no love for Milovych, who

67

made no attempt to conceal his admiration and preference for Natasha Mekhlis, the attractive young stewardess who looked after his cabin. Katutin had confessed to Yenev that the Comissar was, in her book, a dirty old man even if only fifty.

There was a pause before she answered. 'The English-woman has a scalp wound and some bruising. Not serious. But she's still in a state of shock – needs rest. I'd like to keep her here for some hours. The American has abrasions, bruises – mild shock. He should be all right in an hour or so.'

'I see.' Yenev hesitated, fiddled with a pen on his desk. 'In that case we will see him soon after midday and the woman in the evening – if she's well enough. All right?' He turned to Milovych. 'Olga Katutin says the Englishwoman needs a good rest, and the American a couple of hours. You heard what I said. Suit you?'

'Yes. But I wish to have a word with Olga Katutin.'

Yenev handed him the phone.

'Boris Milovych here, Comrade Katutin. The arrangements suggested by the Captain are suitable. But listen carefully. The man is to have the pilot's cabin on Deck One, and the woman the adjoining passenger cabin. Send the American to his cabin as soon as you've finished with him but keep the woman in the sick-bay for the time being. They are *not* to see each other until both have been interrogated. Is that clear?' Milovych paused and put down the phone.

'Why *adjoining* cabins?' asked Yenev.

'It assists surveillance. Standard KGB practice for suspects. Adjoining cells. They always try to make contact. When they do we listen – and often learn.'

Yenev regarded the Commissar with evident dislike. 'Cells? These people suspects? Why?'

'All British and American imperialists on Soviet soil are suspects. The *Antonov* is not only Soviet soil but a ship with a high security rating.'

'If that is how one is to think about survivors, thank God I'm a seaman,' said Yenev. He knew that Milovych would make a mental note of that. The Party did not approve such bourgeois references to the Deity. It was something the Commissar might well mention in his confidential voyage report.

'There are possibly occupations more taxing and helpful to the State than a seaman's,' Milovych was saying.

'Like yours,' suggested Yenev.

'As a matter of fact — yes.' The Commissar ran his tongue slowly round a fleshy lower lip, watching the Captain through half-closed eyes. Yenev recognized the gesture as one of intense satisfaction. Milovych was in effect saying, 'See? It is to be an interrogation. Not a friendly chat. The orders I gave to Olga Katutin are appropriate to the authority I wield here. You may be Captain of this ship but I am its political master. Do you understand?'

'There's another decision to be made,' said Yenev. 'The search for the aircraft will already be in hand. I propose informing Dakar that we have picked up the survivors.'

The Commissar shook his head slowly but emphatically. 'Not yet, Comrade Yenev. Not yet. First we consult Leningrad. But only *after* the interrogation.'

The Captain said nothing. He held this man in the greatest contempt. Their enmity went back to the days when Yenev had commanded the *Zhukov*, one of Russia's most powerful ballistic missile submarines, lost on her maiden voyage due to a structural failure. Milovych had been the *Zhukov*'s Commissar then. On joining *Antonov* Yenev had found that once again he was burdened with this man. Whether this was by accident or design he could not say. He realized that his own appointment to *Antonov* amounted to demotion — there had to be a scapegoat for the *Zhukov* disaster. Possibly Milovych's appointment was for the same reason.

The sick-bay was two decks up in the stern superstructure which housed the bridge, the accommodation and the casing over the main and auxiliary engine spaces. It was divided into three compartments: the forepart, a small four-berth ward with lockers, washbasin, shower and toilet; the central portion, a surgery with operating table, X-ray apparatus and other medical and surgical equipment; the after part, a photographic darkroom and decontamination chamber.

The survivors had arrived on board drenched and shoeless, but pleasantly warm seawater and the heat of tropical morning had done much to lessen their discomfort. They must nevertheless have looked a forlorn couple when Trutin introduced them to Olga Katutin.

When he'd gone she regarded the newcomers with the faintly hostile and uncertain eyes of a host confronted with the problem of providing for uninvited guests. Her first action was to put them into separate compartments with orders to take off their wet clothes. She was an angular woman of middle age with severely brushed hair fastened in a tight bun at the back. Her English was broken but adequate. In spite of her formal rather guarded manner, the crows' feet at the corners of her grey eyes somehow softened an otherwise austere expression.

It was not long before she had examined them and got to work on their cuts and bruises. In the middle of this the telephone rang. They heard her brief conversation in Russian, and gathered it was with the Captain; but they gave no indication of having understood and she offered no explanation. Soon afterwards Trutin arrived with canvas shoes and a change of clothes.

'From the ship's store.' Olga Katutin's manner was tart and businesslike. 'Your own will be returned when they are dry. And the briefcase,' she added with a curious sideways glance at Gallagher.

The examination and treatment completed, Judy was given a sleeping draught and put to rest in the ward. Trutin came back once more, accompanied this time by a blue-chinned man with drooping moustache and a permanent frown. Katutin introduced him as Stefan Lomov, the chief officer. He had no English, she said, but a fair knowledge of French. Did Gallagher understand French? Yes, he did. Good.

'Andrei Trutin, the steward, will show you to your cabin.' The chief officer spoke throaty French with a Slav accent.

'Captain Yenev instructs that you rest until twelve-thirty, when he will see you. Trutin will fetch you at that time. The Englishwoman must rest here until Comrade Katutin decides she can see the Captain — possibly this evening. When she leaves the sick-bay she will go to a cabin of her own. You must not leave your cabin before you see the Captain. Do you understand?'

Gallagher answered wearily in French. 'Yes. But I'd like to send a message to my Corporation. Let them know what's happened. That we're okay.'

'That is a matter you must arrange with the Captain. I cannot authorize it. Come, we go now to your cabin. It is on Deck One.' The chief officer made for the door. Gallagher turned to Olga Katutin, spoke to her in English. 'Thanks a lot for your help. It's greatly appreciated.'

'It is my duty.' She bowed stiffly, no trace of a smile. Gallagher followed the chief officer into the passageway feeling not altogether happy about the way things were working out. But at least he'd anticipated removal and examination of the briefcase. He patted the back pocket of the Russian-type denim trousers, felt the Polo Mints, the pill tube, the ballpoint pen, and was reassured.

# 9

The Commodore (Intelligence) tapped a characteristic beat of irritation on the leather-topped table. 'O'Dowd always late?' His wide ranging stare was intended to give the impression that he was addressing the room at large but it was evident that Rossiter was the target.

The American wriggled uncomfortably in his chair. 'He's new to London,' he said. 'Hasn't sized up transit times, I guess.'

'Taxis can be difficult *after* lunch.' Fothergill's tone left no doubt as to where he thought the trouble lay.

'Can't we begin without him? Up-date him on arrival?' Freddie Lewis glanced from wristwatch to wall clock.

Maltby grunted, looked into the bowl of his pipe. 'Let's get on with it. I've a busy afternoon.'

Rathouse stopped tapping, glared at his fingers. 'I was about to suggest that,' he snapped, his irritation evidently heightened by Maltby's attempt to pre-empt the Chair. 'That first *Aries* signal, Briggs?'

Martin Briggs, deep in whispered conversation with Kitson, came-to suddenly, looked confused. 'That *Aries* what, sir?'

'First signal. F-I-R-S-T signal.'

'Oh, yes of course.' Briggs shuffled through a file, found the signal and passed it to the Commodore.

'Time of origin ten-fourteen today,' said Rathouse. 'I'll read it to you. Begins : *Narwhal* reports November Zero-Four-

Nine-Three Charlie ditched oh-nine-four-one. Exploded and sank few minutes later. Two survivors in life-raft picked up . . .' He was interrupted by the opening and shutting of a door at the far end of the conference room. O'Dowd hurried in. 'My apologies, Commodore. London taxis thin on the ground right now.'

'I trust you enjoyed your lunch.'

'Sandwich at Harrods Dress Circle. That store in Knightsbridge, you know.'

'We've heard of it,' said Maltby, who was flicking tobacco ash from his waistcoat with single-minded determination.

Rathouse gave him a quarter-deck glare. 'Mind if we get on with the meeting?'

'No,' said the fat man. 'Not in the least.'

O'Dowd hung his raincoat and umbrella on the antlered stand and sat down. The Commodore re-read the first part of the *Aries* signal, then continued, '. . . picked up by Soviet bulk-carrier *Antonov* and taken on board. Not possible ascertain survivors' physical condition but they appeared active. Surveillance continues.' He put down the signal, looked at the faces round the table with the deadpan expression of a conjurer who has just produced a rabbit from his hat.

'So they're on board,' said Maltby. 'I must say I had my doubts.'

O'Dowd beamed with pleasure. 'That's great news.'

'We're not sure if it is.' Rathouse was conceding nothing. '*Aries* and Penryhddon radio surveillance report that *Antonov* has exchanged signals with Leningrad. Scrambled ultra-high-speed stuff. Nothing we can decrypt.'

Fothergill's long neck appeared to stretch higher out of his collar. 'Good omen, I imagine. *Antonov* having doubts. Asking Leningrad what next?'

'Do we tip-off the ASR people?' Briggs looked uncertain.

'What?' Rathouse bubbled with disapproval. 'My dear Briggs. How are we supposed to know? Air-sea-rescue and the Soviets would see through that gaff quicker than lightning.'

Briggs managed a cheerful but embarrassed grin. 'Of course. Stupid of me.'

The Commodore's gesture suggested despair. Maltby came back into play. 'Why doesn't *Antonov* admit picking them up?' By way of cover, he added, 'I may say I'm thinking aloud.'

'Presumably because they'd prefer it not to be known. If you remember we canvassed that possibility in the planning stage.'

'If *Antonov* has a secret – and we think she has – the survivors are an embarrassment.'

'A decided embarrassment,' agreed the Commodore.

'What are the Soviet alternatives?' went on Maltby. 'Land them as quickly as possible – Cape Verde or the Canaries – or take them on to Leningrad, or . . .'

'Throw them overboard,' suggested Freddie Lewis.

'Hardly that.' Kitson's mournful eyes reproached him.

'We don't know,' said Rathouse. 'But my money's on Leningrad from what Fothergill's told us.'

Maltby pulled his considerable bulk together, leant forward, pipe in hand. 'And what was that?'

'Discussed and noted at the last meeting,' said Rathouse.

'I was in Washington.' Maltby turned to Fothergill. 'What was the point?'

'I explained that we understood the CIA had taken steps to ensure they would be carried on to Leningrad.'

'What steps, may I ask?' Maltby sat back in his chair, holding his pipe with one hand and scratching his stomach with the other.

'Apparently a CIA double agent passed data on Bort, Garde Optics to Borodin.'

'Who are Bort, Garde Optics?'

Rossiter took up the thread. 'A subsidiary of the Bullock Development Corporation. They lead US research in high performance electro-optics for surveillance satellites. Operate under NASA/Pentagon direction. Located in Phoenix, Arizona.'

'I see,' Maltby nodded with sudden understanding. 'The KGB would like to know what Gallagher knows about BG Optics?'

'Something like that,' said Fothergill with studied vagueness.

'Were the survivors briefed on this?'

'To the extent that O'Dowd told them in Paris that it was highly probable they'd be carried on to Leningrad.'

'That wasn't my question. Were they told about the CIA feed-in?'

'No. We thought they'd sound more convincing under interrogation iֵ they didn't know.'

'I consider they should have been told.' There was a warning glint in Maltby's eye. No one took up the challenge.

The Commodore changed the subject. '*Antonov*'s ETA in the Channel, Kitson?'

Kitson looked at his notes. 'Given normal weather she should pass the Straits of Dover late in the afternoon of the seventh November.'

'Another six days. Long time. Tell me. How is Northwood taking this?'

'Very calmly really. C-in-C Fleet pleased. Called it pretty smooth when I saw him before lunch.'

'*Aries, Jupiter* and Co.?'

'Continuing their exercise between eighty and a hundred-and-fifty miles west of *Antonov*. At intervals they shift position relative to her. Anxious not to alarm Soviet surveillance satellites. *Narwhal*'s still shadowing from astern. She shifts around a bit too but always keeps within sonar range. She has VLR of course. If you remember, these dispositions continue into the Channel. Off Start Point the frigates are to be relieved by RN patrol craft. *Narwhal* packs up then and aircraft and the PCs take over surveillance.'

'WP – weather permitting,' cautioned Briggs.

'Being November it probably will pee,' said Freddie Lewis. Rossiter looked at O'Dowd with a Christ-what-next expression.

Discussion ambled on into the possibilities and exigencies of the second phase should it become necessary. Rathouse, who had a genius for getting to the heart of the matter, summarized with his usual flair. 'There's really not much else we can do now but monitor *Antonov*'s progress. And hope that Gallagher and Paddon find out what we want to know without the necessity for a phase two scenario.'

Maltby came to life. 'Couldn't agree more. I trust they're reasonably treated. Not too happy about this Leningrad business. Might be tiresome politically. Getting them out if things go wrong. Remind me, Ratters. How *do* they initiate the next phase – if they have to?'

'Briggs's "Land Catch" signal. Suffixed "Yarmouth" if there's trouble.'

'I sincerely hope there won't be.' Maltby's mouth puckered in a small reflex of emotion. 'There's something distinctly sacrificial about their role. Don't much like the CIA double agent act. Bloody cynical, I think.'

Fothergill pushed and pulled at the knot of his O.E. tie. 'I can assure you they don't regard their roles as sacrificial.' The SIS man radiated frosty disapproval. 'Fieldmen are well aware how poorly they rate as insurance risks. It discourages them no more than it does Formula One drivers.'

'Poor sods,' said Freddie Lewis. 'Cosier on the planning side.'

The Commodore looked at Maltby and recalled that the fat man was variously described by those who knew him as 'the best brains in the business', 'the biggest shit around for a long time', 'an opportunist genius' and 'that stupid old fart'. He wondered which of those Maltby really was. Probably bits of all of them, he decided.

The cabin Gallagher found himself in was on the after side of the accommodation tower. Its two windows provided a view astern over the engineroom housing; a view partially blocked by the large white and yellow banded funnel and the after lifeboats. It was a generously proportioned room with cupboards, dressing table, twin beds, its own bathroom, and air-conditioning. He was certainly going to be comfortable even if a virtual prisoner. The chief officer, having reminded him that he was not to leave the cabin until called for, made sure he couldn't by locking the door. It had been done discreetly but Gallagher, hearing the click, had tested the door and found it locked.

Was he already a suspect? Was it to make sure he had no contact with Judy, or was it simply to prevent him wandering about the ship? Whatever it was, it fitted O'Dowd's story of unusually strict security precautions in the *Simeonov* class.

The cabin was bare of books or reading matter of any sort. Gallagher had nothing with him but the loaned Russian clothing in which he stood. At a loss for something to do he went to a mirror and examined his black eye. Having exhausted that distraction, he searched the cabin and bathroom for electronic bugs but found none. He looked at his wristwatch. The time was close to half-past ten. At least two hours before he'd see the Captain. He sat in an easy chair, pushed out his legs, closed his eyes and ran through the questions and answers he expected at the interrogation.

The slow roll of the ship, the beat of the twin diesels, the vibrating superstructure with its periodic squeaks and groans, the sibilant hiss of incoming air, and his own nervous exhaustion combined to put him into deep sleep. He was awakened by the sound of the door opening. Trutin had come to fetch him. It was half-past twelve.

The steward knocked discreetly on the outer door of the Captain's suite, opened it and led Gallagher through the office to the dayroom. 'Please,' he said, pointing the way.

Gallagher went in and Trutin followed. It was a large and comfortable room : settee and armchairs at one end, dining-table and chairs at the other. Two men in white uniform stood by a mock fireplace flanked by bookshelves.

'Comrade Captain Sergei Yenev,' said Trutin, adding with evident pride, 'Captain of our ship.' The thick-set man with

pale grey eyes and sandy crew-cut hair nodded gravely, held
out a hand. '*Rat vas vidyet*,' he said.

Gallagher shook his head.

'The Captain is happy to see you,' translated Trutin who
turned next to the plump man with a flabby white face and
deep-set eyes. 'Comrade Boris Milovych, Staff Captain of our
ship.' This time the note of pride was absent.

The plump man nodded, failed to offer his hand. '*Dobri
dyen*,' he said in a squeaky voice accompanied by a self-conscious smile.

'The Commissar says good day,' explained Trutin.

Yenev indicated the armchairs, they sat down and he
kicked off with a formal enquiry about Gallagher's black eye
and other injuries. Having expressed sympathy, he and Milovych got down to the detailed questioning, the latter doing
most of it with Trutin interpreting. Gallagher's briefcase was
nowhere to be seen but it was evident the contents had been
examined because he was not asked his name, nor his passenger's, though both were used. The Russians asked for details
of the flight : type of aircraft; its endurance; purpose of the
flight; why the lady was with him? What had caused the
ditching? Had any distress signals other than the MAYDAY
been transmitted? What emergency action had he taken before
ditching? Why did he think the aircraft exploded? Who
owned the aircraft? Not him? Who then? Where was the
Corporation based? Where had the journey begun? For what
purpose had he spent two days in Lisbon and two in Dakar?
What was his occupation? And his passenger's?

Informed no doubt by the aircraft's logbook, and his own,
the flight papers and other documents in the briefcase, many
of the Russians' questions were, Gallagher realized, put to
check his story. Milovych of the querulous voice and flabby
face was, he decided, the more dangerous of his questioners.

All the questions had, as it happened, been anticipated and
discussed at the Paris briefing and Gallagher was able to
answer them confidently and precisely. After an hour, when
it seemed the interrogation was about to end, Milovych re-

turned to the Bullock Development Corporation.

'You say the Corporation has many different interests. Please tell us about these?'

'Certainly. There are thirty or so subsidiaries in various parts of the United States. Many of those in the mid-West manufacture components for motor vehicle assembly lines; others are in paint and anti-corrosives. Several are in publishing, principally legal and technical books. Other activities by BDC subsidiaries include yacht and boat building, marinas, filling stations, hot-dog chains, and ...'

'Thank you,' Milovych had interrupted. 'What are the Corporation's interests in Sao Paulo?'

'We have a large beef canning operation there.'

'I see.' The Commissar nodded slowly, deliberately, as if trying to read the American's mind. 'You have said your background is aeronautical. For what purpose were you going to Sao Paulo?'

'To discuss a new plant for the canneries.'

'The business in Lisbon?'

'A Portuguese syndicate wants to manufacture BDC diesel injectors for marine engines under licence.'

'And your business in Dakar?'

'To check on the potential for property investment in the downtown area.'

'That does not sound like work for a man on the aeronautical side?'

'I said my *background* was aeronautical. I'm an executive of BDC. Various assignments come my way.'

Milovych thought about that, working his lower lip with his tongue. He then switched with studied casualness to the Allertons; their first names, ages, their house in Sao Paulo, their automobiles, their children. That had been easy – there were none – and so indeed had been all the other questions; the Paris briefing had been thorough.

Milovych changed the subject. 'You are an experienced pilot?'

'Four thousand hours, more or less.'

'Where did you do most of your flying?'

'In the United States Navy.'

'Why did you leave the Navy?'

'Deafness.' Gallagher touched the hearing-aid.

'Battle experience?'

'Vietnam.'

The Commissar's face set in a sardonic smile. 'Your country lost that war, I believe.'

'Politically perhaps, not militarily.'

'Quite so. Even your propaganda-drunk people could not take the United States in her imperialist – colonialist colours.'

'I hope the Russian people feel the same about Soviet activities in Africa.'

Milovych didn't appear to like that. 'My country assists oppressed peoples to liberate themselves,' he snapped.

'Like Hungary and Czechoslovakia?'

Yenev had intervened then; restored calm by suggesting a drink. Trutin went to the pantry off the dining space. He came back carrying a tray with glasses, vodka, lemon syrup and water, put the tray on the sideboard and served the drinks. Yenev raised his glass. 'To your rescue,' he said, bowing to Gallagher.

In the more friendly atmosphere which followed, the American asked if he might send a radio message to his corporation. 'To let them know we're okay,' he explained.

Yenev agreed, gave him a message pad. 'Write it there,' he said. 'I'll have it passed to the radio office.'

When Gallagher had completed the message he put another question to Yenev. 'Where will we be landing, Captain?'

Milovych broke in then. 'We have reported your rescue to Leningrad, requesting instructions. When the reply comes through you will be told.' Again the phoney smile.

Yenev said, 'It is too late for the Cape Verdes. Maybe Tenerife. We shall see.'

Soon afterwards Milovych announced that he had to leave. When the Commissar had gone Yenev pointed to Gallagher's empty glass. 'Another?' he enquired.

The American thanked him. Trutin took the glass and went with it to the sideboard. The phone rang in the adjoining office. Yenev went through to answer it. Gallagher moved over to a window. Trutin's back was towards him and the American was able to glance casually along the length of the maindeck. He counted the hatches. Seven. That over number one hold, though slightly smaller, looked much the same as the others. When he heard Yenev put down the phone he moved back towards the armchairs. It was then that he saw the microphone. In a gap between books on the shelves behind the chair in which he'd been sitting; a small metallic object, gleaming in a shaft of sunlight reflected by the long mirror over the sideboard.

# 10

Back in his cabin, the door once again locked on the outside, Gallagher did some solid thinking about what had happened. Though taping was standard interrogation procedure, the gleaming metallic object in the bookcase had shaken him. The Russians were taking the survivors' presence on board with extraordinary seriousness. The locked cabin, the thoroughness of the interrogation, its secret taping, were quite out of character with the occasion; rescue by a merchant ship of a man and woman from a private aircraft down in the sea. Why were they being treated like prisoners of war? The Russians were notoriously suspicious of foreigners, but surely not to that extent. Unless – the unspoken question seemed to answer itself – *Antonov*'s security rating was so high that exceptional measures were necessary to protect it.

They would now be busy transcribing the tape. The transcription would be scrupulously studied by Milovych who was clearly the ship's political boss, the man to worry about. When Judy's interrogation took place later in the afternoon she would be asked the same questions and her answers would be compared with his. Standard procedure, very thorough, but so fortunately had been the Paris briefing. And on many subjects – the Baron's performance, the Bullock Corporation's activities, his own background and experience – she would be expected to be ignorant. She had met him for the first time in Paris a few days earlier and their relationship – she had been briefed to say – was no more than that of passenger and pilot.

Nevertheless Gallagher was worried. The most thorough of briefings depended always on the memories of those briefed. He had no way of letting Judy know the questions he'd been asked, the answers given. No way of warning her that his interrogation had been taped, that hers would be and the transcripts compared. But she was an experienced operator, well trained and no stranger to interrogation. As to the message he'd asked Yenev to send to the Bullock Corporation, he had little doubt it would not be transmitted until it suited the Russians.

The ship's radio offices were on the after side of the bridge-deck, behind the chartroom. They consisted of an outer office from which a door led to a large compartment where trans-mitters, receivers, generators, scrambling computers and other equipment were housed. There was always an operator on duty in this room. Another door led to a compartment which housed the electronic encrypting machines, tape reels and cassettes of recorded messages. It was known as the cypher-room.

A flaxen-haired young man in white tropical uniform sat at a desk in the outer office. He was working through a stack of message sheets, entering details from them on a printed form. Grotskov, the senior communications officer, had a few minutes earlier gone into the cypher-room and locked the door. He was not to be disturbed, he'd said. The young man would certainly not disturb him. He feared the older man and disliked his body odour which he found peculiarly offensive in the tropics. The locked door usually meant that messages with a top security rating were being handled. There were some that only Grotskov himself dealt with; messages which his assistants never saw except in cryptographic form. The plain language versions were filed in a steel safe to which no one but Grotskov and the Captain had the combination.

On the other side of the locked door Grotskov had taken

off his white uniform jacket, hung it on a peg and set about his task. So busy was he that his pock-marked face, his chest and shoulders soon glistened with perspiration. He sat at the steel work-table, crouched over the cassette recorders. He would press the 'play' tab of one, listen briefly, then do the same with the other. After that he would press the 'rewind' tabs on both and go through the process again. He did it many times, listening intently, his face a study of concentration. At times, having identified sections of tape which particularly interested him, he would press the 'play' tabs on both recorders simultaneously. Sometimes he would shake his head, mutter under his breath and press the tabs with exasperated vigour.

At last he tired of what he was doing, switched off the recorders and removed the cassettes. He took his uniform jacket from the hook, replaced the cassettes in the safe, unlocked the door and went down to his cabin on Deck One.

He would not discuss this with Milovych yet. The theory was too tentative. There would have to be more tests, more recording, before he could commit himself. There was one recording he vitally needed to make. It could be the key to the puzzle. But how to get it? That was the problem which preoccupied him as he sat in his cabin, picking fitfully at his face and frowning at a picture of the Neva in a wintry landscape.

The wall clock in Yenev's cabin showed seventeen minutes past five. At four o'clock that afternoon the Englishwoman had been brought there by Olga Katutin. The interrogation had followed the same pattern as the American's, Milovych doing most of the questioning, Trutin once more acting as interpreter. At no stage had the woman betrayed any nervousness. On the contrary she remained calm and emotionless throughout. At the end she thanked them graciously for saving her life and that of her companion. They had been swift and most efficient, she said.

Trutin had brought tea from the pantry – served in glasses

with lemon and sugar – and after a formal exchange of pleasantries the proceedings ended with the return of Olga Katutin who took the Englishwoman off to her cabin. 'It will be the passenger's cabin,' Katutin said before they left. 'On Deck One. Very comfortable.'

As the door closed behind them Yenev said, 'Well, she and the American seem to tell the same story.'

'I suppose it's all right.' Milovych's concession was reluctant. 'Seems straightforward enough. But it was a necessary and essential precaution. We cannot afford to take chances. I'll compare the transcriptions as a matter of routine. At the moment I must confess I am satisfied. We can inform Leningrad.' Milovych removed the microphone from the bookshelf and began coiling the lead round two fingers. That done, he slid open the door of a cupboard beneath the lower shelf and took out the recorder. 'She's an attractive woman,' he said thoughtfully.

Yenev smiled inwardly. He'd seen the Commissar fall under the Englishwoman's spell. 'Yes. A fine face,' he agreed. 'In spite of the cut on her forehead.'

'She seemed more cultured than the American. Of the two I prefer her.'

I'm sure you do, thought Yenev. He had little doubt what was in Milovych's mind, but he didn't think the Commissar would have much joy there. He was not exactly God's gift to women, either in manner or appearance.

Yenev took a message pad from the bookshelf, settled it on his knee. 'The Leningrad signal. What d'you think?' It always saved time, he'd found, if Milovych had his say first.

The Commissar was thoughtful. 'Yes. The sooner we get rid of them the better. Leningrad already knows from our first signal who they are, what they do. Now I think we say something to the effect that the interrogation is completed, the survivors' stories are satisfactory subject to formal comparison of tape transcriptions. We request permission provisionally to land them at Tenerife by local helicopter.'

Yenev nodded. 'Yes. Something along those lines.' He

paused. 'Air-sea-rescue? Time to let them know we have these people on board?'

'No, no.' Milovych held up an admonitory hand. 'Not without Leningrad's authorization. They must make the decision.'

'Very well.' Yenev handed over the message pad. 'I suggest you write the signal.'

Milovych took the pad. 'I see you wish me to bear the responsibility, Comrade Yenev.'

'You always insist, *Comrade*, that political decisions are your responsibility.'

Gallagher was lying on the settee under the cabin windows when there was a knock on the door, followed by the sound of a key turning. He looked at his watch: it was just after six. The door opened and the chief officer came in. The dark eyes above the black mandarin moustache, the deeply-lined face, combined to give Stefan Lomov a villainous appearance.

'*Comment ça va?*' he enquired.

Gallagher got up from the settee, stretched his arms. '*Ca va,*' he said. '*J'ai faim.*'

'*Et soif?*'

'*Ah, oui. Bien soif.*'

A slow smile transformed Lomov's face. 'In that case,' he continued in French, 'I bring good news. It is to be vodka first, food afterwards. The Captain's compliments. You and the lady please to join him in his stateroom for refreshments.'

Gallagher was suddenly alert, 'Where is she?'

'In the passenger cabin. Next door.'

'Locked in?'

Lomov smiled again. Shook his head. 'No. That was a formality. While we checked credentials, you understand. These things are necessary, unfortunately. A lawless world. Now you are at liberty to move about freely. The only areas out of bounds are the same as they always are for passengers: the bridge, the radio office, the engineroom, the maindeck forward of this tower and the crew's quarters. These restrictions are necessary to protect crewmen.' Lomov waved a hand in a gesture of friendly understanding. 'The presence of strangers distracts them from their duties, you know. Especially if the strangers are beautiful ladies.'

Gallagher said, 'I get the message. At what time does the Captain expect us?'

'As soon as possible.'

'Right. I'll have a quick wash. Change into these.' He nodded towards a chair in the corner. On it were the clothes he'd worn when ditching. They'd been returned to him washed, ironed and neatly folded.

'*Bon*,' said Lomov. 'I see you later.'

Gallagher knocked on the outer door of the adjoining passenger cabin. Judy answered. 'Who is it?'

'Me,' he said, and she let him in. She'd already changed back into her own clothes.

As soon as the cabin door was closed she turned to him. 'Oh, Ben,' she whispered and he thought she was about to burst into tears. He put a warning finger to his lips, took her in his arms, held her tight. It was an unrehearsed emotional response, tension released; but it was dangerous. He broke the spell by holding her away. 'How's the forehead?'

She nodded understandingly. 'Nothing much. Just a headache. Soon be better. How's the eye?'

'Black, I guess. Otherwise okay.'

'Were you questioned?' She winked.

'Yes. At length.' He returned the wink.

'Me too. I wonder why?'

'The Russians are very thorough. Normal procedure I guess. Nothing to worry about. We've nothing to hide.'

'No. Of course.'

He whispered in her ear. 'There was a mike in the bookcase. The interrogations were recorded.'

Raising his voice again he told her of the Captain's invitation.

'Nice,' she said. 'Give me five minutes to do my face.'

87

'So you got back your vanity bag.'

'Of course. And you. Your things?'

He knew she was thinking of the briefcase. 'Yes . . . clothes, shaving gear, the lot.'

The Leningrad reply came through earlier than expected; on no account were air-sea-rescue or any other authorities or persons to be informed of the survivors' presence on board. Gallagher and Paddon were to be brought to Leningrad. They were to be told they would *probably* be landed at a French or British Channel port, weather and other circumstances permitting. The message went on to record that Bort, Garde Optics, a subsidiary of the Bullock Development Corporation, was involved with NASA and the Pentagon in research, manufacture and supply of high technology components for surveillance satellites. The message concluded with *– the existence and work of the BGO subsidiary is not to be discussed with the survivors who are to be treated in friendly and sympathetic fashion. It is of the utmost importance they should not suspect what we know nor our intentions. Acknowledge.*

For a number of reasons the final paragraph had driven Milovych to a high tide of indignation. First, the American never mentioned, even hinted at, Bort, Garde Optics. It was gross deception; highly suspicious. Second, Milovych took the peremptory hands-off warning in the message as a vote of no confidence. It clipped his wings in no uncertain fashion. Third, Leningrad would certainly have noted his failure to elicit information about Bort, Garde Optics during the interrogation – more particularly since he'd already sent a signal confirming that he was, after comparison of the transcripts, satisfied with the survivors' credentials. Fourth, it meant they'd have these people on board for at least another ten days; that complicated his security problem. Finally, the suffix coding indicated that the message had been signed by Borodin personally. Borodin was the KGB's senior man in Leningrad. His name was enough to make more important people than Milovych shiver.

The Commissar admitted none of this to Yenev. He was not going to give the Captain the satisfaction of knowing how humiliated, upset and insecure he felt. When Yenev had first read the Leningrad message and passed it over he'd said, 'You'll find it interesting, Boris Milovych.'

Milovych realized now that the way Yenev had said that, the quizzical half-amused stare, was a measure of the Captain's satisfaction at his discomfort.

And it hadn't helped when Yenev had added, 'I shall invite them to drinks this evening.' Particularly since Milovych had shortly before remarked that the American's deviousness was typical of an effete bourgeois pig.

'Drinks! This evening. Why?' Milovych's voice squeaked and he was uncomfortably aware that it was pitched too high. But how could he help that? He was upset.

'Because, *Comrade* Milovych, your master in Leningrad has commanded that the survivors be treated in friendly and sympathetic fashion.'

Milovych simmered with inward anger. One day, he resolved, he would make Yenev pay dearly for his patronizing manner and studied lack of respect. The only comfort he could draw from the Leningrad message lay in Borodin's injunction that the survivors' presence on board should not be made known. That fully justified his instruction to Grotskov not to transmit the personal messages from Gallagher and Paddon informing their people that they were safe and well on board *Antonov*.

# 11

When she came from behind the mooring winches he was at the stern rail, no more than a dark shadow in the moonlight. Despite her rubber soles and stealthy approach he must have heard her for he called, 'Hi, there,' in a low voice before she reached him.

She gave an answering 'Hi.'

He came forward, took her arm, led her to the rail where they looked down over the stern along the luminous path of the moon. Behind them the engineroom housing loomed white and cliff-like; beyond it the radar mast swung slowly across the night sky, starboard to port, port to starboard, a giant pendulum marking the rhythm of the swell.

The silence was broken by the sound of water along the sides and the distant rumble of the diesels. The stern, vibrating to the beat of the propellers beneath it, was harshly alive. Wafts of diesel exhaust, warm and acrid, drifted down from the funnel and sullied the night air.

It was a wonderfully secluded spot, suggested by him when they'd made the whispered assignment on their way to the saloon after the Captain's party.

Now they spoke in whispers.

'Interrogation okay, Ben?'

'Sure. Yours?'

'Straightforward. I didn't know about the mike, but I don't think I boobed.'

'That's great. I figure this is a safe place.'

'Bugs in the cabin, you think?'

'We have to assume that,' he said.

'How did you enjoy the party?'

'A bit forced. Everybody being polite. But a good sign. They seem to be happier about us now than at the start.'

'I thought so too. Even the asides in Russian were not unkind.'

'Yeh. Difficult to remain deadpan when they chat away in Russian and you're expected not to understand.'

'I know what you mean. I could have hugged Dave O'Dowd when they were interrogating me. That briefing was so good. What do you think of the Captain and his Commissar?'

'Yenev's a nice guy. Milovych's a creep.'

'A dangerous creep,' she said.

'That's right. Need to watch him.'

'And Stefan Lomov. What about him?' She inclined her head towards Gallagher, trying to read his expression in the moonlight.

'Not as sinister as he looks, I'd say. Seems to fancy you.'

She laughed self-consciously. 'I thought you might say that. Very attentive, wasn't he?'

Gallagher made a noise somewhere between a snort and a dry laugh. 'Attentive? You could fool me. Did you hear his aside about you to Grotskov?'

'No. What was that?'

'Just as well. Not repeatable. Even in Russian.'

She laughed gaily. 'Bad as that. Milovych shooed him away from me.'

'No. How did he do that?'

'Reminded Lomov in a rather nasty way of some returns he'd failed to put in. Told him to get busy. That did it.' She paused. 'Learn anything?'

'Not at the party. They were guarded with each other. I guess. As if they thought one of us *might* understand Russian.

I heard something at supper afterwards. From the table right behind us. Remember? Two young engineers, the third officer and a couple of radio operators were there.'

'What did you hear?'

'The third officer – Grigor Ivanovitch – was telling some joke about a passing-out parade at Kaliningrad.'

'Clean I hope.'

'That wasn't the point. *He* was in the parade. Got the seamanship prize.'

'So?'

'It was at the Higher Naval School. A training academy for naval officers. Not for the merchant navy.'

'I see.' It was a long-drawn-out *see*. 'What did you make of the civilians' table, Ben? Doctor Linovsky and company?

'I spoke to him at the party. The Captain introduced us, said Linovsky and his assistants were on board for this voyage only. Linovsky is a refrigerator expert from the Baltic Shipyard in Leningrad where *Antonov* was built. He speaks good English. Interesting man. Studied physics at Trinity College, Dublin, for five years. Has a good sense of humour. He told me that the plant for the refrigerated cargo space had been giving teething troubles. He and his assistants are on board to sort it out before arrival in Leningrad.'

'Did he say where the refrigerated space was?'

'No. I didn't follow up. Unwise to appear interested. But I guess it's number one hold.'

A cloud drifted across the moon and darkness closed in on the night like a drawn curtain. A light breeze touched them and she teased back strands of hair which had blown over her face. His shoulder pressed lightly against hers.

'Wonder if it will be worthwhile,' she said. 'Our venture, I mean.'

'I guess what we've seen so far confirms that this is no ordinary merchant ship. That alone justifies the effort.'

'We'll be off Tenerife the day after tomorrow. There's not much time left if they decide to land us there.'

'O'Dowd thought that unlikely.'

'Yes, I know. I didn't really understand why he was so certain. But . . .'

They heard footsteps on the steel deck behind them. Two men talking in Russian were coming down the starboard side. They'd not yet reached the mooring winches. Gallagher grabbed her arm, led her in the darkness to the port side. They moved silently past the winches, reached the after end of the engineroom casing and walked on until they came to the door to the accommodation tower. They were soon in their cabins.

The stooping man with the domed head and myopic eyes behind pebble lenses went back to his desk, picked up a sheet of paper, held it close to his face and resumed his restless pacing. As he moved up and down the large office he read and re-read the message many times. It was from the *Antonov*.

A younger man, notebook in hand, stood by an old-fashioned fireplace, his back to the electric fire. He watched the pacing figure in silence, knowing that when Borodin concentrated interruption was not permitted. What was it, the young man was thinking, in the mind of this man which lent to his instincts and judgement the quality of genius; a genius which had taken him into the highest echelons of the KGB hierarchy?

His thoughts were interrupted by Borodin's voice. He had stopped pacing and gone to a window which looked out over the Neva. 'Very well,' he said enigmatically. 'We shall find out. Take a message to Muelher in Washington. Begins: Benjamin Dwight Gallagher aged forty-three, US Navy Airforce, now employed as executive Bullock Development Corporation Inc. Saint Louis, USA. Stop. A subsidiary of the corporation – Bort, Garde Optics of Phoenix, Arizona – is employed on research, development and manufacture of high technology components for surveillance satellites. Stop. Obtain without delay full information about this man, the BD Corporation and BG Optics. Message ends.'

Borodin left the window, stared at his assistant through the steel-rimmed lenses. 'Classify that "Most Secret". Prefix it "Immediate action". Put my name on it.'

The young man finished writing, read back his shorthand.

'Good,' said Borodin. 'Take another message. This time for the *Antonov*.'

# 12

On the morning of the second day the survivors were again sent for. Trutin brought the message and accompanied them to the Captain's office. There they were greeted in friendly fashion by Yenev and Milovych. Had they slept well? Enjoyed their breakfast? They had. Good. Now there was news for them.

Yenev shuffled the papers on his desk, picked up a message sheet, put it down again, spoke to Trutin. He'd not gone far when Milovych interrupted. Yenev held up a peremptory hand. Milovych squeaked some sort of protest. Yenev frowned, admonished the Commissar in a low voice and went on talking to Trutin.

When Yenev had finished the steward turned to the survivors. 'The Captain says he has received a reply from the management in Leningrad. There are difficulties if you are put ashore in Tenerife. Technical and cost problems. For this reason the management has decided you must remain on board at present. The Captain says you will probably be landed by shore-based helicopter at a British or French Channel port. It will depend on weather and other circumstances. The help of the British and French authorities will also be necessary and we are not sure of this.' Trutin's tone suggested little confidence in British and French authorities. 'So you will be with us for another six days.'

Gallagher looked at Judy, turned to the steward, smiled, cleared his throat. 'Please tell the Captain we understand. We are grateful for all that is being done for us.'

Trutin translated and Milovych, not to be outdone, had his say. The steward's expression as he watched the Commissar, the flicker of his eyes, were unsympathetic though he nodded submissively when the plump man had finished.

'Staff Captain Milovych says,' interpreted Trutin, 'that you are very welcome on board. He hopes you will relax and enjoy yourselves. He hopes you will please remember that it is not permitted to visit the bridge, the engineroom, the radio office or the maindeck forward of this accommodation tower. He says the quarters of the crew on Decks Three and Four are also out of bounds. He hopes you will understand this. The crew understand only Russian, therefore passengers must not speak to them except through an interpreter. He hopes also that you enjoy the voyage.' With a wry smile, Trutin added, 'You can see the Staff Captain hopes for many things. Thank you.'

Gallagher said, 'Tell the Staff Captain that we are grateful for his kind and helpful remarks. Tell him also that we hope – ' Gallagher grinned – 'that we do not give him any cause for complaint.'

Trutin translated and the Commissar arranged his small eyes and putty-like face in an affable smile.

Yenev looked at the clock on the bulkhead, remarked that it was almost noon and asked to be excused. He would be required on the bridge.

The survivors took the hint, thanked the Russians once again, and the party broke up.

In the radio office late that afternoon Grotskov handed two envelopes to Salpern, the junior of his four assistants. 'Put these in their cabins, Salpern. I will be busy here for the next hour.'

The envelopes contained 'replies' to the radio messages he

was supposed to have transmitted for Gallagher and Paddon. Milovych had said, 'Make the replies brief. No more than an acknowledgement and an expression of relief that they are safe. The less said the better.' So Grotskov had composed brief messages and to ensure the quality of their English he'd asked Doctor Linovsky to look through them. The Doctor had done so and made some alterations.

When Salpern had gone Grotskov went into the cypherroom and locked the soundproof door. He took a number of cassettes from the safe, examined them carefully, chose two, placed them in the recorders and switched on.

The more he listened the more certain he became that his theory was correct. But he lacked the means of proving it; a vital link in the chain was missing. He switched off the recorders and sat head in hands glowering at them, wondering by what means he could possibly obtain the evidence he needed. He recalled the conversation with Linovsky after the doctor's game of chess with the American. But he didn't want to take Linovsky into his confidence. He disliked the man and knew it was mutual. The phone on the table rang. It was the Captain. 'What news of the air-sea-rescue search, Leonid Grotskov?'

'It is still active, Captain. We have monitored several messages. Aircraft, ships and shore stations reporting. All recorded negative results – but the search continues. Some of the international broadcasts have given the story as a news item. You know – private aeroplane lost in sea on flight from Dakar to Brazil. Man and woman missing. Ships and aircraft searching for them. So far without results.'

'It would be surprising if there were results,' said Yenev, 'but thank you.'

Grotskov replaced the phone, scratched thoughtfully under a bare armpit, frowned at the recorders. Where was he? Oh yes. The missing link. If only . . . quite suddenly the answer came to him. The ship's concert, of course. He would go and see Olga Katutin. Discuss the matter with her. Ask for her co-operation. She was on excellent terms with Simyon Linovsky. He might do it for her. It was still too soon to tell Milovych. The Commissar would want proof. Now if all went well, he would get it.

'Muelher doesn't waste time.' Borodin got up from the desk, the Washington message still in his hand, and began pacing his office.

The young man by the fireplace waited patiently. Borodin peered and read, peered and read, lifting his head at times as if searching the distance for inspiration.

He's thinking, weighing the words, thought the young man. For Borodin it's a game, like chess or a crossword puzzle.

The tall man stopped. 'Muelher confirms that our information on Gallagher is correct. Both as to background and present function. He *was* in the US Navy; he *is* an executive of the Bullock Development Corporation; one of their subsidiaries *is* Bort, Garde Optics Inc.; they *do* work in close co-operation with and under the direction of NASA and the Pentagon – and they have contracts with them for satellite components. But Muelher gives a new angle. Listen to this.' Borodin held the message close to his eyes, focused intently upon it. 'BGO have developed certain electro-optical components for surveillance satellites. These components have an exceptionally high security rating. Regret efforts to obtain more specific information through NASA/Pentagon sources unsuccessful.'

Borodin stroked his chin. A prominent, outward-jutting blue-shadowed chin.

The young man said nothing, knowing that Borodin was thinking aloud rather than addressing him.

Borodin began pacing again. The thinking aloud continued : 'So Gallagher is a man we should talk to. And if he doesn't wish to talk – well.' He thrust his arms out like the wings of a vulture about to fly. 'Well,' he repeated, 'we know how to make him talk.'

98

The young man smiled dutifully. 'We certainly do, Comrade Borodin.'

For Gallagher and Judy the second day had seen life on board assume a settled pattern. In the morning, anxious for exercise and an opportunity to be alone, they walked on the lower bridge-deck. They would have liked to have sat there, too, for the weather was perfect but deck chairs were conspicuously absent; probably deliberately, decided Gallagher. There was nothing in English for them to read; loud-speakers in the main lounge relayed news bulletins in Russian, and a daily news sheet, in Russian, came from the radio office. Much as they would have liked to read it they dared not. So they talked and philosophized, carefully avoiding the subject uppermost in their minds for fear of bugging. Another subject they avoided, also much on their minds, was the changing nature of their relationship. Each was aware of a growing dependence upon the other, but conscious that emotional involvement could be the kiss of death to a mission as dangerous as theirs neither admitted it.

In the dining-saloon they sat at the Captain's table. Milovych, Zhakas the chief engineer – a shrivelled wizened little man with a lipless mouth – Lomov and Olga Katutin were others at the table. But either because their hours of duty varied or they chose not to attend all meals, it was only at *uzhin*, the evening meal, that most of them had been present.

Trutin who served at the Captain's table, having established a proprietary interest in the survivors, would explain the menus to them with paternal concern: *kaputsa*, he had pointed out, was cabbage soup, but cabbage was *shechi*: *pitoche myasneye* were meatballs, meat being *myasa*; and *kisyel* was a cold, fruit flavoured jelly-like substance, whereas jelly was *zhelye*. He himself much favoured *kisyel* but of course if they wished there was always *marozhenaye* which was ice-cream – and so on. Trutin's good-natured but laboured explanations of these culinary linguistic variables –

amplified by Olga Katutin or Stefan Lomov if they happened to be present – would be listened to with patiently simulated interest by Gallagher and Judy who would then cap them with splendid but deceitful mispronunciations.

It was on the way to the evening meal, going down the stairway to the dining-saloon, that Gallagher stopped, took her arm and whispered, 'The reply came this morning. Found it in my cabin.'

'Same here.'

'Mine's phoney.'

'Mine, too.' She gave him a startled sideways glance as if she'd just seen something rather unpleasant, and he knew she was wondering what had led the Russians to this deception. He'd been worrying about that too.

After the evening meal Olga Katutin told them there would be a cinema show in the main lounge that night. 'At a quarter past eight,' she said. 'It is the story of a peasant girl who wishes to be a ballerina. She reaches Moscow. Then the story is very tragic. But I shall not tell you.' Katutin tossed her head with schoolmarmish authority. 'Yes. It is sad. But very good. I have seen it already in Leningrad.'

During the cinema Gallagher fell asleep and had to be awakened by an embarrassed Judy because of his snoring. Afterwards they joined Stefan Lomov and Olga Katutin for coffee and a nightcap in the lounge. Lomov, eyes and teeth flashing, concentrated his attention on Judy with whom he conducted a verbal flirtation in animated French; Gallagher and Olga Katutin were discussing the film when Grotskov came into the lounge and looked casually round before joining them. Once or twice after that Katutin turned to him for an opinion but he declined to be drawn. 'My English is not sufficient for such talk,' he protested.

Whether it was laziness or boredom, or simply the man being honest, Gallagher could not say; but whatever the cause the radio officer took little part in the conversation, though he listened intently, his pale yellow eyes darting from one speaker to the other.

The conversation flagged, Grotskov looked at his watch, pleaded duty and left. Olga Katutin followed, having reminded them to call at the sick-bay the next morning. It was some time before Judy, on the grounds that she was tired, was able to shake off Lomov. She and Gallagher left the lounge together. Out in the passageway she yawned, said, 'Let's get some fresh air. I'm almost asleep.'

'Go ahead.' Gallagher fingered his bruised eye which was changing from black to green. 'Same place, I'll join you.'

A few minutes later he was with her at the stern-rail. It was later than on the previous night and the moon rode high in a sky filled with stars and fleecy ranks of cirrus clouds. The trade wind blew more strongly and small white frilled seas rolled in from the north-east, slapping the ship's sides and throwing up wisps of spray, the superstructure creaking and groaning in protest.

Judy mentioned the radio messages. 'How did you know yours was a fake, Ben?'

'The project authentication was missing. A single word. Should have been included in the text of the message. It wasn't. Yours?'

She nodded in the darkness. 'Same thing. I knew at once.' She darted a puzzled, apprehensive glance at him. 'Think our cover's blown?'

'I guess not. We'd be under lock and key if it were. More likely they don't want the world to know we're on board. Not yet anyway.'

'Why not?' she challenged.

He was silent for a moment, anxious not to tell her what he really thought. Instead he said, 'They're cagey people, Judy. Good poker players.'

'There's something strange going on, Ben. I don't like it. Frightens me.'

Gallagher decided it was time to change the subject. He switched to the other events of the day: the Leningrad message; the changing images of Olga Katutin and Stefan Lomov who had lent them items of clothing and showed other kindnesses. They spoke of Katutin as 'the Kat' – of Grotskov as 'the Grot' and agreed he was sinister. Milovych was already 'the Creep'.

'In Yenev's office this morning,' Gallagher spoke in little more than a whisper, 'while he was telling us about the Leningrad message, I could watch the maindeck through a forward window. Saw something interesting. Doctor Linovsky and his three assistants went along to number one hold followed by two sailors carrying deck-buckets. The assistants had what looked like large briefcases hanging from shoulder straps. Linovsky unlocked a watertight door under the break of the focs'le immediately ahead of the hatch to number one, and led the party down below. The two sailors remained on deck, began washing paintwork close to the watertight door.'

'That makes sense, doesn't it, Ben? The trouble with the refrigerator plant? Wouldn't they be seeing to that?'

'Yeh. Could be. One thing sure doesn't make sense though. After the cinema – in the lounge less than fifteen minutes ago – two of Linovsky's boys were chatting. Sitting right behind me. One of them was belly-aching. Ship's library list same as last voyage when he'd read the lot. Said they damn well ought to change it for the next voyage.'

'Sorry, Ben. Don't follow.'

'Linovsky told me that he and his assistants joined the ship in Leningrad for *this* voyage only.'

'Maybe you misunderstood him.'

Gallagher shook his head. 'I don't think I misunderstood. This voyage *only*, he said. To deal with teething troubles in the refrigeration plant. Yenev said the same thing.' The American was emphatic. 'Something queer about this ship. A sick-bay bigger than a frigate's, with X-ray apparatus, an operating table, decontamination unit, the lot. Unusual aerial configuration. Five radio operators instead of the one normal in a bulk-carrier. Difficult to keep count, but from what I've seen I reckon the crew to be nearer seventy than the thirty-five we would have in one of these. The ship swarms with them. You tell me why?'

She touched his hand on the rail. 'I'm no sailor, Ben, so I wouldn't know. Have to take your word for it.'

'Thank you, ma'am.' Gallagher laughed quietly, ignored the hand that touched his. 'Pretty flimsy I agree. More hunch than anything else. Maybe it's just Russian overmanning. They do that. Gives full employment.'

'I think,' said Judy, 'we've got to be careful not to make what we see fit our assumptions. Better to do it the other way round.'

'You're dead right. Thanks for the reminder. You should get into instructing at Camp Peary.'

'Are you, Mr Gallagher, telling me that I'm lecturing?'

He cleared his throat. She'd begun to recognize that signal of tension. 'We need evidence, Judy. Solid evidence. Have to get busy and find it, I guess. Suspicion isn't enough. Only five or six days left.' They had a long discussion on ways and means then, after which they returned to the subject of the Leningrad message.

She said, 'You know, what puzzles me is why Dave O'Dowd said nothing about the possibility of our being landed at a French or British Channel port.'

'He must have thought that contingency didn't figure. He was strong on the possibility that we'd be carried on to Leningrad. Said the ship's staff would want to leave final responsibility for our discharge to the authorities ashore.'

'I suppose you're right.' She was dubious. 'But I'm still puzzled. Everything else about that briefing was so thorough.'

# 13

'Has Simyon Linovsky decided yet?' Grotskov sat astride a surgical chair in the sick-bay watching Olga Katutin's back as she rearranged sets of bandages in a cupboard.

'He says the only song like that he really knows is *The Mountains of Mourne.*'

The communications officer frowned. 'Do you know it?'

'He played it for me on the guitar. I have not heard it before. Simyon says it's an Irish folk song. Very well known in the English-speaking world.'

'That is good. Now we must hope he also knows it.' Grotskov's yawn drew taut the skin of his pock-marked face; it was the colour of parchment, a good match to his strawlike hair.

'Tired?' Olga Katutin regarded him quizzically.

'Yes. I worked for hours last night after I left the lounge.'

'What work, Leonid Grotskov?'

'It concerns what we have been discussing.'

'You talk in a strange way. So mysteriously. Can't you tell me what it is? And this business with Simyon Linovsky. Why is it so important?'

'I cannot tell you now. Later I will. You must accept that I have good reasons.' The pale eyes, yellow as lemons, stared at her like a cat's without the trace of a flicker.

'I'm sure you have,' she said. 'Otherwise I would not help you.'

They reached the forward end of the bridge-deck, Gallagher stopped, looked at his watch. 'Eleven o'clock. We've done three miles. Know what?' He lowered his voice. 'I'm going to the cabin. Throat's dry. I need a Polo Mint.'

'Bring me one please.'

He watched her for a moment in silence, thought what a remarkable woman she was, admired her calmness. She'd rearranged her hair so that the small red scar scarcely showed and he smiled inwardly at the display of feminine vanity. It was at moments like this that he would remind himself that she was an operative, an accomplice on a difficult assignment; then he would push sentiment and emotion from his mind and become brusque and businesslike. Sensing that she was the more easily swayed emotionally he was determined to keep their relationship free of involvement, at least until the mission had been accomplished. After that? Maybe a brief affair; then no doubt they'd go their separate ways. Espionage was not an occupation for the married.

Once in the cabin he locked the door, produced the tube of Polo Mints from an inside pocket, opened it and shook four on to the table. He took the next two from the tube. At first glance they looked like the others; but they were flat, without holes and heavier. From each he peeled white coats of poly-thene to reveal minute microphone transmitters. He took one, released its adhesive suckers and went through to the bathroom where he pressed it against the bulkhead some distance from the washbasin.

With the basin half-filled he adjusted the tap to a steady drip, took off his spectacles and worked on the micro-receiver in the hearing-aid. Satisfied with the adjustment he went back to the cabin, shut the bathroom door and stood as far from it as possible. The drip could not be heard. He put on the spectacles and listened again. The drip-drip of the tap sounded loud and clear and he knew the 837-Sr was transmitting. It was the standard bug used by CIA agents in communist-bloc countries. Though made in the United States it was of Soviet design, an exact replica of the bug most commonly used by the KGB.

After he'd tested another 837-Sr he put them in his pocket, replaced the mints in the Polo tube, dropped it into a drawer and left the cabin.

Judy was on the bridge-deck leaning over the rail looking out to sea when he rejoined her. They chatted casually, their hands touched and he passed her an 837-Sr. While they talked she blew her nose in gently feminine fashion after which he saw the bug go into her pocket with the tissue.

'Look out,' he warned, 'the boy-friend's coming. This could be your chance. I'll try to keep him talking.'

'*Ah, bonjour, madame, m'sieu. Comme ça va?*' Lomov took Judy's hand and kissed it in an extravagant imitation of French gallantry.

'*Ca va,*' they replied.

He came to the rail, pushed himself between them. They exchanged small talk during the course of which she told Gallagher that while he'd been in his cabin the *Antonov* had passed a fishing fleet.

'Look,' she pointed astern. In the distance the large bulk of a factory ship could be seen heading south; around the big ship, spread over many square miles of ocean, were the black dots of her catchers. Gallagher counted eleven of them.

'Are they trawling?' he asked.

'No. Line fishing,' said Lomov. 'Long lines with thousands of hooks. When the fish-holds are full they transfer their catches to the factory ship for processing. The flesh is canned. Bones, offal, skin are made into fertilizers. Nothing is wasted.' Lomov explained the importance of the fishing industry to Russia's economy. That led to a more general discussion, to comparisons of the USSR and USA economies.

It was interrupted by Judy. 'Economics aren't my subject,'

she declared, pushing away strands of hair the wind had blown across her face. 'I'll leave you men to it. Must do some washing.'

Lomov protested, white teeth flashing under the darkly drooping moustache. 'Madame. You leave us so soon?'

'I'm afraid I must. Some other time we'll talk, you and I. But please – not economics.' The gently mocking eyes, the half-open mouth, the tips of milk-white teeth above moistened lips were sensuous and provocative.

Lomov watched her move away until she'd disappeared. He turned to Gallagher with a sigh. 'A beautiful woman.'

'Yes, indeed,' said Gallagher as if passing the topic in review. 'You were saying . . . ?'

Lomov frowned, seemed lost for a moment. 'Ah, what was it? Yes. I was saying that the West has higher standards of living but the USSR has stronger defences.' He paused, smiled. 'You know, the West has mountains of butter. We have mountains of guns. You cannot defend a state with butter.'

Five minutes, Gallagher was saying to himself, she needs five minutes. I must keep this going.

It took Judy little time to get to her cabin, write the note and place it in the vanity bag with some coins, a lipstick, a keyring and tissues. After that she went down the passageway to Lomov's office and once in shut the door behind her. Everything now depended on how long Gallagher could keep the chief officer talking. Though she was keyed up, nerves taut, her judgement was cool and detached. Sound training had contributed to that.

She made a quick inspection of the office. It was simply furnished. A desk in the centre, behind it a chair with its back to the forward windows through which came daylight. There were two chairs on the near side of the desk. Book-shelves and cupboards lined the port bulkhead, beneath them stood two easy chairs and a small table. A door on the star-board side led to Lomov's day-room : beyond that lay his sleeping cabin. To the left of the door a cargo-loading model of *Antonov* surmounted a computer; on the bulkhead above it there was a framed sectional plan and a large coloured photograph of the ship on her sea trials. To the right of the loading model stood two steel filing cabinets. Judy concentrated first on the model and sectional plan, but the quick examination was unrewarding. The caption on number one hold – both on the model and the plan – spelt out two words in the Cyrillic characters of the Russian alphabet. They translated simply as 'refrigerated space'.

She went to the desk. It was a large one : kneehole in the middle, banks of drawers to left and right, cupboards on their reverse sides.

Now, she asked herself, where do I put the bug? The best places were always the most obvious so she rejected in quick succession the bookcase, the underside of the desk top – either in the kneehole or along the edges. The underside of the computer on which stood the loading model was about eight inches above the deck. That, she decided, would do. Holding the open vanity bag in one hand and the tissue-wrapped bug in the other, she knelt in front of the computer. She was about to place the bug when she heard the sound of a door opening. Someone was coming in from the day-room.

She dropped the purse, scattering coins, lipstick and key-ring on to the deck where she knelt. Seconds later Natasha Mekhlis, the blonde stewardess who looked after Lomov's cabin, came in through the door. She regarded Judy with a worried frown, questioned her sharply in Russian. Judy shook her head. 'I don't speak Russian. *Je ne parle pas la Russe.*'

The stewardess shrugged her shoulders. '*Ya ni gavaryu angliski pa frantsuski*' – I don't speak English or French.

They stared at each other in silent hostility until Judy broke the stalemate. Indicating to the Russian girl that she must watch, she re-enacted her own entry into the office; first she went to the loading model, looked at the coloured photograph of the *Antonov* above it. Then she stepped back, dropped the open vanity bag, knelt and collected its scattered contents. Finally she went over to the desk, took the sheet of folded notepaper from her bag and laid it on the blotter.

The stewardess joined her at the desk, looked at the note, seemed to sense then what had happened and nodded. Judy managed a forced smile. 'Thank you,' she said and walked out of the office with her heart pounding so hard against its rib-cage that she feared the stewardess might hear it. Throughout the incident her left hand had clutched tightly the tissue with the bug in it.

She made for the bridge-deck, cursing her luck. Not only had she failed to place the bug but she'd very nearly been caught in the act of trying to. The only thing that pleased her was the planning, the precautions she'd taken; the note to Lomov, the vanity bag, had probably saved the day.

Gallagher and Lomov were still on the bridge-deck when she rejoined them.

'Washing done? So quick?' Lomov's ample eyebrows arched in surprise.

'Yes. One pair of tights.' She laughed. 'You see there are advantages in travelling light.' Then she frowned, became serious. 'That French novel I said you must read, Stefan?'

'Yes. I remember.'

'I've written down the title and the author's name. Put the note on your desk. I tried to explain to your stewardess but she doesn't speak French or English.'

'Ah. Natasha Mekhlis. She speaks only Russian. But a very good stewardess.'

'Dangerously attractive, I'd have thought,' she teased.

'Ah, so.' An unabashed Stefan Lomov's eyes settled on her casually-buttoned shirt where the round of her breasts pressed against the Sea Island cotton. 'Beauty is often dangerously attractive.'

'Stefan Lomov, you are a wicked man,' she said. The chief officer's eyes gleamed with pleasure at the mischievous smile which accompanied this rebuke.

Shortly before noon Pico de Teide, the peak of Tenerife, was sighted at a distance of more than seventy-five miles. At first it seemed no r.ore than a pale blue shape on the horizon, scarcely visible in the shimmering heat of late morning; but as time went on and distance diminished the peak could be seen for what it was: a soaring thrust of mountain, its summit a volcanic cone more than twelve thousand feet above the sea, its sides rising steeply from Las Canadas.

Lomov had left and Judy and Gallagher, alone at last, watched the peak in silence, enjoying its remote grandeur. It was the centrepiece of the huge canvas of sea and sky through which they were moving, the ship brushing aside indigo seas which rolled in from the north-east, their crests ruffled like old lace. The wind blew fresh and keen, seagulls wheeled and screamed and a school of dolphins kept station on the bow, leaping and diving.

'It's gorgeous,' she said. 'Wish the circumstances were different.'

'Just as well they're not.' He was offhand. 'Could be problems.'

She brushed back wayward strands of hair in a familiar gesture, looked up at him affectionately. 'Nice problems I hope.' She added in a whisper, 'I boobed.'

It was not at once clear to him what she meant. When the penny dropped he enquired, quite casually, 'Disastrous?' For the benefit of a passing sailor he pointed to the distant peak. 'Great, isn't it?'

She waited until the sailor had gone. 'No. I don't think it was disastrous. But I've still got it.'

'You must be careful.' He spoke with uncharacteristic severity. 'Don't take chances.'

She sensed in his tone a measure of disapproval, an innuendo of reproach, and it irritated her. *Don't take chances.* What utter rubbish. They'd been doing nothing else since leaving Paris.

From the bridge above came the sound of eight bells followed by a blast on the ship's siren.

'Noon,' he murmured. 'I must go.'

She nodded curtly, watching him with mixed feelings as he walked away.

In the afternoon *Antonov* passed through the channel between Gran Canaria and Tenerife and by late evening the Canaries were no more than dark smudges on the southern horizon.

# 14

After the evening meal they gathered in the lounge for coffee : Lomov, Gallagher, Judy and Olga Katutin. She raised the subject of the ship's concert. 'Of course,' she said in a manner which brooked no opposition. 'You will do something. The other passengers – Simyon Linovsky and his assistants – they have already agreed.' The mock disapproval with which she regarded Gallagher and Judy was belied by the smile in her eyes.

'When is it?' asked Gallagher.

'Two days from now – Thursday night. In the recreation room.'

'Maybe I could do a Cossack dance.'

'No, Mister Gallagher. You are not a Cossack.'

Judy said, 'I'm hopeless, Olga. Can't do anything. Let alone speak Russian.'

'Nonsense.' Olga Katutin put on her severe look. 'With that face and body you don't need to speak. Just be yourself. The sailors will be very happy to look.'

'Mime,' said Judy. 'That's a brilliant idea.'

'Mime? What is mime?' With the tip of a finger Olga Katutin pushed her steel framed spectacles higher up the bridge of her nose.

'Miming. No words. You just act the part.'

'That? Yes I know. We do it also in Russia . . .'

Lomov interrupted in French. 'You could be a statue. The

Venus de Milo. Statues don't speak.'

'I don't fancy myself as an armless nude, Stefan Lomov.'

'Then we make an exception.' He chuckled wolfishly. 'The Venus de Milo *with* arms.'

Olga Katutin pointed an accusing finger at Gallagher. 'You can sing, Mister Gallagher. Such a deep voice. Bass? Yes?'

Gallagher said, 'How did you know. As a matter of fact I sang in the Metropolitan State Opera for years. Until this happened.' He patted the hearing-aid.

Olga Katutin's eyes widened. She looked at the others. 'Is this true?'

'No. He's a liar,' said Judy. 'But he croons. Not very well. I've heard him.'

'Thanks for the compliment,' said Gallagher.

'We have a very good guitar player. He can make music for your song.'

Gallagher shook his head. 'I don't know any Russian songs, Olga.'

'Simyon Linovsky knows many songs. Not only Russian. Ask him. He will tell you. Now,' she turned to Judy. 'What will you do?'

'I've been thinking. Couldn't I mime a fashion model. I used to be one once.'

'In those clothes?' Gallagher shook his head. 'You must be joking.'

'Natasha Mekhlis has the same shape and size.' Olga Katutin's eyes travelled over Judy's shapely body. 'She will lend you something. A beautiful evening gown she has, I know.'

Conversation was interrupted by the chief steward's announcement that the film *War and Peace* was about to be shown in the recreation room.

As they left the lounge Lomov took Judy's arm. 'Keep the seat next to you for me,' he whispered. 'I'll be along soon.'

The lights were still on when they got to the recreation room. Gallagher estimated the audience to be close on fifty. Olga

Katutin led them to the front row where Yenev, Milovych, Dr Linovsky and the chief engineer were sitting. She took a seat between Judy and Gallagher, the lights went down and the film began. Soon afterwards Grotskov arrived, and took the seat next to Judy. It was the only one left in the front row.

'Sorry,' she whispered. 'This is the chief officer's. He asked me to keep it for him. He'll be here any minute now.'

Grotskov grunted something, moved into the row behind. The chief officer arrived shortly afterwards and plunged down next to her. Rather too close, she thought, but it suited her purpose.

Gallagher's eyes were on the screen, but not his mind, and that wasn't only because he'd seen the film before. He had a great deal to think about. In a few whispered snatches of conversation he'd got the gist of Judy's failed attempt to place a bug that morning. She seemed pretty sure that Natasha Mekhlis had been satisfied with the mimed explanation. But he wondered.

His own task had been successfully accomplished. Knowing that Yenev would be on the bridge for the ritual of the noon position, Gallagher had gone to the Captain's suite with a radio message for transmission to the Bullock Development Corporation. Whether or not it was sent was of little importance; its purpose was to give him a reason for being in Yenev's office at midday.

He'd left the message on the desk, having fixed an 837-Sr on the underside of the Captain's desk chair. That operation had taken less than fifteen seconds and there'd been no interruptions.

During the afternoon, as was his custom, Gallagher had exercised on the bridge-deck, the one on which the Captain's suite was situated. The 837-Sr had worked well. In the course of an hour the micro-receiver in his hearing-aid picked up Yenev's end of two telephone conversations, a discussion between Yenev and the chief engineer, and another between Yenev and Trutin. Nothing of consequence had emerged from these but at least they'd demonstrated to Gallagher that he was able to exercise a degree of surveillance – and that represented real progress. Other thoughts which occupied his mind were the faked radio messages he and Judy had received and the knowledge – gleaned from a conversation he'd overheard in the saloon between Gallagher and Doctor Linovsky – that the search for the missing Beechcraft and its occupants was still proceeding. So Yenev had not yet admitted having the survivors on board. That must have been done on the instructions of Leningrad. What lay behind these deceptions? Soviet security precautions were notoriously tortuous but surely not to that extent? He recalled Dave O'Dowd's words at the Paris briefing: 'I figure you'll most likely be carried on to Leningrad. The Captain won't want to accept responsibility for landing you before then. He'll know that once the ship is in Leningrad it's their problem. That suits him and I guess it suits us. The longer you're on board the better the chances of learning something. Right?'

There was at least one other problem on his mind. He and Judy had now on successive nights met in the stern to exchange news. They'd agreed it would be dangerous to make a habit of this, dangerous to establish a pattern. They'd decided for the time being to make do with low key asides on the bridge-deck. But these had to be in a sort of verbal shorthand and that was not easy and could lead to misunderstanding.

During the afternoon when the ship was making the passage through the Canaries there'd been a brief exchange which worried him. She'd whispered, 'Suppose I'll have to do the beastly bait bit.'

'I don't follow,' he'd replied.

'For the Polo Mint, I mean.'

'Lomov's cabin?'

She'd nodded, looked at him curiously, said nothing.

What exactly she'd meant by 'the beastly bait bit' he wasn't quite sure, but he had a shrewd idea and didn't like it.

After the cinema they gathered as usual in the lounge for coffee and a nightcap. Both were more often than not combined in the form of coffee laced with vodka. It was apparent that the use of alcohol in *Antonov* was well controlled. Deck and engineer officers going on watch at night were not permitted spirits though beer was allowed; even so there was no suggestion of excessive drinking at any time. In general it was the senior officers – those who did not keep watches – who made up the nightcap parties. With the ship homeward bound, moving steadily to the north and due in Leningrad in a week's time, the atmosphere on board had grown increasingly cheerful and this mood was reflected in the lounge where Judy was used to hearing herself discussed in Russian. In general the remarks were kindly, often flattering, and though at times they were of the sort women were supposed not to hear – 'wouldn't mind sharing a bed with her'; 'Lomov's after her. Think he'll make it?' – they, too, were in a sense complimentary.

She had no doubt that Lomov was 'after her' and she'd have been surprised, perhaps hurt, and certainly disappointed if he hadn't been because she'd been casting her fly in his pool now for some time, deftly and with unmistakable feminine guile.

Towards midnight only Gallagher, Lomov and Judy were left in the lounge. Long before that the steward had rolled down the bar shutters noisily enough to remind those present of the time and the exodus had begun.

Gallagher looked at his watch, yawned widely, spoke in French. 'Quarter before twelve. It's bed for me.'

Lomov looked pleased. *'Bonne nuit. Dormez bien,'* he said with almost indecent haste.

Gallagher glanced at Judy. 'Coming?'

She looked embarrassed, shook her head. 'Not just yet, Ben.' She switched to English. 'Stefan and I are discussing music.'

'Great. I guess he'll want you to hear his.' For her the sarcasm was softened a little by the concern in his eyes.

'Funnily enough he's just suggested that.'

'I'm sure he has. And I guess it'll be the hi-fi in his cabin. Not this one.'

'Yes. How did you know?'

Gallagher shrugged his shoulders and left the lounge.

Lomov chuckled. 'I think your friend is jealous, Judy.'

'He's no right to be. A nice guy but there's nothing between us. Just pilot and passenger.'

'I don't blame him. Who would not be jealous with a woman like you.' Lomov stood up, took her hand. 'Now you must hear Tchaikovsky. Please.' His eyebrows gathered in a puzzled frown, the dark eyes searching hers, the drooping moustache adding a touch of stagelike villainy.

'It's late,' she protested. 'Don't you go on watch tonight?'

'No. I don't keep watches. The first officer has the morning watch. Come on. I will not keep you long. Please.' He pulled her from the chair.

'All right,' she said with feigned reluctance. 'I shouldn't. But I can't stay long.'

Lomov's eyes were bright with excitement.


O'Dowd looked at the portrait over the fireplace – Howard of Effingham, he'd now learned. A man to be envied, great days those must have been. Wooden ships, canvas sails, iron men against wind and sea. At long intervals set-piece battles at point blank range; but mostly sailing to strange places, voyages of discovery and exploration, with piracy in the name of the Monarch thrown in for good measure. What a life. The Brits had built up a great tradition, there was no denying that. But Paul Jones hadn't done too badly, tweaked their noses in no uncertain fashion and set the pattern for the United States Navy, the world's greatest. The Japs thought they'd finished it at Pearl, but what battles the USN had fought in the long come-back after that: Midway, the Coral Sea, the Java Straits – and a whole lot more.

Now there was another great fleet, the USSR's; fine ships, superb weaponry, as sophisticated as any in this electronic age. But no one would know how good the Soviet Navy was until the shooting started. That was the problem which always confronted strategists. The Italians had shown in World War Two that fine ships were just not enough. The way you fought them was what counted when the crunch came. O'Dowd was feeling pleasantly relaxed on that score when his thoughts were interrupted by Rathouse's abrasive, 'What is your view on that, O'Dowd?'

Since he'd no idea what *that* was, O'Dowd was in difficulties. 'I'm afraid I don't follow, Commodore.'

Rathouse directed a red-eyed stare at the American. 'Presumably you heard Briggs report that *Antonov* passed through the Canaries this afternoon. Abeam of Salvagens Island at 2200.'

'Yes, sir. He was giving us *Aries*'s signal.'

'He was. I then remarked that *Antonov* had still not reported picking up the survivors. I asked what your view on that was?'

O'Dowd scratched his head with a tentative forefinger. 'I guess the project is coming along according to plan, Commodore. The CIA feed-in has paid off.'

Maltby, eyes half-closed, blew smoke at the ceiling. 'I don't like it. Ominous.'

The Commodore regarded those round the table with a jaundiced eye and switched into his table-tapping routine. 'There seems to be a tendency to overlook phase two in this discussion. The Russians' silence about the survivors suggests that the ship *has* got an important secret. By the time she reaches the approaches to the Channel, Gallagher and Paddon may well have found out what it is. The initiative is theirs. If they consider the next phase necessary they will inform us.'

'If they don't,' said Maltby, 'it's a fair assumption there's been a balls up. Or our intelligence has been weak.'

Fothergill's eyes expressed disapproval of this flippancy and his head swung from side to side as if to ease his neck out of its starched collar. 'With respect, Sir James, not necessarily. What they learn will, one hopes, preclude the need for phase two.'

The Commodore looked at a slip of paper on which scrawled hieroglyphics evidently meant something to him. 'Kitson. The commercial units? What's their state of readiness?'

'Both have been requisitioned. The COs have attended two preliminary sessions and have had dummy runs in *Huntress*. We'll have a final briefing on the seventh. All very satisfactory. They go to two hours' notice at midnight. *Antonov* should be approaching the Lizard by then.'

'Are they happy about their assignment?'

'Surprisingly so. Very keen in fact.' Kitson, eyes downcast, ears prominent, became suddenly lugubrious. 'A little worried, perhaps, that the weather may not be suitable.'

'Who's ever been happy about the weather in the planning stage?' challenged the Commodore.

'Nelson,' said Maltby firmly. 'He always assumed God would do the right thing by the British.'

'Quite right too,' said Freddie Lewis. 'Remember Dunkirk?'


When she'd accepted Lomov's pressing invitation to hear Oistrakh playing Tchaikovsky, Judy had few illusions about the Russian's intentions. Which was just as well.

When they got to his day-room he had insisted on more vodka. 'Then we can really appreciate the music,' he'd observed enthusiastically. So he poured the vodkas and put on the cassettes.

She knew the music and enjoyed it, but long before the finale more vodkas had been poured and Lomov had begun to show his paces. The long and exhausting struggle which followed had been interrupted by the ringing of his office phone. What he thought about that he'd said in a few brief but well-chosen Russian words. She'd been waiting for the interruption for some time, wondering why Gallagher was taking so long about it.

The moment Lomov left the day-room she got busy, slipped the 837-Sr from her vanity bag, leant forward and pressed it into the underside of the steel-framed settee on which she was sitting. Lomov came back to say with a guilty grin, 'Your friend Gallagher. Wants to know why you've been so long. I said you were enjoying the music.'

'What cheek,' she protested angrily. 'Phoning like that. I don't have to account to him for my actions.'

'Or do you?' demanded Lomov, sitting down next to her and resuming his groping tactics which once again involved her in a Judo-like defence. He paused, breathing heavily. 'He seemed to be expecting you,' he said, biting her neck playfully and doing more positive things lower down. Judy, who was no weakling, pushed him away. 'No, Stefan,' she said. 'He was not expecting me. If he was he is going to be disappointed. Just like you are.' Lomov's cry of surprise coincided with the final strains of the Tchaikovsky concerto and the need to switch off the hi-fi. When he'd done that he came back, hair dishevelled, uniform in disarray, and stared at her in shocked disbelief. Her first instinct was to laugh because he looked so ridiculous; but that gave way to other feelings and she felt sorry for him.

'Sleep with me, Judy,' he pleaded. '*Please*. I want you.'

She shook her head emphatically. 'No, Stefan. It's impossible. I like you, you are kind, but there is somebody else.'

His expression changed, the mandarin moustache dropped more dismally, the dark eyes clouded, the thick eyebrows knotted in dismay. 'Is it Gallagher?' he asked.

She shook her head. 'No. Someone in England whom I've known a long time.' It was a double lie. Of course there *was* someone in England – widowhood didn't entail celibacy – but mutual attraction not love was involved in that sort of relationship. On the other hand she suspected that she *was* in love with Gallagher.

Nevertheless the way in which Lomov accepted defeat won her admiration. There were no tantrums, no reproaches, just a sad aside: 'I'm sorry. You are so beautiful. I wanted you and I thought . . .' He threw out his hands in a gesture of helplessness, smiled apologetically. 'I thought you could want me.'

She looked at the photograph of his wife and children on the mantelpiece above the mock fireplace. 'They would be pleased, Stefan. That it is like this. That we are just good friends.'

'Yes,' he said. 'That is true. But it is also true that I would like to sleep with you.'

She kissed him lightly on the cheek. 'You are a nice man. Now I must go.'

He nodded dejectedly, opened the door, led her into the passageway and along to her cabin. 'Good night,' he said sadly. 'Sleep well.'

She opened the door, went in, waved to him, shut and locked it and began to undress. She smiled at her thoughts : Gallagher would have been listening to the 837-Sr transmission from Lomov's cabin and he'd know what had happened. That, she realized, was of importance to her. And she had succeeded at last in placing a bug in the chief officer's cabin. That was even more important.

# 15

With the ship past the thirty-fifth parallel of latitude and the tropics far behind the wind blew with increasing vigour, whipping up seas which rolled in across the swell left by an Atlantic gale a thousand miles to the northwest. Banks of cumulus filled a sky patchworked with blue, their shadows scurrying over the sea so that sometimes the ship was in shade at others in sunlight. Caught between the opposing forces of sea and swell the *Antonov* described a gentle corkscrewing motion, her bows throwing up fine spray which misted back over the maindeck.

The latitude of Madeira, a hundred and twenty miles to the west, had been passed soon after dawn; below the horizon, more than two hundred miles to starboard, lay the coast of Morocco, beyond it the Sahara. Crewmen could be seen about the ship scraping and painting, working on windlasses and winches, attending to running gear and those other tasks which occupy the days of men at sea.

Gallagher and Judy were looking down on this scene from the lower bridge-deck when Trutin arrived with a message from the Captain. Would they please go to his stateroom.

'When?' enquired Gallagher.

'Now,' said Trutin. 'Come with me.'

The Captain rose to greet them, pointed to the armchairs which stood with their backs to the bookshelves on the forward bulkhead. Gallagher imagined the hidden microphone was still there. With Trutin interpreting the conversation proceeded through the conventional stages of social enquiry: were their cabins comfortable? Was the food to their liking? Were they being well looked after? How was the cut on Mrs Paddon's forehead? Healing? Good. And Mr Gallagher's bruised eye? Yes, indeed. One could see it was better.

He's taking a long time to get to the point, thought Gallagher. We've not been brought here just for this.

Yenev went through to his office and came back with sheets of typed paper; he spoke to Trutin before passing them to Gallagher.

'The Captain says he has had a summary made in English of our daily newssheet. He apologizes if the English is not good, but Doctor Linovsky has done his best. We hope you will find it interesting.'

Gallagher examined the newssheet briefly. 'Tell the Captain, please, that we very much appreciate his kindness. It is good to be in touch with what is going on in the outside world.'

Trutin translated and Yenev nodded genially. For the next half hour he discussed the news with them, sometimes addressing Judy, at others the American. Trutin worked hard at translating and didn't always get it right. It was on such occasions that the pretence that they couldn't understand Russian became particularly frustrating; there was no alternative, however, for it was the strongest weapon in their armoury.

During a laboured interpretation by Trutin, Gallagher's wandering eye was caught by movement in the long mirror above the sideboard. It reflected the view of the maindeck through the forward windows. Yenev, sitting opposite the survivors, had his back to it.

What Gallagher had seen was a group of men walking aft from the direction of number one hold: Linovsky, his three assistants, Lomov and a petty officer. As on the previous occasion, large black satchels hung from the assistants' shoulders and as before two sailors with deck-buckets and scrubbers brought up the rear.

It was the inspection party he'd observed two days earlier. Then, too, he and Judy had been with Yenev in his day-room. Was it coincidence or planning that ensured they were not on deck when the inspection party moved to and from number one hold? Probably the latter, he decided, when a few minutes later Yenev brought the conversation to an end and they left the day-room.

In the lounge before lunch that day Gallagher played his third game of chess with Linovsky. It was a therapy to which the American had often resorted in his naval flying days; a game he really enjoyed. As usual he was no match for Linovsky who had him check-mate in fifteen moves. 'You like another game?' the doctor asked.

Gallagher looked at his watch. 'Not right now,' he grinned. 'You're too good, Doctor.'

He suggested a beer. They went across to the bar, the lager was poured and they raised their tankards to each other. 'Thanks for the English newssheet,' said Gallagher. 'It's very welcome.'

Linovsky shrugged his shoulders. 'Not very good English. But we try to make it interesting.'

'It's fine. Wish I could speak Russian.'

'If you have the same opportunity you can.'

'You mean like Trinity, Dublin?'

'Of course.'

The conversation moved on, the two men exchanging information about their work, their countries, the voyage and the *Antonov*. Gallagher made some enquiry about the refrigerating plant in number one hold – had the doctor and his team solved the problem?

Linovsky looked up quickly from his tankard, the dark glasses he wore masking his expression. 'I think we make good progress. The problem is more a matter of design than main-tenance.' With that he switched the subject to aviation. Why, he wanted to know, was the United States so far behind in the development of supersonic commercial flight? After all the Soviet Union, Britain and France already had their super-sonics in service. That subject kept things going until Judy arrived and they went in to lunch.

For close on two hours during the afternoon Gallagher was on the lower bridge-deck, mostly walking at a vigorous pace. He'd found that reception of the 837-Sr transmissions was better there than in his cabin, and for a man who attached as much importance as he did to keeping fit the exercise was more than welcome.

In the late afternoon Judy found him. Daylight was fading as they went down ladders and along the maindeck to the stern. In the west the sun moved behind a bank of cumulus, edging it with gold and daubing the western sky with pastel shades of rose and salmon : across this backdrop wisps of cloud drifted like golden feathers. Soon the sun dropped be-neath the cumulus and the bronze disc balanced on the horizon before slowly sinking.

'Wish there was a swimming pool,' said Judy. She wore a light woollen jersey and a head scarf borrowed from Natasha Mekhlis. 'We've had such marvellous sun. Could have got a super tan. Too late now. The weather's getting bleak.' As if to match her words the wind freshened.

'Your face is nut brown. You look fine.'

'My body's a ghastly white.'

'I'll take your word for it. Tell me. How did Tchaikovsky go last night?' His searching look, the evident train of thought, made her smile.

'You must have heard most of it.'

'Some of it. *After* the Polo Mint job. Before that I mean?'

'Usual male groping scene. Roger Beamish would have been delighted. After all, that's what I'm here for, isn't it?'

'At least Lomov didn't sleep with you.' It was close to a question.

'It wasn't for want of trying.'

Gallagher cleared his throat. 'Is there really someone in England?'

'Actually there are *two* someones in England.'

'Two.' His voice rose in surprise. 'What are they to you?'

'Is that really anything to do with you, Ben?' Her calm eyes outstared his.

'No, I guess not.'

'If you must know,' she said, 'I like them both very much – go to bed with them occasionally – but do not love them. Happy?'

Gallagher looked glum. 'Happy, hell. Why should I be? But I guess I asked for it.'

She said, 'Let's talk about something else. Polo Mints helping you?'

'Not much yet. I aim to take them regularly. Should help. We'll see.'

He told her briefly about his pre-lunch chat with Linovsky, and went on to discuss the ship's concert. They agreed it was a bore but that they must co-operate. 'The friendlier we get the better,' said Gallagher. 'I've a date with Linovsky in the games room at eight-thirty tonight. We have to find something we both know. He's optimistic.'

'Splendid. Can't wait to hear you. That resonant bass.'

'Thank you, lady. Maybe I'll give them "Old Man River". And your act? Modelling? The Paddon body, if I may say so, is made ...'

'What about my body?' she demanded.

Gallagher examined it with admiration. 'It's fabulous, Judy. Made for modelling. And above it there's a lovely face. You'll have them fighting in the aisles. When does Natasha kit you out?'

'Tonight,' she wrinkled her nose watching him with uncertain eyes. 'You're quite a Roger Beamish, aren't you?

Only he's more subtle. Let's go. It's getting cold. I must fix my face and hair.'

Back in his cabin Gallagher switched on the micro-receiver in the hearing-aid. He looked at the time: 6.12. Each evening since they'd been on board Linovsky had gone to the Captain's suite about then. It was some sort of ritual. Maybe to have a chat over a drink, Gallagher decided as he stretched himself out on his bed and hoped the ritual would hold up that evening. It did. Minutes later the voice of Yenev greeting Linovsky came through on the micro-receiver.

YENEV: Sit down, Simyon Linovsky. Vodka?

LINOVSKY: Thank you, Sergei Yenev. Always good at this end of the day. (Sound of ice clinking in glasses, liquid pouring.)

YENEV: There. Your good health, Doctor.

LINOVSKY: Good health, Captain.

YENEV: This morning's inspection. Satisfactory?

LINOVSKY: Yes. Everything in order. Warning systems checked, found correct and logged. Position by inertial and electronic navigational systems compared, checked and recorded. Release control and arming systems tested and locked. Computers run, checked and tested. Communication systems checked and tested. Usual routine.

YENEV: Good, now let's relax. Have you seen today's news-sheet? Yes. What d'you think of Leo   . Brezhnev's reply to Carter on the Cuban intervention in Southern Africa?

LINOVSKY: Logical, rational. The West cannot controvert the facts. And if they could what can they do? The American people will not stand for United States intervention in Africa. Carter can talk. But only talk.

After that, the discussion between the two men continued along general lines and nothing of further interest had emerged by seven o'clock when Linovsky took his leave and there was the sound of a door closing.

What Gallagher had heard was crucial. The responsibilities

of Simyon Linovsky and his assistants had little if anything to do with refrigeration plants. There was enough now to confirm that the suspicions of British and US Naval Intelligence were justified. *Release control and arming systems?* Release what? Arm what? *Positions by inertial and electronic navigational systems – checked.* What had that to do with refrigeration? And why should all this activity be concentrated in number one hold?

Gallagher was faced with a critical decision. There were sufficient grounds, he believed, for transmission of the executive signal – LAND CATCH. *Aries* and *Jupiter* were, he knew, within a hundred and fifty miles to the west; *Narwhal* was shadowing from somewhere astern, always within radio range. He could transmit the signal that night, or hold on for another day. The 837-Srs had only just come into operation. If he held on there was the possibility, the probability, of more information, particularly as he'd not yet monitored transmissions from Lomov's cabin. For some time he weighed the pros and cons. The decision that the next phase was necessary rested solely with him; it was a responsibility made more difficult by his ignorance of the form that phase would take. He knew it meant that further investigation was necessary but how, when and where were unknown to him. In Paris O'Dowd had said it involved political and practical implications of a serious kind but achievement of its objective would, he'd said, justify the risks involved.

After some hard thinking Gallagher decided that it would be sensible to delay transmission of the signal for another twenty-four hours. During that time the 837-Srs might provide evidence so conclusive that further investigation would be unnecessary.

That night the American went along to the games room for the rehearsal with mixed feelings. It was all rather childish and the thought of performing before an audience of Russian seamen embarrassed him. On the other hand it was important to be friendly and to co-operate. As it happened the rehearsal was more amusing than embarrassing and by its end he was enjoying himself.

Olga Katutin was there to give moral support and her good-humoured bantering soon broke the ice. The doctor had turned out to be a useful guitar player. They began on a trial and error basis: Gallagher would name a song, hum or whistle it, and Linovsky would shake his head and strum an alternative. At last common ground was found. Linovsky strummed a refrain, hummed an accompaniment, Gallagher joined in, sang the words. Linovsky smiled, looked at him enquiringly, Gallagher nodded, they found a key and took off, the chords of the guitar harmonizing with Gallagher's deep voice.

The American stopped singing, laughed. '*The Mountains of Mourne*. You learnt that in Dublin?'

'Of course.'

'Great,' said Gallagher. 'Let's try it again.'

And they did, several times, until it was really quite well done. They went back to the lounge after that. At the bar Linovsky suggested beer. It was poured and the doctor held his tankard aloft. 'To our success.'

'To our success,' repeated Gallagher, raising his.

Towards midnight Yenev closed the file of confidential radio messages, locked it in a desk drawer and stood up. As he did so the ship lurched to starboard and he knocked over the swivel chair. It was while picking it up that he saw the small metallic object on the underside of the steel bracket into which fitted the spindle on the chair's cruciform legs.

He prized it loose with a paper knife, put it on the blotter and examined it with a magnifying glass. It was easily recognized: an 837-Sr – the type commonly used by the KGB. His first reaction, one of extreme anger, gave way to sober thought. He had long suspected Boris Milovych of placing a bug somewhere in his suite. Of course the office was the logical place, but Yenev's searches in the past had been fruitless. It had never occurred to him to examine the underside of the chair. For that oversight he blamed himself.

He went through to the bathroom, filled an empty medicine bottle with water, placed the 837-Sr in it, replaced the screw top and locked the bottle in his personal safe. He was not at all sure what steps he would take; confront Milovych with the discovery now or wait for a suitable opportunity.

His instinct suggested the latter.

# 16

At dawn on the fifth November the *Antonov* was off the coast of Portugal, almost one hundred and twenty miles west of Lisbon. It was the beginning of the survivors' fifth day on board. During the night the barometer had fallen, the wind had backed to the north-west and by daylight was blowing half a gale. The maindeck, wet and glistening, mirrored the greys of a lowering sky as the ship plunged into seas rolling in from the wide spaces of the North Atlantic.

The motion of the ship became harsher, less predictable, the superstructure straining and creaking in protest, its vibrations reflecting more urgently the forces unleashed by powerful engines and thrashing propellers.

After breakfast Gallagher suggested a walk on deck.

'In this weather?' Judy questioned.

'Yes. It's great. What being at sea is all about. You can have your tropics, flat calms, flying fish. That's not seafaring.'

'It is for me.'

'Come on,' he urged. 'Do you good.'

Something in his manner told her that more than a walk was involved. 'Right. Just let me fix this.' She took from her neck the scarf she was wearing, put it round her hair and tied the ends under her chin. Natasha had lent her the scarf. 'Now. Let's go.'

They went to the lower bridge-deck, chose the lee side,

walked its length unsteadily several times before Gallagher
led her to the rail at the after end. He moved close beside her.
'Polo Mint's gone on the blink,' he whispered.

'Which one?'

'The boss's.' That meant Yenev's.

'Power failure?'

'Hopefully. But unlikely so soon.'

'So?'

'Could've been located. Maybe they've got a ferret.' He
was alluding to the electronic sweeper used in counter espionage for detecting the presence of bugs.

'Oh God. Hope not. What time?'

'Don't exactly know,' he said. 'Nothing through since six-
thirty when I woke up.'

'What'll you do?'

'Wait and see.'

'Anything on Stefan's?'

'Nothing worthwhile. It's still alive. Heard him chatting
up Natasha last night. He fancies her.'

'Unfaithful brute. Thought it was me he loved.'

'She's quite a dish.'

They became serious after that. In brief verbal shorthand
he told her of the Linovsky-Yenev conversation; of his intention to transmit the Land Catch signal at midnight.

'Oh,' she turned to him with a worried frown. 'Sure that's
a good idea?'

'Yeh. Absolutely.'

'I'm frightened,' she whispered. Her hands were tightly
clenched on the rail, the knuckles white. He pressed a shoulder
against hers, touched her hand. 'Of course,' he said, 'but take
it easy. It's going to be okay.'

The pressure of his hand and shoulder, the whispered
Southern drawl, reassured her.


An excited Grotskov ushered Milovych into the cypher-room
and locked the soundproof door behind him. He unlocked
the safe, took from it two cassettes and put them into the

recorders on the worktable. 'Sit down, Comrade Milovych.'
He and the Commissar took chairs opposite each other.

'Now,' he said, pressing the 'play' tab of a recorder, 'I give
you the first exhibit.' There was the electronic swish of blank
tape turning, the sound of a man clearing his throat, followed
by MAYDAY . . . MAYDAY . . . MAYDAY.

Though inflected with unusual urgency it was unmistak-
ably Gallagher's voice : *Fire in starboard engine. November
Zero-Four-Nine-Three Charlie preparing to ditch. My position is* . . . The voice cut off suddenly.

Grotskov's yellow eyes sought the Commissar's and cool
though the air-conditioned room was his face glistened with
sweat. 'That's exhibit One,' he said turning to the second recorder. 'Now for exhibit Two.' He switched on and the two
men waited, tense with expectation. Again the sound of
throat clearing, then *Foxtrot Seven-Nine . . . this is Five-
Three-Seven.* There was a pause, another voice answered, *Go
ahead Five-Three-Seven . . .*; again a pause, then, *Have
sighted Danbuoy*, replied the first voice; *Bravo Zulu*, came the
response; after that there was nothing but the sound of blank
tape.

Grotskov switched off, turned to the Commissar. 'How
would you describe the pilot's accent?' he asked.

'How can I tell? I don't speak English.'

Grotskov nodded. 'Exactly. I speak some English yet I can't
identify these accents. But Simyon Linovsky is fluent in the
language and he tells me that is an Irish accent. Now listen
to this.' He took a third cassette from his pocket and put it
in the recorder from which he'd taken the MAYDAY message.
'I give you exhibit Three,' he said solemnly.

There could be no doubt that the radio officer was enjoying
the drama in which he was playing the sole and only role
before an admiring audience of one man – but that man was
the political boss and for Grotskov the most important person
in the ship.

He switched on. The sound of blank tape was interrupted
by the thrum of a guitar, followed by throat clearing and a

man's voice breaking into song. Accompanied by the guitar, he sang in a deep bass. It was a folk song, *The Mountains of Mourne*, and the Irish brogue of the unseen singer clothed the words with all the warmth, humour and pathos of his race. When three verses had been sung Grotskov switched off the recorder. 'Wait,' he said and his voice trembled with excitement. 'We'll have exhibit Two again.' He pressed the 'play' tab of the second recorder and once more they heard the Irish voice calling Foxtrot Seven-Nine.

At Milovych's request the radio officer played the cassettes several times more until at last the Commissar held up a hand. 'That's enough, Leonid Grotskov,' he said. 'You have convinced me. The identical throat clearing. The same voice with the accent you tell me is Irish.' He put out a congratulatory hand, patted the radio officer on the shoulder. 'You have done well. A brilliant piece of detection. You may be sure you will be rewarded for this.' Milovych rose to his feet, his podgy face bulging with importance, his eyes gleaming triumphantly. 'We will report now to Sergei Yenev. Leningrad must be informed without delay.'

'That will do. I've heard enough.' Yenev got up from his desk, went to a window and stared ahead into the gathering storm. Grotskov switched off the recorder, took out the last of the cassettes and put it in his pocket.

On the far side of the desk Milovych sat like a bullfrog, his eyes, fixed on the Captain's back, glinting with concealed triumph. 'Leonid Grotskov deserves congratulations does he not, Comrade Sergei Yenev?'

Yenev turned away from the window. 'Yes. A clever piece of work.' He looked at the communications officer. 'Tell me, what alerted you to this?'

'The throat clearing, Captain. In accordance with standing instructions we were monitoring and recording signals between the British frigates and their helicopters on the naval frequency. We had another receiver tuned to the frequency used by civilian aircraft. So we had this helicopter Five-

Three-Seven talking to Foxtrot on the one channel and soon afterwards the MAYDAY signal on the other. At the time I wasn't suspicious. The pilot of the civilian aircraft had an American accent, the pilot of the navy helicopter quite a different sort of voice.' Grotskov's tone was almost apologetic. He moved away from the desk, stood with his back to the forward bulkhead, legs apart, bracing himself against the movement of the ship, his cat-like eyes bright.

He went on. 'When Gallagher came on board I noticed he often cleared his throat before speaking. In the lounge – I think it was on the second day – he was playing chess with Simyon Linovsky. I was watching. When Linovsky had him check-mate Gallagher cleared his throat – erm-herm – just like in those transmissions. Then he made a remark in a dialect I couldn't understand. Afterwards I asked the doctor about it. He said that Gallagher knew he'd studied in Dublin and occasionally put on the Irish accent when joking.' Grotskov's eyes seemed to be searching the faces of his listeners for appreciation. 'That was when I got suspicious.' He hesitated. 'Anyway I was sure I'd heard the voice before. But for a long time I couldn't recall where. Then I remembered the helicopter pilot. I found recordings of the Foxtrot and MAYDAY transmissions and played them over many times. The more I did so the more convinced I became that it was Gallagher's voice in both transmissions.'

'Why didn't you report to me at once?' Yenev's frown was a mixture of bewilderment and displeasure.

'It was only a suspicion. I hadn't any proof. Problem was how to get it. Then I thought of the concert. I wasn't sure but I felt there was a chance it might work. It depended on Simyon Linovsky and Gallagher knowing the same song. When they rehearsed in the games room I had a concealed mike and recorder there.'

'You did well. Very well indeed.' Yenev sat down, a hand supporting his forehead, deep in thought. Milovych began to speak. Yenev shook his head. 'Wait. Let me think.'

There was silence after that but for the distant rumble of

the diesel engines and the creaking of the ship as she moved in the seaway. At length Yenev said, 'So Gallagher and Paddon were planted. A well-planned, complex operation which included the frigates.'

'They're still there, Captain,' put in Grotskov. 'We continue to monitor their signals.'

'And why this complex operation?' It was a rhetorical question which Yenev at once answered. 'Because they are determined to probe the secret of these ships.'

'We were warned of that when we commissioned,' said Milovych. 'It's no surprise. Not to *me*, at any rate.'

Yenev knew that the Commissar was thinking 'I told you so', but he ignored the innuendo and instead asked, 'Anything interesting from the bugs in their cabins?'

Milovych stared at Yenev in a curious dead-pan way. Perhaps he thought the question had something to do with his reputation as a voyeur. 'Nothing,' he said. 'Only once has Gallagher been in her cabin as far as we know. That was on the first day. *After* the interrogation.' He gestured with his hands. 'They are well trained of course.'

'Talking of bugs,' Yenev was watching the Commissar's face closely, 'I found one in this office last night. Attached to the base of that chair.' He pointed to the swivel chair.

'Why didn't you tell me, Comrade Yenev?' Milovych's humourless smile became a frown.

But Yenev didn't smile and there was nothing humorous about the menacing glint in his pale eyes. 'It was a Soviet bug, *Comrade* Boris Milovych. An 837-Sr to be exact.'

The Commissar looked bewildered, turned away from the Captain's stare. 'You thought I placed it?'

'I repeat. It was a Soviet 837-Sr. Who do *you* think placed it?'

'The American, of course.'

'The American. A Soviet bug?' Yenev shrugged his shoulders, dropped the subject. 'There are more important things to discuss now. The action to be taken.'

About that there was no dispute and the matter was

quickly settled; Borodin was to be informed at once and his permission for the arrest of Gallagher and Paddon requested. In the meantime they were to be treated as if nothing had happened.

When Grotskov left the Captain's office he took with him the message they'd drafted for Borodin. He lost no time in scrambling it by computer and transmitting it to Leningrad. Its time of origin was 1155.

The reply from Leningrad came within the hour: Gallagher and Paddon were to be confined to their cabins under close arrest. They were not to be given any reasons for this step.

When Yenev and Milovych had finished discussing the signal, Trutin was sent for.

'Go at once to the American and the Englishwoman,' said Yenev. 'Tell them I have important news. Bring them here immediately.'

The steward acknowledged the order and hurried away.

Trutin knocked on the door, opened it and ushered Gallagher and Judy into the Captain's office. Yenev was at his desk writing; Milovych sat on a chair beside the desk reading the daily newssheet. Gallagher knew at once that something was wrong. Both men looked up as he and Judy came in, but neither stood nor was there any greeting; the Russians simply stared with blank faces as if seeing the survivors for the first time. Yenev did not, as was his custom, invite them to sit down.

The tense silence was broken by Gallagher. 'I believe you have important news for us, Captain.'

Trutin translated, the Captain nodded and his mouth closed in a firm line as he turned from the steward to the American. 'You and the woman will be confined to your cabins for the remainder of the voyage,' he said. 'Food will be brought to you. Under no circumstances are you to leave the cabins. An armed guard will be on duty outside to ensure that my order is observed. That is all.'

By the time Trutin had finished translating this the American had recovered from his initial shock at what Yenev had said. He put on a show of astonishment. 'Tell the Captain we wish to know the reason for this extraordinary decision.' The Russians watched them with stony stares as Trutin translated and Yenev gave his reply. The steward, visibly shaken by what had happened, looked at them with puzzled, questioning eyes. There was a bond of friendship between him and the survivors, tenuous but nevertheless real, and he was obviously hurt and embarrassed. 'The Captain is not prepared to give reasons or make explanations,' he said. 'The interview is over.'

Gallagher began a further protest but in the middle of it Yenev and Milovych walked through to the day-room, closing the door firmly behind them. Trutin said, 'I must ask you to follow me.'

In a voice thick with emotion Judy said, 'What on earth has happened, Ben?'

He looked blank. 'You heard what the Captain said. "No reasons. No explanations".'

'What are we going to do?'

'For Christ's sake. What can we do with a situation like that.' He took her by the arm. 'Come on. We've no option. Let's go.'

Trutin said, 'I go first. Please follow.' He led them into the passageway where two petty officers were waiting. Gallagher saw the revolvers and that more than anything Yenev had said brought home to him the reality of their situation. Trutin spoke briefly to the petty officers after which he turned to Gallagher. 'These are your guards,' he said. 'You must go with them to your cabins.' His rueful expression would have been amusing had the situation not been so serious.

Gallagher said, 'Thank you, Ivan Trutin. I'm sorry this has happened. I guess it's a misunderstanding.'

The steward looked miserable, turned away. One of the petty officers beckoned to them to follow and with the other bringing up the rear they moved along the passageway. The leading petty officer stopped at Judy's cabin, opened the door and gestured to her to enter. Before going in she gave Gallagher a last despairing look and her eyes filled with tears. He called out, 'It'll be okay, Judy. Our people will put it right in Leningrad.' She smiled wanly and he knew he'd failed to reassure her.

The petty officer took Gallagher by the arm, opened the door of his cabin, pushed him in, and shut it. Then, revolver in hand, he frisked the American but found nothing other than a wallet, a few coins and the plastic tube of antacid pills, all of which he transferred to his own pockets. He made Gallagher take off his shoes and trousers and with these under his arm left the cabin, locking the door behind him.

Gallagher looked round : the lights were on, there was a smell of burning and the steel deadlights had been lowered over the windows and secured so that daylight was shut out. He tried to open a deadlight by unscrewing the cleats but found they'd been fixed with spot welds which were still warm to the touch. Must have been done in the last five minutes, he decided. He checked through his few possessions : the odd items of clothing, the pyjamas Lomov had lent him were there but the briefcase had gone and with it the pocket calculator.

He put on the pyjama trousers, went into the bathroom and opened the cupboard above the washbasin. His toothbrush and toothpaste and the Remington shaver were still there. He sighed with relief. Next he went to the airvent in the lavatory, turned the butterfly cover, thrust his fingers into it and felt around. The tiny cadmium batteries for the microreceiver were still where he'd secured them with Sellotape.

He sat at the bedside table thinking. First about Judy. The petty officer had not gone into her cabin but had closed the door behind her and locked it. Of course the cabin would have been searched. Not that she'd anything to hide. He was worried about her. Wondered how tough she was. Okay, she'd chosen to live dangerously but he knew her well enough already to realize that fear was often her companion. The situation they were in was worse for a woman than a man.

His thoughts switched to more urgent things. Their cover was blown. No doubt about that. Was it a slip, a leak in the planning stage, or was it something else? Whatever it was he'd now have to add 'Yarmouth' to the Land Catch signal. Send it at eight o'clock, he decided. No point now in waiting for midnight. The more he thought about it the more likely it seemed that it was the bug in Yenev's cabin that had given them away. Maybe they knew the CIA used the Soviet 837-Sr. They'd be checking the pocket calculator, examining the printed circuits, the battery compartment, looking for a micro-receiver. And they'd be disappointed. Like they must have been when they searched the cabins. They'd know he could have hidden a receiver almost anywhere in the after end of the ship. That would give them a problem. Unless they thought of the hearing-aid he would still be able to listen to the chat from Lomov's cabin. But they'd be on guard now. And if they had a ferret they'd find the bug in Lomov's cabin. He didn't think the micro-receiver was going to help much from now on – but it had done a great job.

# 17

Borodin's personal assistant, Vladimir Ilyitch, stood by the fireplace, his back to the electric fire, watching in silence the pacing figure. The long feline steps, soundless on the thick carpet, reminded him of a wild animal padding its cage; an animal dangerous if disturbed, despite its apparent docility.

While others found this restless pacing an irritating habit it was for Borodin essential stimulus to his thought processes. As he paced his brain performed the basic functions of a computer; taking in data, processing it by means of systematic rejection and acceptance, moving with precision to logical conclusions. At the moment the complex mechanism of that brain was concentrated on a problem as intriguing as it was unusual.

Gallagher and Paddon : a US citizen and a UK citizen. CIA and SIS? The facts pointed to a US-UK liaison operation, set up to break the security net around the *Simeonov* class. Liaison operations called for joint planning. Where would that planning have taken place? Pentagon or Whitehall? At either or both, but the British element appeared to predominate in this instance. Thus probably MOD Whitehall and US Navy HQ, Grosvenor Square. That meant Gryzan.

Borodin stopped at the window, looked towards the Neva. It was early afternoon but darkness was already closing in over the wintry landscape, compounding the mist which obscured the view of the river. Without turning he said, 'Take this message for the Embassy in London. Classify it "Most Secret". Prefix it "Immediate action – attention Khazarov".'

Khazarov was head of KGB operations in the United Kingdom. The message would be computer encrypted, squirt transmitted from KGB's Leningrad transmitters to the radio station in the Soviet Embassy in Kensington Palace Gardens.

Borodin went on: 'Gryzan to provide immediately any information relevant joint US-UK naval operation involving US Beechcraft Baron aircraft November Zero-Four-Nine-Three Charlie, departed Orly airport Paris October twenty-eight for Lisbon – Dakar. Departed Dakar November first bound Sao Paulo. Ditched deliberately approximately one-eight-zero miles west Dakar. Pilot US citizen Benjamin Dwight Gallagher. Passenger UK citizen Judy Paddon. Registered owners Bullock Development Corporation of Saint Louis, USA. British frigates *Aries* and *Jupiter* and US submarine *Narwhal* allegedly exercising in the area assisted operation which placed Gallagher and Paddon on board Soviet ship *Antonov* in role of survivors. *Antonov* departed Luanda October twenty-six due Leningrad November eleven. Stop. Gryzan to proceed with utmost urgency, Borodin.' The domed head turned from the window and the eyes behind the pebble lenses focused on the younger man. 'Get that off immediately. The message to be repeated to Muehler in Washington.'

It was a seaman, not a steward, whom the armed guard admitted to Gallagher's cabin with a tray at 6.30 that evening. The meal was basic: black bread, cabbage soup and a mug of weak tea. Very different to the *uzhin* served in the officers' saloon.

At 7.30 the same seaman came to the cabin and removed the tray. He left, the door was locked from the outside and Gallagher heard him talking to the guard in the passageway.

It was the moment the American had been waiting for. It was unlikely he would be disturbed again for some time. He went through to the bathroom, shut the door behind him and took the electric shaver from the cupboard. Removing the spray-head from the flexible tubing on the bathroom shower he shook out the stainless steel ballpoint he'd concealed there during his first day on board. He unscrewed the cap at the top of the pen and pulled out a telescopic aerial. Then he unscrewed and removed the cone at the writing end and prized open a concealed panel on the shaver to reveal a micro transmitter-receiver. The shaver bore the Remington mark but it was of CIA design and manufacture. Gallagher fitted the aerial spigot and with the volume control turned down checked that the transmitter was functioning.

Standing on the WC seat he turned the knurled knob on the airvent until its apertures were open. The vent gave out on to the after side of the accommodation tower; it was for use in the event of air-conditioning failure or shutdown. He looked at his watch. Seven minutes to eight. Though the movement of the ship suggested that wind and sea had moderated it was still dark and blustery outside. At eight o'clock the watches would change, men would be moving about, exchanging reports with those they were relieving. It was the time when alertness in the ship was at a low ebb. Gallagher waited patiently.

When eight o'clock struck on the ship's broadcast he poked the aerial through the aperture in the airvent, held the shaver to his lips and called, 'Greensleeves, this is Gravestone.' He waited, ready to repeat the call, but it was not necessary.

'Go ahead Gravestone,' was the immediate response.

'Will land catch Yarmouth.'

'Okay, Gravestone. Roger.'

That was all and that was enough. If Grotskov's operators or Soviet radio surveillance picked that up it didn't matter, decided Gallagher. *Antonov* was in an area where there were many trawlers. He climbed down, removed the aerial, restored it to its ballpoint format, replaced it in the shower tubing, and the razor in the washbasin cupboard. He flushed the toilet, opened and shut the bathroom door noisily and went back to the cabin. There he tapped three times on the bulk-head to Judy's cabin. There was a short delay before three taps came in reply.

That will puzzle the Russians and help her, he thought. She would know the Land Catch signal had gone and been acknowledged.

Dog-tired, he lay on the bed and shut his eyes. It was the tiredness of nervous exhaustion, the sort that precludes sleep. For Christ's sake, he thought, how did they blow our cover? It was a question which had kept flashing through his mind like a bright light ever since Yenev's bombshell earlier in the day. Was it the bug? He gave up. Can't be helped, he decided. We've done all that's possible. It's up to the planners now. He spent the rest of the time until he fell asleep trying to settle in his mind where the ship was and where she would be twenty-four hours later. The first answer was, he reckoned, about thirty-five miles south-south-west of Cape Finisterre. Twenty-four hours later they should have almost crossed the Bay of Biscay to a position about fifty miles south-west of Brest. Four hours after that they should have entered the English Channel. With that thought he fell asleep.

The woman in the hooded blue raincoat walked slowly along the footpath skirting the Knightsbridge side of the Serpentine. It was a dismal night, dark, the south-west wind blowing low cloud over Hyde Park, the rain beating down in prickling swathes. At a landing stage a man stood watching the lights reflected in the muddy waters of the lake. As the woman drew level with the landing stage he threw his unfinished cigarette away, stepped on to the path beside her and they walked on together, talking in low voices.

'I have been trying to get you for hours, Jan Gryzan. Where have you been?' She spoke heavily accented English.

'My day off duty. At the pictures. I'm still human.'

'We wanted you urgently. Time is very short.' She was a plain, rather severe-looking woman whose voice matched her looks.

'Too bad, Anna Mursk. How was I to know I'd be wanted today?'

'You could not know. But Khazarov says every minute is vital.'

'For what?'

'A message from Borodin. It came hours ago.'

'You have it?'

She shook her head in the darkness. 'No. But I have memorized it.'

'Tell me then, Anna. What is it?' He stopped on the path, lit another cigarette.

In the flare of the lighter she saw the burn-scarred face. She repeated Borodin's message, word for word. A formidable woman, she had a degree in linguistics from Moscow University, a photographic memory and three years' service as personal assistant to Khazarov. A woman to be treated with respect.

They discussed the message briefly.

'I'll check the duty roster,' he said. 'See what watches I kept round about those dates.'

'You'll have to work quickly, Jan. This is very urgent. I can't stress that too much.'

'I'll do my best. From memory I can't think of anything connected with this. I'll have to examine the call-record sheets and my duty notes. Maybe they'll bring back something. They often do.' There was a rough harshness about his voice as if his throat was dry.

'Phone me as soon as possible. Let us meet on the bridge over the lake next time.'

'Right. Leave it to me. See you.'

He pulled up the collar of his raincoat and moved away in the direction of Hyde Park Corner. She watched until he was lost to sight in the darkness. Only then did she begin to walk at an unhurried pace in the opposite direction. She liked Jan Gryzan, would like to have seen more of him. He was the sort of man she could have had an affair with if he'd shown any interest, but he hadn't. His ugly manliness, his intelligence, determination and dependability, his total commitment were qualities she admired. Having seen his KGB history sheet she knew a good deal about him. Born in Brooklyn of Polish parents – post-1945 refugees – Gryzan had served in the US Navy for eight years, most of which time he'd been in the communications branch. Two years in the Navy Department at the Pentagon had been followed by a posting to USN Headquarters in Grosvenor Square for telecommunication duties. He'd been there for almost a year. The KGB had netted him in Guantanamo, the US naval base in Cuba, some years before that. Always inclined towards the political left, he'd got too friendly with a Cuban girl and passed her classified information. She was a dupe used by the KGB to get the tapes and photos which would have earned him a life sentence in the US. That had been pressure enough. He'd been resentful at first but mellowed later. As a result of being rewarded well and appreciated generously, commitment had followed. Because of the nature of his USN duties in Grosvenor Square – teletype and confidential switchboard operator – his value to the KGB was considerable. She knew that Khazarov thought a lot of him.

The minute hand on the wall clock in the conference room moved to 1135. Rathouse examined the faces round the table with a bucolic stare. 'Sorry to get you out at such short notice. And on such a filthy night.' He paused. 'I imagine you realize that something important has come up.'

'Not a *crise de guerre*, I trust,' interjected Maltby.

Glancing at the fat man as if he were something the cat had brought in, Rathouse took a message sheet from the file. 'It's from *Antonov*. Our people,' he said. 'I'll read it. Begins: Will land catch Yarmouth. Message ends. Transmitted at five minutes past eight tonight.'

The silence which followed was broken by Maltby. 'So they *are* in trouble.' The tone suggested he always knew they would be.

'What seems to me rather more important,' corrected the

Commodore, 'is the indication that phase two is necessary. That, may I remind you, is the significance of Land Catch.'

Maltby stopped in the act of lighting his pipe. 'We're well aware of that. What I'm worried about is the Yarmouth bit. They *are* in trouble. What sort of trouble? We don't know, do we. Nor can we be sure it won't compromise the project.'

'Unlikely I think. Gallagher and Paddon don't know the details of phase two.' The Commodore spoke to O'Dowd. 'Perhaps you would confirm that. You did the briefing.'

'Yes, Commodore. I can. All they know is that they had to send the Land Catch signal if what they'd seen on board persuaded them that *Antonov* required closer examination. That's all I guess. In Paris they asked for details of phase two. I said I had none. Presumed it meant a fuller investigation. That was all. No doubt they've thought about it, made their own assumptions, but they know nothing of OPERATION PETTICOAT.'

Maltby took his pipe from his mouth in order to voice a low rumble of disapproval. 'Why have we given this cat-and-mouse treatment to these people? First we don't tell them we've tipped off the KGB about Bort, Garde Optics and Gallagher. Next we get them to initiate the second phase without their having the faintest idea what it's all about. Bloody unfair, I think.'

Rathouse shook his head in despair. 'My dear Sir James — with the greatest respect — you are Chairman of the Intelligence Co-ordinating Committee. You know as well as I do that it's not policy to give clandestine operatives the whole picture. *The more they know the more they blow,*' he quoted with evident relish, no doubt pleased to have caught Maltby off balance.

'I don't question that policy in general. In this instance I believe its application to be inappropriate. The *Antonov* isn't the Lubianka prison. Her crew are not professional interrogators. That task would be reserved for Leningrad.'

'To coin a phrase,' said Rathouse. 'Exceptions make bad rules.'

Maltby grunted uncompromisingly. The Commodore looked with heavy emphasis from the wall clock to his wristwatch. 'I would remind you,' he said, 'that the purpose of this meeting is to launch OPERATION PETTICOAT.'

He turned to Kitson. 'Where is *Antonov* now?'

'She was abeam of Finisterre at 2217. Now in the Bay of Biscay. The weather there has improved. She should be off Brest in twenty-four hours. Off the Lizard about three hours later – say 0100 on Friday – and in the Dover Straits about 1700 that day.'

'Up-dated ETA for position X-ray?' The veins on Rathouse's forehead pulsed with more than usual vigour.

Kitson consulted the single sheet of paper in his file. 'Northwood give it as 0530 on the eighth – that's Saturday.'

'Time of sunrise?'

Kitson looked at his notes again. 'Oh-seven-two-one.'

'Right. I propose we now make the executive signal for Petticoat.' Rathouse's outward calm did little to deceive Briggs who knew from the rat-a-tatting on the table that the Commodore's tension was struggling to get out. 'Is that agreed?'

It was. The Commodore spoke to Kitson. 'When do you and Rossiter join *Cyclades*?'

'We fly to Newcastle tomorrow morning. Arrive there at ten-fifteen. A helicopter will transfer us to the ship. Should be on board before noon.'

'Good.' He turned back to face Maltby at the far end of the table. 'Northwood will keep us abreast of developments. Fothergill will keep you informed, Sir James. In the meantime I propose we meet again at eight o'clock tomorrow night – unless the situation calls for an earlier get-together. Is that agreed?'

It was.

# 18

Borodin's message to the Soviet Embassy in London was received there in the late afternoon. Khazarov's reply reached him during the forenoon of the following day and gave him the clue for which he was searching. It recorded that in the course of a phone conversation on 27 October between Lieutenant-Commander Briggs (RN Intelligence), Whitehall, and Commander Rossiter (USN Intelligence), Grosvenor Square, the latter had been asked by Briggs to *get Dave O'Dowd to confirm the baron's ETD*. At that point, at Rossiter's urgent request, Briggs had switched to a scrambler phone and all further conversation had been lost. Khazarov's reply went on to explain that 'Dave O'Dowd' was Commander David O'Dowd of US Naval Intelligence; that he had been absent from US Navy HQ, Grosvenor Square, for the period 26/28 October during which time calls had been put through to him in Paris; that he was now back in London, whereas Rossiter had left that day for an undisclosed destination in Scotland, possibly the Polaris submarine base on the Clyde.

Borodin paced and the wheels of his mind turned as he marshalled the facts: O'Dowd had been in Paris for the period 26/28 October. *Confirm the baron's ETD* – the baron's expected time of departure? It *must* be the Beechcraft Baron. It had left Paris for Dakar on 28 October. Rossiter and O'Dowd were both commanders in the United States Navy, both served in US Naval Intelligence. On the evidence available both were probably involved in the planning which had placed Gallagher and Paddon on board the *Antonov*. Rossiter, now somewhere in Scotland, was not immediately available but O'Dowd, back in London, was. As one of the planners of the operation he would know a great deal more than Gallagher and Paddon, whose briefing would have given them only that which they had to know as operatives – the essential minimum. Their interrogation would present him with only a part of the picture; O'Dowd's would give it all. British and United States Intelligence had resorted to extraordinary measures in this operation. The KGB would do the same. O'Dowd must be brought to Leningrad. On that score he had no doubts. Nor apparently had Khazarov for his reply had ended with: *Abduction O'Dowd feasible if you can arrange collection by helicopter at location Ezra 0600 tomorrow 8 November.*

Borodin stopped pacing and stared at Vladimir Ilyitch as if he had just become aware of his presence. 'Take this message for the London Embassy,' he said. 'Begins: Your 1053 refers. Proceed with abduction. Helicopter will be at location Ezra at 0600 tomorrow 8 November. Ends.'

He moved his steel-rimmed spectacles, blinked owl-like at Ilyitch, took a tissue from the desk and began to clean them. 'Classification "Most Secret",' he said. 'Prefix it "Immediate action – strictly personal to Khazarov." '

Borodin went to his desk, picked up the phone, dialled the internal number of the Director of Operations. A voice answered and Borodin moved the scrambler switch to 'on'.

As he poured himself his second vodka of the evening Boris Milovych hummed a refrain from Tchaikovsky's *Little Russian* and made snapping noises with his fingers. He was in high spirits for he had just left the Captain's cabin after a discussion during which Yenev had not only apologized but had acknowledged that he, Milovych, had been right from the start.

The apology had, it was true, only come after Milovych had said, 'You may possibly recall my remarks, Comrade Yenev, the day we picked them up.'

'What remarks?' Yenev had been gruff, offhand.

'You asked why these people should be treated as suspects. I replied that all British and American imperialists on Soviet soil were suspects. I pointed out that *Antonov* was not only Soviet soil but a ship with a high security rating.'

Yenev had thought about that and then he had after some delay and to Milovych's surprise said, 'You were right. I apologize.'

It was that in part which accounted for the Commissar's euphoric mood, but there was more to it. He felt that he had now rehabilitated himself in Borodin's eyes; a congratulatory message had come in from Leningrad bearing the great man's name. Admittedly it was addressed to Yenev and himself, but he had already completed drafting the confidential report which would go to Borodin and which would leave no doubt as to who was primarily responsible for what had been accomplished. Milovych had of course mentioned Yenev's over-conciliatory attitude towards the survivors, and his own insistence that they be thoroughly interrogated and their cabins placed under radio surveillance – this he had done, he stressed, in spite of the Captain's opposition.

Needless to say he had mentioned the part Grotskov had played, though he'd been at pains to avoid giving too much credit to the communications officer. In this Milovych had been influenced by his own disappointment – bordering on anger – at Grotskov's failure to confide in him at the outset. It was most reprehensible that he, the ship's political officer, had not been informed of Grotskov's suspicions and of the tape tests he'd been conducting. Milovych's report had stressed Grotskov's failure in this respect.

Rolling a mouthful of vodka round his tongue, the Commissar reflected how important it was to be objective in these matters; to give credit where credit was due, to censure where censure was justified. If there was one thing more than another – and there were many others – on which he prided himself it was his objectivity.

During the night the weather in the approaches to the Bay of Biscay moderated, wind and sea dropped though the sky remained overcast. Despite the north-westerly swell *Antonov* made good progress; Cape Finisterre was abeam soon after ten o'clock that night; twenty-four hours later Ushant had been left astern and the crossing of the Bay completed. Not long afterwards course was altered and the ship headed up into the mouth of the English Channel. She was off the Lizard at one o'clock in the morning; Start Point was abeam, distant thirty miles, some hours later.

Traffic in the Channel was as usual heavy and though *Antonov* kept to the north-bound lane those on board constantly sighted the lights of south-bound ships on the port side and ferries and other vessels crossing from port and starboard. There were, too, the lights of trawlers, yachts and various small craft, and this abundance of maritime activity showed up on *Antonov*'s radar displays as luminous specks which glowed like hatches of fireflies. At times there came the roar of aircraft passing overhead, and the lights of those flying low would drift across the sky. Among these constantly moving lights and radar echoes, distant and anonymous, were those of the frigates *Aries* and *Jupiter* and the submarine *Narwhal*, now surfaced; all were making for Portland having been relieved of their task of shadowing *Antonov* off Start Point by two *Bird* class patrol craft from Portland and a Westland Wasp helicopter from the Royal Naval Air Station there.

Unaware of the presence of these uninvited escorts, the men on *Antonov*'s bridge concentrated on navigating the Soviet bulk-carrier safely through the busy waters of the English Channel.

# 19

Whirls of gathering fog shrouded Admiralty Arch, slowing the pace and blurring the lights of traffic along the Mall. In the conference room on the southern side of the old Admiralty building a meeting had just begun. Kitson and Rossiter were notable absentees.

'It was necessary,' said the Commodore, 'to call you together earlier than planned. Northwood have come up with a problem. The latest report from the Met. people predicts fog in the North Sea in the early hours of tomorrow morning.' He gestured towards the windows overlooking the Mall. 'Not surprising. We seem to have the beginnings of it here.'

'If it's not surprising what's the problem?' Maltby exposed his teeth in a humourless grin.

The Commodore ignored the intervention. 'Northwood want us to reconsider the position. *Antonov* will reduce speed if she encounters fog. That introduces certain complications most of which, fortunately, have been foreseen.'

'What wasn't foreseen?' challenged Maltby.

'Fog in the North Sea,' said the Commodore. 'Most unusual in November.'

'Is it?' Maltby examined the bowl of his pipe with elaborate care. 'Not unusual here.'

'This is not the North Sea.'

'Sorry. Do carry on.'

'Thank you,' said the Commodore. 'Northwood point out

that if the ETA of 0530 at position X-ray is to be maintained, it may be necessary to shift X-ray south. Possibly as much as thirty-five miles.'

'Alternatives?' asked Maltby.

'Amend the ETA to a later time. Northwood are not keen. Sunrise is at seven-twenty-one and daylight is not our friend. X-ray *can* be shifted to the south, but a big shift complicates ship dispositions – particularly if the need arises at short notice. For these reasons Northwood want us to assume there *will* be fog and agree now to move X-ray thirty-five miles south, fog or no fog. If we agree that, they will revise time and disposition schedules and pass them to *Cyclades* without delay. Less than twelve hours left. That is the situation.' He looked round the table. 'Do we agree to the shift?'

'Don't see that we have any option,' said Maltby. 'Let's agree and get on with it.'

There was general assent.

'Good,' said the Commodore. 'Those are my feelings. Pass that to Northwood, will you, Briggs.'

Briggs hurried away. The Commodore got on with outlining developments since the previous night's meeting. *Antonov*'s position at four o'clock that afternoon was, he said, midway between Boulogne and Dungeness; the shadowing units were remaining at long range, periodically changing position relative to the Soviet ship. The helicopter from Portland was, he'd been told, maintaining a low profile.

'Horrible cliché,' objected Maltby.

'In fact,' concluded Rathouse, 'everything's proceeding according to plan.'

'Except the weather.' Maltby's chair groaned alarmingly as he heaved himself into a more comfortable position.

'Surely fog's rather a help?' Freddie Lewis, having made one of his rare contributions, smiled amiably, leant back and folded his arms across his chest.

'In some ways,' said the Commodore. 'But we'd be happier without it. Ships can cope. Aircraft have problems.'

'So I believe.' The group captain was at his mildest. He

had well over four thousand hours in his RAF logbooks. The Commodore's frown suggested that the irony had not been lost on him.

Later Briggs returned to announce that he'd passed the decision to Northwood. After a number of other aspects of OPERATION PETTICOAT had been discussed the meeting broke up at 5.20 pm.

O'Dowd checked out through security, walked down the steps of the old Admiralty building and arrived on the pavement to find the darkness of early evening made worse by a damp and chilling fog. A stranger to London, uncertain what to do, he hesitated. Find a cab in Trafalgar Square? Sure. That was it. He turned left and started walking. He'd not gone far when a taxi drew up a few yards ahead of him. The passenger got out, paid the fare.

'You free?' O'Dowd asked the driver.

'Depends where you want to go. Fog, see.'

'Not far. Grosvenor Square. US Navy offices.'

The driver nodded. 'Okay, guvnor. But it'll take time. Traffic's slowed right down.'

'Sure has. I'll accept the delays as long as I get there. I'd walk it, but I'm a stranger to London.'

'American aren't you?'

'I guess so.' O'Dowd opened a door, climbed in and the taxi moved off into the Mall. As it pulled away from the kerb a yellow-helmeted rider sitting astride a Suzuki revved up his engine, spoke into the mike of a two-way radio, let out the clutch and followed. On the metal saddle-boxes of the Suzuki a stylized arrow appeared above the inscription ARROW EXPRESS DELIVERIES. Beneath that there was a London telephone number.

The taxi moved forward again, kept going slowly for a minute or so before jolting once more to a stop.

O'Dowd looked out of the misted windows. The fog was thicker, visibility down to about thirty feet he decided. All he could see were the vehicles close at hand and at times the shadowy outline of people along the pavements, and the blur of street and traffic lights. He had no idea where they were. He looked at his watch – 5.50 pm. They'd already been twenty-five minutes on the journey. He leant forward, tapped on the glass partition. 'Much farther to go now?'

The driver opened the sliding panel. 'Not far, guvnor. Once this lot gets moving.'

The traffic crawled forward again and they moved with it, edging into the nearside lane, hugging the kerb, until at the next traffic light they turned into a narrow side street. The driver half-turned his head. 'Short cut, guvnor. Had to get away from that lot.'

At its end the street turned ninety degrees. The taxi followed the turn and pulled up alongside a Post Office telephone booth just beyond it.

'Got to phone the old lady, guv,' the driver explained. 'Be home late tonight. Won't be a sec.' He went into the lighted box and through the mantle of fog O'Dowd could see the dim shape dialling. While he was watching he heard the door on the off-side of the taxi opening. A gruff voice said, 'Take it easy, man.' He switched his head right, saw the short barrel of the Smith & Wesson .38 pointing at his chest and decided discretion was the better part of valour.

The man got in and sat down, the barrel of his revolver pressed into O'Dowd's side. The newcomer was breathing heavily, a stale smell of beer and cigarettes hanging about him like an unseen cloak.

The driver came back, got into the driving seat. As he started the engine the near-side door opened and another man, small and wizened, climbed in. He, too, had a revolver and once seated beside O'Dowd he pushed its barrel into the American's left side with a pressure matching that on the right. The two intruders didn't speak to each other.

They take care of the heart and liver, thought O'Dowd; very considerate. But he didn't feel anything like as flippant as the thought suggested.

156

'What's going on here?' he demanded, realizing it was a futile question. Whatever the answer, there was little he could do about it.

'Nothing,' said the gruff voice. 'Just keep your mouth shut, look straight ahead and you'll be okay.' The language was English but the accent was foreign.

The taxi pulled away from the kerb and resumed its journey through the fog. After a series of left and right turns they joined a busy traffic stream on a main thoroughfare. Two blocks later they stopped again at a traffic light.

While the taxi waited for the lights to go green, the yellow-helmeted Suzuki rider following it once again spoke into his two-way radio.

To O'Dowd the journey seemed interminable. His only point of reference was the time and this he consulted sparingly for fear of alerting his captors. The last fleeting glance he'd had at the luminous dial of his wristwatch told him it was 6.30 pm. They'd been going for more than an hour, but that didn't involve much distance under those conditions. From what he could see through the fogged windows they were now in an industrial part of London : broad, winding thoroughfares with more lorries and trucks than before. Changed though its nature was, the traffic still moved slowly and stopped often.

O'Dowd saw a motorcycle with a yellow-helmeted rider overtake on the off-side, slow down and drop in ahead. Soon afterward it turned right at a traffic light and the taxi followed. There were several more turns, the motorcycle leading until they were in an area of high brick walls interspersed with warehouses, an occasional pub and empty building sites. The taxi turned once more and passed under a brick archway on to an unlit cobbled road bordered by warehouses. The taxi's headlights did no more than illuminate the Suzuki rider and thirty or forty feet of roadway. Beyond that there was a wall of fog. O'Dowd managed to read the Suzuki's registration number and he made a mental note of it. The taxi stopped, the off-side door opened and the gruff-voiced man got out. O'Dowd heard the sound of a ship's siren. It was followed by an answering wail. The Thames he decided. The deserted docks area. His thoughts were interrupted by the gruff voice. 'Put it on, Vasily. I'll keep him covered.'

The small man on the left turned towards O'Dowd. He was holding something in his hands. The American felt the blindfold being drawn tight over his eyes. After that a wad of cotton wool was pushed into his mouth, and his lips were sealed with strips of plaster.

'Okay. You're fine now,' said the gruff voice.

O'Dowd was pulled out of the taxi while he was still thinking that the remark sounded very much like a dentist reassuring a patient after a difficult extraction. With a man holding his arms on either side, he was led some sixty paces down a shallow incline until they stopped, one of the men knocked on the door several times – a coded knock, decided O'Dowd – and there was the sound of unlocking, followed by the squeak of hinges. One of his captors released his arm, the other led him through what was presumably a doorway.

'Watch your feet,' commanded the gruff voice.

They walked on gingerly, O'Dowd's feet at times encountering what felt like slats of timber, at others brushing against litter. They stopped at last and he was made to sit on a hard surface, from the feel of it a packing case. His hands were then tied behind his back and his ankles bound together, so that he felt remarkably like a trussed chicken. There was no longer the damp chill of fog on his face, and from the musty smell of rotting matter and the occasional lap-lap of water he assumed they were in a warehouse facing the river.

Once O'Dowd and his guards had left the taxi and disappeared down the lane between the warehouses the driver got out, lit a cigarette and walked at a leisurely pace to where the Suzuki rider sat motionless on his machine.

'Everything okay, then?' enquired the taxi driver. He was

a big, blue-jowled man with a large moustache and a hoarse boozy voice.

The Suzuki rider took an envelope from the inside pocket of his leather jacket and handed it to him. 'Two hundred pounds. Count it if you like.'

The big man took it. 'Always do,' he said. 'Not that I don't trust you. Just habit.' He opened the envelope, flipped through the ten £20 notes. 'Okay,' he said. 'It's dead right.'

'It always is. You're suspicious aren't you, Brewster. I don't know why. *We* trust you.'

'It's habit, like I told you.'

'We trust you,' repeated the Suzuki rider, 'because you know you'd be a dead man if we couldn't.'

'No need to threaten, mate. This isn't the first job I've done for your lot. Haven't ever let you down, have I?'

'Better keep it that way. Healthier for you. 'Bye now.'

' 'Bye,' the taxi driver went back to his cab, climbed in, started the engine and drove away.

Not long after the taxi had disappeared the blurred headlights of an approaching car came up through the fog. They belonged to a black Mercedes which pulled up short of the Suzuki. The driver got out and opened the rear door. Two men emerged; a thin man carrying a briefcase and a short thickset man wearing dark glasses and a black coat with a fur collar. They joined the Suzuki rider who was standing beside his machine. The thickset man said, 'Good evening. Everything I hope is in order?' The stilted English, the deep voice, were foreign.

'Yes. He's given no trouble. They've taken him inside.' With his head he gestured towards the warehouse. 'I paid Brewster. He drove off just before you arrived.'

'So. It is his lights we see before the corner. Yes?'

'Sure. That's right.'

'Better that way. Now we make business.' He turned towards the thin man with the black briefcase. 'You can go to them,' he said. The thin man left them, disappeared down the lane between the warehouses.

'The other arrangements. Okay?' The Suzuki rider was pulling on his gauntlets.

'Yes. At midnight the motor launch *Pamir* takes him from here. The tide will be right. Six hours later they will be at location Ezra. The helicopter lifts him from there.'

'What about the fog? Maybe there'll be fog off the Outer Gabbard?'

'If it is so a surveillance trawler will take him on board.'

'I see. Well organized.' The Suzuki rider lowered the vizor of his crash-helmet. Somewhere in the distance a clock chimed seven. 'Must get back to Grosvenor Square. I'm on duty at eight.'

'Yes. Of course.' The thickset man patted him on the shoulder. 'You have done well, Jan Gryzan. Borodin will be pleased.'

'Thank you, Comrade Khazarov. I did no more than my duty.' He climbed astride the Suzuki, started the engine, let out the clutch, waved to Khazarov and rode slowly down the cobbled road. The tail-light was swallowed by the fog long before the sound of the powerful engine had faded.

# 20

The Captain of the frigate *Cyclades* frowned at the three men in his day cabin. 'So that's it?' he said. 'Usual cock-up.' He passed the Northwood signal back to Kitson. 'How does fog affect your braves?'

Kitson gazed gloomily at the chart on the table between them, did things with dividers and a parallel ruler. 'Not seriously. Could help. We still have eleven hours and there's no sign of fog yet. Much better to make the shift now while we have time. Last minute scrambles are usually disasters.' He looked up with the mournful expression of a bloodhound. 'This involves shifting X-ray and the units concerned thirty-five miles south. Nothing more. The operational plan isn't affected. When we simulated this thing in *Huntress* with the skippers and patrol boats' COs we allowed for a shift of X-ray. Not because of fog but on the assumption that for one reason or another *Antonov*'s course and speed might alter materially. After all her course is based on a prediction — standard routing to the Skaggerak — but it's still only a prediction. She may always alter course and speed. Since we have to maintain an ETA at X-ray of five-thirty, the only way to deal with these contingencies is to shift it as necessary.'

The Captain of *Cyclades* looked at the chart, ran a hand through a mop of dark hair. 'I imagine top priority now is to pass the new position to those concerned.'

'*Huntress* has already done that,' said Rossiter.

'Good.' The captain nodded approvingly. 'Before we pack up I'd like to have another look at your games board, Kitson.'

Kitson looked mildly pleased, took a hinged board from his briefcase and unfolded it on the table. From a small box he produced six plastic arrows of different colours, each an inch long. The hinged board was overprinted with a half mile grid, its centre occupied by a compass-rose from which concentric circles ran out at two mile intervals. 'The centre of the compass-rose is X-ray,' he said. 'With its shift thirty-five miles south our point of reference – the Dan Oil rig – will be sixty miles to the north.'

He placed the arrows on the concentric circles. 'Those are the approximate positions of each unit when *Antonov* is ten miles to the south of X-ray. The stern trawler *John Henry D.* and the survey ship *Huntress* on the ten mile circle are approaching from the south-west and north-east respectively. *Auxoil*, the oil-rig tender, also on the ten mile circle, is approaching from the north-west. The red and yellow job at the bottom, approaching from the south, is *Antonov*. She is exactly ten miles south of X-ray.'

'What about the patrol boats?'

'I've not shown them – the board only goes up to ten miles – but *Kittiwake* will be two miles astern of *Antonov* steering the same course – that is a northerly course. *Plover* will be on *Antonov*'s starboard quarter, coming in from the south-east. Incidentally *Plover* will rendezvous with us at midnight to take Rossiter on board. After that she'll take up station to the south-east of *Antonov*.'

'Sounds complicated,' *Cyclades*'s captain looked doubtful.

'Extraordinarily simple really,' defended Kitson. He was a navigator and the operational plan was his brainchild. 'Each unit will be heading for position X-ray. Each will have the entire picture on radar. *Kittiwake* will, ostensibly, be doing a survey – running a line of soundings from south to north, passing the readings to *Huntress* by voice radio. Every tenth sounding will be followed by the word 'reference' followed by seven digits. They will represent *Antonov*'s bearing and distance from Dan Oil, the distance to one decimal place. That will look after any problem of identification which might arise. Should be particularly useful in fog, if any. *John Henry D.* and *Auxoil*'s principal task will be to adjust course and speed as necessary to maintain *Antonov* on a steady bearing.' He looked up from the board. 'You already know the rest of the scenario.'

'What about other traffic? Quite likely to be some.'

'That's right,' Rossiter said. 'We allowed for that. It helps, I guess.'

'Confusion worse confounded,' suggested Kitson.

*Cyclades*'s captain got up, walked round the cabin, looked at the painting of his wife over the electric fireplace, went back to the settee. 'These chaps, the skippers of *John Henry D.* and *Auxoil*. Are they absolutely to be relied upon?'

'D'you mean professionally or the other thing?'

'The other thing. Security.'

'Absolutely. They're both RNRs with about twenty years in. First rate men, double-dyed patriots. Professionally, they are highly competent.'

'I've never doubted that. It was the security aspect. Any of their crews in the picture?'

'None, only the skippers. *John Henry D.* is outward bound from Hull to fish. *Auxoil* is en route from Aberdeen to load equipment for a new oil-rig south of the Argyle field. The movements of both are tailored to the requirements of Petticoat. But that's known only to their skippers and the owners' MDs – both, like the skippers, long involved with us on surveillance work. The price they'd have to pay for indiscretion is beyond contemplation. No problem there. The other units are RN, and only their COs are in on this.'

Rossiter said, 'I guess you've forgotten the *Belknap* frigates, Paul.'

'That's right.' Kitson was apologetic. 'Stupid of me.' He spoke to *Cyclades*'s captain. 'The USN have two *Belknap* frigates exercising south-west of the Dan Oil field. They are there for muscle if needed. Like *Cyclades*. Their captains are, of course, in the picture.'

'Very much so,' confirmed *Cyclades*'s captain. 'They dined with me here last night. By the way, Rossiter, hope you've a stomach for small craft.'

Rossiter grinned. 'Guess I'll manage.'

Kitson put away the board and arrows. 'I think that's really all I can give you by way of a pre-run.'

'Thank you, Paul. That was very good. Now what about a drink?' *Cyclades*'s captain pressed a bellpush.

A steward appeared from the pantry, took the order and left.


Martin Briggs stayed on in the old Admiralty building after the meeting of the *Antonov* committee. Rathouse had decided that he and Briggs would remain there until the conclusion of OPERATION PETTICOAT on the following morning. The Commodore's office had direct and confidential telephone and teletype links with Northwood, with MI5 and 6, the Special Branch, US Naval Headquarters in Grosvenor Square and several other key authorities.

For the time being Briggs was on his own, Rathouse having gone off to the In and Out to keep an appointment which he said could not be deferred. 'Back within the hour,' he'd reassured Briggs. 'Fog or no fog.'

At about seven o'clock the phone on Briggs's desk rang; he picked it up. 'DNI's office,' he said.

'That you, Martin? Dan Hellinger here.' Hellinger was Briggs's opposite number at Grosvenor Square.

'Hullo, Dan.'

'Is Dave O'Dowd with you?'

'No. He left some time ago. About five-thirty.'

'You don't say. He was due back here after the meeting. Had to report to Burwell. We tried his flat in Belgravia. Wife said he's not there.'

'Could be the fog, couldn't it?'

'An hour and a half to get here? No way. He'd have been in a hurry. He knows Burwell doesn't like waiting. More likely a road accident. Anyway the Admiral's on the warpath. Know how we can find out real fast?'

'Yes. Leave it to me. I'll speak to Scotland Yard. Call you back soon.' Briggs got through to the Yard and spoke to the Chief Superintendent (Traffic). The Super kept his promise. Phoned back in fifteen minutes: casualty wards, ambulance services, police stations in the area had been checked. There was no record of O'Dowd or anyone like him. Briggs's next move was the Special Branch. Dugald McGann took things in a low key. In Briggs's experience he always did. A man without a decent sense of urgency, he'd long decided. McGann said, 'Leave it with me, will you? No need for alarm, I should say.'

Briggs phoned Grosvenor Square again. No joy there yet, reported Hellinger, but they were still trying.

At seven-thirty Rathouse returned, tired and irritable. 'This bloody fog,' he complained. 'Gets up my nose. What's the latest from Northwood?'

'*Antonov*'s approaching the North Hinder. Should be off the Outer Gabbard at about twenty-one hundred. *Cyclades*, *Huntress* and the other units involved are adjusting their deployment in relation to the amended position for X-ray.'

'Cumbersome sentence, Briggs. Why not "the Petticoat lot are redeploying for the X-ray shift"?'

'Sorry, sir. Staff course, I'm afraid.'

'Pity, Briggs. Should have got it out of your system by now. The weather?'

'Fog patches in the Thames Estuary. None so far in the Channel or North Sea, but the Met. people think it's increasingly likely.'

Rathouse said, 'On this occasion I agree with them. You'd better be off now and get something to eat. Make it snappy.'

'There's a problem, sir.'

'There always is.' The Commodore became irascible. 'What's it this time?'

'O'Dowd has disappeared.' Briggs delivered his punchline with some satisfaction. 'Failed to report back to Grosvenor

Square after the meeting.'

The Commodore stopped in the act of opening the door of his office, stared. 'Good God. What's being done about that?'

Briggs told him: no news as yet; the Yard and Special Branch would keep checking; Grosvenor Square busy too, so far without success.

'Very odd,' said Rathouse. 'Tart, d'you think? He's new to London. Could've been picked up. They're remarkably persuasive, I'm told.'

'Hardly likely, sir. He had orders to return to Grosvenor Square as soon as possible. To report personally to Admiral Burwell.'

'Very odd,' repeated Rathouse. 'I wonder . . .'

The phone rang on Briggs's desk. He picked it up. 'Briggs here.'

'Fothergill here, Briggs. I hear from Dugald McGann that you're fussing about O'Dowd.'

'We are. So is Grosvenor Square. He's disappeared.'

'So I believe. May I suggest you lower the temperature. The Special Branch are on to this. One gathers they have the situation well in hand. McGann's taking it with commendable calm.'

Fothergill's plummy primness triggered something in Briggs's more homespun make-up. 'Bugger McGann's calm, Fothergill. We want to know where O'Dowd is.'

'I suspect we shall shortly.' The SIS man's tone was icy. '*Good*bye.'

Briggs heard the phone click off, looked with disgust at the instrument in his hand. 'Bloody hell,' he said and replaced it noisily.

'May I ask what all that was about?' Rathouse eyed him with disapproval.

# 21

The first car to arrive – a Rover 2300 – nosed through the fog into Prussom Street and parked; the third and fourth parked in Wapping High Street; the fifth and sixth in Glamis Road. The driver and his two passengers remained in the Rover. From time to time one of them gave terse, monosyllabic orders by radio in a voice as rough as gravel.

Fog had slowed down and complicated things but by eight minutes past seven all cars had parked in the positions allocated and Fagan, the rough voiced man in the Rover, launched the operation with the words 'Butterfly proceed' repeated three times. Walking singly and in twos and threes, they approached Wapping Wall from three directions – from Glamis Road, from High Street and from Garnett Street. Anyone seeing these anonymous shapes in the fog would have put them down as local men going about their business, walking to and from home or the pubs, or visiting friends. Their clothes, almost everything about them, was ordinary; but none had women with them and under their jackets all carried guns in shoulder-holsters.

At 7.15 Moynihan reported to Fagan by radio, 'Sunbeam Five ready and waiting. No change.'

Fagan at once replied. 'Roger, Sunbeam Five. Standby.' He turned to the man beside him. 'The warehouse is surrounded. The Mercedes still parked outside, driver still at the wheel.

Maybe a long wait, Wilson.'

'Likely it will be,' said Wilson. 'I'll give my lads a call.'

The Rover had two radio sets on different frequencies. Because of the possibility of monitoring they were not frequencies normally used, nor were the call-signs. Wilson picked up the handset, spoke into it. 'Moonshines. Situation static. No change. Over.'

Acknowledgements came in quick succession. Some from patrol cars, some from motorcyclists, and three from police launches lying in the Thames off Wapping Wall. Between them these units formed the outer cordon which covered every approach to the warehouse.

O'Dowd had been sitting on the packing-case with his captors for the best part of fifteen minutes when two more men arrived on the scene; they came singly, a short interval between them. They spoke what O'Dowd presumed was Russian, though he could neither speak nor understand the language. On their orders the plaster and gag were moved but not the blindfold nor the lashings on his hands and feet. Then the questions began, one putting them, the other acting as interpreter. O'Dowd, who'd done the anti-interrogation course and periodical refreshers, had no great difficulty in dealing with this verbal probing. He gave the minimum of information, dissembling, denying, misleading, acknowledging, refusing to answer as circumstances demanded. From the increasingly rough tone of the questioner he assumed that his refusal to co-operate was not appreciated. But he was well trained and, stubborn by nature, not a good subject for interrogation. He was expecting them to resort to more basic methods when the proceedings ended abruptly. The questioner said a long piece which the interpreter rendered as, 'You will shortly be taken to another place —' O'Dowd thought that sounded very much like a judge pronouncing the death sentence — 'where we think you *will* co-operate. If you don't —' The interpreter's sibilant hiss suggested something like neck slitting.

O'Dowd said nothing, the recent arrivals left, and the plaster and gag were replaced.

The call 'Sunbeam Five' on Fagan's receiver halted Wilson in mid-sentence. Fagan picked up the handset. 'Go ahead, Sunbeam Five.'

'Alert. Two repeat two out and embarked. Proceeding west. Standby.' It was Moynihan's voice, as richly Irish as ever.

Fagan acknowledged, spoke to Wilson. 'Two of them have come out, now in the black Mercedes going west.'

Wilson at once passed the message to all Moonshines, adding, 'Apprehend.'

Fagan said, 'Good. As soon as your lads have got them I'll give Moynihan the word to go in.'

To Fagan and Wilson time after that seemed to stand still; but the seconds ticked away and less than a minute later Wilson's receiver came alive again; 'Moonshine Three calling Moonshine.'

'Go ahead, Moonshine Three.'

'Driver and passenger now in custody. Proceeding to station.'

There was the sound of knocking on the door. One or more of the Russians returning, thought O'Dowd. His captors discussed matters in urgent undertones. The knocking turned to hammering. There was more discussion, sounds of disagreement, then silence. With appalling suddenness it was shattered by the explosive crackle of several shots fired in quick succession. O'Dowd threw himself sideways off the packing-case and landed heavily on the floor. He heard a man screaming, wood splintering, footsteps coming towards him; two more shots, the *spaang* of a passing bullet and the thump of a body close at hand. With enormous relief he heard British voices. Someone picked him up. 'We're Special Branch, Commander,' said an unseen voice. 'Not to worry. Everything's under control.'

The blindfold was taken from his eyes, the plaster and gag removed, and his hands and ankles were freed. He blinked owlishly, adjusted his vision to the dim light, stretched his arms and legs gingerly and felt the circulation returning. He looked for his helper and saw two men in front of the packing-case. The light of torches made a patchwork of the darkness but he saw enough to confirm his belief that he was in a deserted warehouse.

Near the packing-case a man lay in a grotesquely un-natural position, legs drawn up, knees against his chest, eyes staring at the ceiling, blood trickling from his mouth. O'Dowd could see dimly two other bodies lying by the shattered door where more men with torches and guns were entering. Near O'Dowd someone was talking into a two-way radio, asking for an ambulance.

A man left the group at the door and came across to O'Dowd. He shone his torch in the American's face. 'You okay, Commander?'

'Bit stiff. Fine otherwise. Who are you?'

'Chief Inspector Moynihan. Special Branch, Scotland Yard.'

O'Dowd shook his head. 'How in hell did you know where I was? And get here so quick?'

'We have ways and means, Commander.'

'Goddam – and to think I always reckoned the Brits were . . .' he hesitated, momentarily embarrassed. '. . . well, a bit slow. Bit old-fashioned, you know what I mean?'

'I know exactly what you mean.' Moynihan took him by the arm. 'Better come along now. There's a car waiting.'

O'Dowd said, 'There were two Russians interrogating me. Left about five minutes ago. Know what's happened to them?'

'We've got them.'

'You have. That's great.'

They moved towards the doorway. The Chief Inspector shone his torch on the bodies slumped near the broken door. The face of one was visible. With his foot he turned the head of the other until the face could be seen. 'Recognize them?' he asked.

'Yes. The guys who got into the taxi. The big one came in

first. He did the talking.'

'Good. We'll be taking a full statement from you at the Yard.'

O'Dowd looked at the dead bodies. The thickset man with the gruff voice who'd smelt of stale beer and cigarettes; near him the small wizened man who'd not spoken a word in the taxi. Somehow he felt sorry for them, shared vicariously the violence of their deaths. He looked at Moynihan. 'You had to do a lot of killing?' It was tentative, a concealed question.

The Chief Inspector settled the beam of his torch on the body near the packing-case. 'Had to kill *him*,' he said. 'Or he'd have got you. Shooting at you when we fired.'

'Guess I'm still some more in your debt then.' O'Dowd paused. 'These guys?' He looked at the bodies by the door.

'Both shot in the back of the head by the chap who was after you.'

'Christ. Why did he shoot his buddies?'

'The game was up. He killed them first, then tried to get you. He'd have killed himself after that. Dead men can't talk.'

'Yeh. I guess that's right.'

By the time O'Dowd had finished making his statement in Fagan's bleak office it was close to ten o'clock. Fagan and Moynihan then took him down a pasage, up some stairs and along another passage to the larger and lusher office of Assistant Commissioner Dugald McGann. A stocky Scot, bald with brown eyes and a high complexion, he looked more like a publican than supremo of the Special Branch. His manner was abrupt and he rarely smiled. Fagan introduced O'Dowd, McGann pointed to a chair and they sat down. In the discussion which followed it was evident that McGann had been well briefed.

When the opportunity came O'Dowd asked a question which both Moynihan and Fagan had refused to answer. 'Who were the two guys who questioned me? Cleared off in the Mercedes before your people broke in?'

McGann thought about that, his eyes on the paper-knife balancing on the back of his hand. The knife fell on to the blotter and he looked up. 'Sorry, Commander. Can't disclose that. It's a matter for the DGSS.' The Director-General of the Security Services was the shadowy figure who headed Britain's Intelligence services. He was never referred to by name and few people knew his identity.

'Let me ask you a question?' McGann's sharp eyes stared into O'Dowd's. 'It's one I'll precede with a statement: we think the KGB have a man in Grosvenor Square. Any idea who he could be?'

O'Dowd's face showed doubt and surprise more eloquently than could words. 'You sure about what you're saying?'

'Sure? No. But we have reason to believe that's how the KGB got on to your track.'

'What are those reasons?'

McGann shook his head. 'Sorry. That's another thing I can't disclose. I only mentioned it because I thought you might have someone in mind. Perhaps you could think about that. MI5 will be checking with your people.'

'I certainly will, Commissioner. Right now I figure it can't be that way. Our security screening's really tough.'

McGann said, 'There's no screening tough enough. No shortage of Philbys and McLeans at this end of the twentieth century. Every country has them. When ideologies tangle with patriotism anything can happen.'

'Another thing I'd like to ask,' said O'Dowd. 'The guy on the Suzuki – the one with the yellow crash helmet. There's no doubt he was leading that taxi to the warehouse. Reckon you'll get him?'

'There's not much to go on. The registration number you gave Moynihan was a phoney. If we get him we'll find the taxi driver.'

'Can't you get a lead on that from the big boys you're holding? The Mercedes passengers? When you interrogate?'

McGann resorted to the paper-knife balancing act. 'Maybe. But there are problems.'

'What sort of problems?'

'Diplomatic immunity maybe. That sort of thing you know.'

'Diplomatic immunity. With all those dead bodies?'

'They didn't kill them. Accessories after the fact, maybe. But these are problems I prefer not to discuss.'

'You're not going to release them?'

'*I'm* not. DGSS will decide that.'

There was a knock on the door and a sad-looking man in a check suit came in with a tray of coffee.

That effectively ended the night's discussion.

# 22

Something woke Gallagher. He listened intently but there was nothing but the steady beat of the diesels, the hum of auxiliaries and the scarcely audible hiss of the air-conditioning. *The beat of the diesels?* He realized then that the engines were turning more slowly than usual. Speed had been reduced. That was what had woken him. He was wondering why when he heard the muffled sound of a siren. He switched on the cabin light, looked at his watch – 4.10 am. Two minutes later the distant rumble of the siren came again. This time he checked with the second-hand of the watch: six seconds. He waited, timing the interval. It was two minutes before the next six second blast sounded. The international signal made by ships under way in fog. Six second blasts every two minutes. They were using the auto-siren on the stump mast forward in the bows. That was why the sound was so faint; that and the sealed windows.

So *Antonov* was in fog. That explained the steadiness of the ship, the absence of movement, of pitching or rolling. Fog came with calm weather. He gathered his thoughts. Four o'clock in the morning. Where were they now? The beat of the engines suggested that speed had been reduced to something like two-thirds of normal. By his reckoning they'd passed through the Straits of Dover between five and six on the previous evening. The ship had been steaming at sixteen knots. Say 5.30 pm off Dover. That was almost eleven hours back. Eleven hours at sixteen knots : one hundred and seventy-six miles. In his mind's eye he saw the coastline of the southern part of the North Sea. They'd be closer to the Dutch and German coasts than Britain's; well up in the North Sea now, probably in the latitude of Cuxhaven or Bremerhaven; somewhere off the Weser. Unless the fog was widespread *Antonov* would be back to full speed before long. By noon they'd be off Jutland on the Danish coast; through the Skaggerak and into the Baltic soon after that. Within the next three days the ship should be in Leningrad.

His thoughts turned to the cabin next door. Judy would be thinking the same things, coming to the same conclusions, worrying desperately. It was tough for her sitting there alone, not knowing what was happening, unaware that the bug she'd planted in Lomov's cabin had gone on the blink within hours of their arrest. The Russians must have used a ferret. Okay, he told himself, it was a Soviet bug with Soviet markings, but they could be wise to that CIA dodge – it was an old one. And they'd reckon she'd planted it. Too bad he decided that a woman like Judy had got caught up in such a dangerous and messy business.

His thoughts switched. What were O'Dowd and the people behind him doing? They'd had the Land Catch Yarmouth signal for more than twenty-four hours now. They'd not only know that the *Simeonovs* merited closer investigation but that he and Judy were in serious trouble – and it wouldn't require a very intelligent guess to decide what sort. What would they do about it? He remembered O'Dowd's warning at the Paris briefing : 'You are, I'm afraid, expendable. I figure it's unlikely the situation will arise. The planning's been very thorough. But if your cover's blown, make no mistake – no way can we stage a rescue operation. I guess matters would have to follow their normal course.'

*Their normal course*. Gallagher had no illusions about that. Repudiate, disown, deny, leave the clandestine operators to their fate. What was politely known in the Craft as 'plausible denial'. Maybe – but only maybe, and years later usually –

if you were important enough you might be included in an exchange of spies. It wasn't the sort of future he cared to think about. He pushed the thought away, decided to be positive. At least the project had paid a dividend. They'd been able to confirm that the *Simeonov* class had a covert naval function which required closer examination. It was too bad there was no way they could pass RN and USN Intelligence details of what they'd already seen and heard. He thought about the interrogation which lay ahead. The starting point would be the bug in Yenev's cabin. That wouldn't compromise the whole operation; wouldn't reveal RN-USN participation. Or would it? How would Judy stand up to interrogation? It would be long and rigorous. The Soviets were experts. They'd throw in everything: psychological pressure, drugs, lie detectors, the lot. No doubt she was well trained; anti-interrogation courses and refreshers – all that stuff. But how tough was she?

Yakunin, *Antonov*'s first officer, took over the morning watch at 0400. The second officer gave him a course of 024°, a speed of sixteen knots, reported the ship's position and drew attention to traffic in the vicinity.

'There's a forecast of fog,' he said. 'You'll see in the Captain's Night Order Book that he is to be called at once if we encounter it.'

'I hope we don't,' replied Yakunin. 'Would happen in my watch.'

'Rather you than me, Peter Yakunin.' The second officer stayed chatting for a minute or so then made for the chartroom.

At the radar Yakunin switched to the twelve mile scale. There was a fair scatter of ship echoes on the display though no more than usual for the southern reaches of the North Sea. Satisfied, he moved to a bridge window. It was dark, a night of no moon, the sky bright with stars. He went on to the bridge-wing and searched the darkness with night glasses. The only lights he could see were those of ships broad on the bow and abaft the beam though radar had shown a number ahead. He searched there again but there was no horizon, sea and sky had merged into a wall of darkness. It's the fog, he thought. It's come.

He went back to the wheelhouse, spoke to the quarter-master. 'There's fog ahead, Mikhailovsky.'

The first tenuous swirls soon appeared and Yakunin saw the halo round the foremost steaming light. The mast which supported it, the windlass beneath it, were almost hidden by smokelike whorls. Beads of condensation were already form-ing on the wheelhouse windows so he switched on the clear-screen and automatic wipers and phoned through to the watchkeeper's standby room to order two men to the bridge for lookout duty. Having pressed the button which started the auto-siren he picked up the phone and dialled the Captain.

'What is it?' came Yenev's voice.

'Yakunin here, Captain. The ship is in fog. I've started the siren and posted extra lookouts.'

'Right. Reduce speed to twelve knots. I'm coming up.'

There were six men in *Cyclades*'s operations room : the Cap-tain, Kitson, the weapons electrical officer (WEO), the navi-gating and communications officers, and Hammond, a chief petty officer. They were the only men on board who knew that the frigate was involved in OPERATION PETTICOAT – indeed the only men on board who knew there was such an operation.

Four of them were at the scanning and data console dis-play with the WEO and CPO Hammond who was maestro of this orchestration, its components silent save for the ticking of gyro repeaters, the hum and click of radar and data dis-plays and other electronics. A digital clock over the console showed 0424. The communications officer sat at another console wearing a single-sided headphone; above him a loud-speaker relayed a North American voice reporting on visibility.

The communications officer cut him off, selected another frequency. 'That was one of the *Belknap* frigates,' he explained. 'They're still in fog.'

The loudspeaker came alive on the new frequency. '. . . twenty-four decimal three – twenty-four decimal eight . . .' twenty-four decimal three – twenty-four decimal eight . . .' four – twenty-four decimal seven . . .'

'*Kittiwake*,' said the communications officer. 'Reporting a line of soundings to *Huntress*.'

'Remain on that frequency, please.' Kitson had his eyes on the clock.

'Twenty-five decimal zero,' continued the droner. 'Twenty-five decimal nine . . . reference . . . one-seven-three-seven-two decimal three.'

'That'll do for the moment,' said Kitson. 'The seven digits after "reference" were *Antonov*'s bearing and distance from the Dan Oil rig.' He moved over and stood behind Hammond. The others joined him. 'That's position X-ray.' He pointed to it on the display. 'There you see *Huntress*, *John Henry D.*, *Auxoil* and *Antonov* – CPO Hammond has put markers on them – each ten miles plus or minus from X-ray. Remember the board game I showed you yesterday? Well, here it's actually happening. The three unmarked ships are nothing to do with our lot. Not necessarily a nuisance.' He pointed to the display again. 'These are the two patrol boats : *Plover*, approximately fifteen miles from X-ray coming in from the south-west, and *Kittiwake* two miles astern of *Antonov*, steering the same course. Hope Rossiter's taken his Avomine tablets.' He chuckled uncharacteristically before going on. 'Each unit is doing something between ten and twelve knots, except *Plover* which is bowling along at about sixteen. All our lot are adjusting course and speed as necessary to keep *Antonov* on a steady bearing.'

'Seems to be working out nicely,' said *Cyclades*'s captain. Kitson turned sad eyes to him. 'So far, yes.'

A light flickered on a console. The lieutenant picked up a phone. 'Communications officer here. Go ahead.' He replaced the phone. 'Senior officer of *Belknap* reports two Soviet KRIVAK I class guided-missile destroyers escorting an

AMUR repair and submarine depot ship in position zero-four-two degrees from the Dan Oil rig, distant twenty-seven miles. Steering two-zero-five, speed fifteen knots.'

'Well done the *Belknaps*,' said *Cyclades*'s captain. 'In this fog identification must have been by sonar and radar signatures.'

Kitson disagreed. 'Don't like it really. They could make a shambles of Petticoat.'

'Presumably you planners reckoned something like this might happen. Anyway, they're well north of X-ray.'

'We did,' agreed Kitson. 'But it's a confounded nuisance. Could cut things rather fine.'

'Have we acquired the Soviet ships on sonar or radar yet, WEO?' asked the Captain.

'No, sir. Still out of range.'

'Put that KRIVAK and AMUR position on the plot, Pilot, and give me their distance from us.'

'Aye, aye, sir.'

There was silence after that until the navigating officer reported, 'The KRIVAKS and AMUR are seventy-one miles from us, bearing zero-three-seven degrees, sir. Combined speed of approach twenty-eight knots.'

'How far are they from X-ray, Pilot?'

The navigating officer did some more measuring. 'Eighty-three miles, sir. By five-thirty that should be down to sixty-eight.'

The Captain said, 'About two hours from X-ray if the KRIVAKS go to full speed at that time. Should be all right.'

'I hope it is.' Kitson looked gloomily at the clock on the console. It showed 0440.

# 23

In the half-hour or so since Yenev had come up the fog had grown denser. Now it swirled across the bridge shutting out the wheelhouse, isolating him on the starboard wing, a moist and chilling mantle pouring over him, condensing in his hair and eyebrows.

From time to time he heard the thrum of sirens, some distant, others close. In the intervals between them the background of silence grew deeper, amplifying sounds which would normally have passed unnoticed : the slap and gurgle of water passing down the side far beneath him, the distant hum of machinery in the engineroom.

The ship was now without a point of reference, a vast steel structure, most of it invisible to him, floating in a sea of fog, its forward motion no longer apparent since there was nothing to relate it to.

Somewhere out on the port bow a siren sounded. It was followed by others, each with a different note, some to port, some to starboard. Fog did strange things with sound but he believed that one of the ships to port was uncomfortably close. It would be the ship he'd seen on radar coming in on a converging course from the north-west. *Antonov* didn't have to worry about ships on the port bow. It was her duty under the Regulations for Preventing Collision at Sea to give way to those on her starboard bow. But nowadays with so many poorly manned ships, so many inexperienced and uncertificated officers, one had to be careful. His thoughts were interrupted by *Antonov*'s siren: a deep trembling blast engulfing all other sounds. It reminded him that there was nothing to be gained out there on the bridge-wing; nothing to be seen but the blanket of fog; he'd better get back to the wheelhouse. Another siren sounded, a high-pitched note this time, somewhere on the port quarter. He didn't have to worry about ships overtaking, that at least was something.

In the wheelhouse he found Yakunin at the anti-collision radar.

'There's a ship close to port,' said Yenev. 'See it?'

'Yes, Captain. Four points on the bow at one point seven miles. A small echo. Coaster maybe. Closing on a converging course. I've put a relative motion marker on it – and on several others approaching to port and starboard. They're farther away but all within critical range. We may have to alter course for those to starboard. I'll watch them closely.'

Yenev went to the navigational radar, pressed his face into the aperture in the display hood. Moments later he said, 'Reduce to eight knots. We'll have to let this infernal cowboy to port cross ahead of us.'

Yakunin removed the Perspex safety cover on the engine-control panel and depressed the eight knot button. A light glowed in response. Almost immediately the beat of the diesels slowed and the RPM counters clicked down to the reduced revolutions.

'The rule of the road means nothing to this idiot,' complained Yenev. 'How do such people get certificates of competency?'

As he spoke a man came puffing and blowing into the darkened wheelhouse. Yenev could not see who it was but the voice and commotion were enough.

'Fog, I see,' announced the newcomer in a shrill voice. 'I was not called.'

'Fog is not a political matter,' said the Captain dryly.

'I presume, Comrade Yenev, that we are taking all necessary precautions?'

'You presume correctly, Boris Milovych.' The Captain's eyes remained fixed on the radar display.

'What is happening?' insisted the Commissar.

'A number of things. But please keep your questions for later. There are many ships in the area and we have to concentrate.'

Milovych muttered something under his breath, went to a forward window and stood there breathing heavily.

Yenev went back to the display. Five ships to port. Two well clear on parallel courses. Two crossing from port to starboard, one of them the ship at four points on the bow; another, a small echo on the port quarter, two miles astern and steering much the same course as *Antonov*. Three ships to starboard. Two crossing from starboard to port. One coming up on the starboard quarter, evidently overtaking. From its speed it could be a ferry.

There was urgency in Yakunin's report. 'Captain – that cowboy to port is now on a collision course. Distant just over a mile.'

'Bring the ship's head twenty degrees to starboard,' Yenev at once ordered. 'Sound one blast on the siren.'

Mikhailovsky repeated the order, turned the wheel and the gyro-repeater clicked off the degrees as the bow swung to starboard. Later he reported, 'Ship's head twenty degrees to starboard, sir. Now on zero-six-zero.'

'Steady her on that,' Yenev ordered from where he bent over the radar.

There was silence then in the wheelhouse but for the hum of the radar sets, the whirr of clear-view screens, and the click-click of automatic wipers; these background sounds were soon smothered by a six second blast from *Antonov*'s siren.

Yakunin called out, 'The new course puts us in the way of two ships to starboard, Captain. One a point forward of the beam, a small echo coming up fast, range just over a mile. The other a large echo at four points, distance two miles.

Both ships are crossing from starboard to port – both are on steady bearings.'

Yenev snapped. 'Stop engines,' and took Yakunin's place at the anti-collision radar. The display presented a disturbing picture. *Antonov* was boxed in between the two ships approaching on the port side and the two coming in from starboard. The relative motion markers Yakunin had placed on the threatening echoes showed that a critical situation had developed, due largely to failure of the ship on the port bow to give way as she should have done.

Yenev realized that his action in stopping *Antonov*'s engines would enable the two ships to starboard to cross ahead of him, but a serious hazard had arisen to port where the closer of the two echoes, the ship which had altered course to pass astern of him, was now less than half a mile away. Its manoeuvre – correct when initiated – had been confused by *Antonov*'s reduction of speed. While he concentrated on this problem, evaluating actual and potential threats, crucial time was passing. He realized that with the speeds of approach involved he had no more than a minute or so left in which to avoid a collision. 'Emergency full astern,' he ordered sharply. 'Sound three blasts.'

Yakunin pressed the emergency full astern button with one hand and the siren button with the other. Yenev knew that his ship was now committed, there was nothing more he could do but watch and wait and trust that the other ships would somehow keep clear. Taut with apprehension he concentrated on the radar display, almost mesmerized by the unfolding drama. The two ships to starboard were turning away and increasing speed to pass ahead of him; the ship to port – the ship which from the first had failed to alter course – had at last woken up and was turning away to port; but the other ship to port, the one which had manoeuvred correctly, was now dangerously close to *Antonov* and on a collision course. Yenev realized that its captain had heard *Antonov*'s three blasts – *I am going astern* – had seen movement of the Soviet ship's echo slow down on his radar display and was now making a last minute alteration to starboard and increasing speed in a desperate effort to pass astern.

'Why didn't he stop engines long ago – go hard-a-starboard?' Yenev muttered to himself – but he realized that *Antonov*'s movements had complicated things for the other vessel.

At the navigational radar Yakunin, too, had seen the danger. 'The ship on the port beam, Captain,' he shouted. 'On a collision course now. Very close.'

'Stop engines, wheel amidships.' Yenev grabbed the handset of the ship's broadcast system. 'This is the Captain speaking – proceed at once to collision stations – repeat collision stations.'

He put the phone down, ran out of the wheelhouse to the port wing of the bridge. He'd no sooner reached it than two ear-splitting blasts came from a siren no more than a hundred or so metres away. Two blasts – *altering course to port*. For God's sake, what's the man trying to do now? The thought had no sooner passed through Yenev's mind than a dark blur showed up through the fog on the port side. In the few seconds of agonizing suspense which followed he saw the blur take shape as the bows and bridge of a ship. His brain was telling him that a collision was inevitable when his ship lurched, shuddered convulsively and he heard the muffled but chilling sound of steel tearing steel.

The unknown vessel had struck *Antonov* abreast of number seven hold, just forward of the foot of the after superstructure.

# 24

Yenev rushed to the wheelhouse, called to Yakunin. 'Tell Grotskov to broadcast a MAYDAY. Give him the ship's position. Inform the engineroom we have been struck abreast of number seven hold.'

From Milovych came a plaintive, 'What is happening, Comrade Yenev?'

Yenev ignored him. 'Call Doctor Linovksy and Trutin on the broadcast, Yakunin. They are to report to me immediately. Switch on maindeck floodlights.' Yakunin, who'd now been joined by Ivanovitch the third officer, repeated the order. The Captain took a loud-hailer from the rack and made his way to the bridge-wing. Through the swirling curtain of fog he could just see the white superstructure of a ship, the bows of which had penetrated *Antonov*'s side. In that limited visibility he couldn't see anyone on its bridge nor in the wheelhouse. It was a small vessel, probably a stern trawler of about three or four thousand tons, its bridge superstructure well forward; but it had been travelling fast and the impact had been severe. Through the loud-hailer he shouted in Russian, 'Keep your engines going ahead. Do *not* go astern.' There was no response. He used the loud-hailer again. This time a reply came back through the fog in a language he couldn't understand. It sounded like English. It was vital to the safety of *Antonov* that the unknown ship should keep her bows pressed into the hole she'd made in the bulk-carrier's side. Yenev had no doubt it was a very big hole, big enough perhaps for a bus to pass through, and it was dangerously close to the watertight bulkhead between the engineroom and number seven hold. His thoughts were interrupted by a voice behind him. 'Linovsky here, Captain.'

Yenev said, 'Good, go back to the wheelhouse at once, Doctor. Speak to this ship by radiophone. Tell the Captain in English that he *must* keep his engines going ahead.'

Linovsky had no sooner left than Trutin appeared. Yenev handed him the loud-hailer, pointed down to the dim shape of the vessel embedded in *Antonov*'s side. 'Tell him in English he *must* keep his engines going ahead. He must *not* go astern. Look sharp.'

Trutin took the loud-hailer, passed the message in English.

'What's that? Can't hear you,' came the reply.

Trutin repeated the message.

'This is the *John Henry D.* from Hull,' announced the unseen speaker. 'What ship is that?'

The sound of metal tearing came from the deck far beneath the bridge-wing. With sickening alarm Yenev saw the battered bows of the unknown vessel backing away till they and the white of its bridge superstructure were lost in the fog. His emotions were too much for him. He snatched the loud-hailer from Trutin. 'Maniac,' he shouted in Russian. 'You ram us. Then you go astern. You are a mad dog.' Yenev handed the loud-hailer back to Trutin, ran to the wheelhouse, picked up a two-way radio. 'Captain calling. Second officer to report to me at once.'

There was a quick response. 'Second here, Captain. Coming to the bridge now.' Soon afterwards he arrived, and at Yenev's request went to the chartroom and checked and double-checked the ship's position.

The list to port which was developing confirmed Yenev's belief that the damage to the hull was severe. He phoned the engineroom, spoke to Yuri Zhakaz, the chief engineer. 'Have you got the pumps going, Chief?'

'Yes. We are concentrating on the bilges to the engineroom and number seven hold. But it makes little impression. The engineroom is flooding through the forward bulkhead. It has been breached on the port side. The position is very serious.'

Yenev said, 'Number seven is loaded with chrome ore. Two-thirds of the area of the hold is free space above the ore. The bows of the British ship must have opened up the side above the ore level and strained the after transverse bulkhead. Concentrate your pumping on the engineroom, Chief. We can accept the flooding of seven hold, but not of the engineroom.' The Captain put the phone down.

Yakunin reported, 'Ship is listing fifteen degrees to port, Captain.'

'Fifteen degrees.' Yenev was not surprised, it felt like it. 'Continue to watch it. Let me know if it increases.' His two-way radio bleeped.

It was Lomov speaking from the maindeck. 'The impact is just forward of the transverse bulkhead between the engineroom and seven hold. Seven's flooding fast.'

A cold shiver ran down Yenev's spine. If the pressure of water in the hold became too much for the damaged bulkhead it would collapse, the engineroom would flood and the ship would sink.

With the broadcasting of 'collision stations' *Antonov*'s large radio office had at once been fully manned. One of Grotskov's assistants was controlling the high speed transmitters and receivers on Soviet naval frequencies, another was at the transmitters and receivers operating on the 500 kc international frequency for merchant vessels, a third was looking after the electronic cypher machines and yet another was busy on the radiophone system. Grotskov himself, lean and saturnine, stalked round the office checking, controlling, encouraging.

Within minutes of the collision the MAYDAY had been transmitted on 500 kcs, Leningrad and Soviet naval vessels at sea had been informed by high speed transmissions, and the position of the ship, the nature of the emergency and other essential data had been broadcast. Almost immediately the replies came flowing in and the radio office was soon buzzing with activity. Grotskov picked up a phone and dialled the wheelhouse. Yakunin answered.

'The Captain,' demanded Grotskov. 'Urgent.'

Yenev's voice came on to the line. 'Captain here.'

Grotskov glanced at the notepad on his desk. 'Replies coming in fast now, Captain. Nearest ships are the *Huntress*, a British Navy survey vessel, and the Danish ferry *Oska Laertes*. Both are closing our position at maximum speed. British Navy patrol boat *Kittiwake* on survey duty with the *Huntress* is also close, and the oil-rig tender *Auxoil*. These vessels should be here soon, some within the next few minutes. '*But –* ' Grotskov put heavy emphasis on the word – 'two of our KRIVAK destroyers, *Retivy* and *Dostoiny* – escorting an AMUR repair ship – are sixty miles to the north. The KRIVAKS are closing us at thirty-five knots. Signal just received from the senior officer in *Retivy* reads : "You are to refuse all offers of salvage assistance from other vessels." '

Yenev said, 'That goes without saying. Inform *Retivy* that number seven hold is fully flooded, the engineroom is flooding, we have a list of twenty degrees and the ship is down by the stern. The watertight bulkhead between seven and the engineroom has been breached. If we can control flooding to the engineroom we should remain afloat. Confirm that we will reject all offers of salvage assistance.'

'Very good, Captain.' Grotskov's voice was unusually hoarse.

'Any news of the ship that collided with us?'

'Yes. The *John Henry D.* of Hull sent out a MAYDAY. Said she'd been in collision with a big ship in fog. Has badly damaged her bows. Making for Hull at three knots but requires assistance.'

Judy was awake when the collision occurred. The change in

188

the rhythm of the ship's engines when speed was first reduced
had broken her sleep. She'd heard then the muffled thrum of
a siren, a sound which was repeated at regular intervals and
she guessed they were in fog. Speed had again been reduced
and eventually she'd heard the engines stop. After that had
come the message in Russian over the ship's broadcast:
*Proceed at once to collision stations*, followed by sounds of
people running along the passageway and men calling to each
other.

She switched on the light, glanced at her watch – 0531 –
and was putting on clothes when the ship shuddered and
lurched and she knew a collision had taken place. She ran to
the cabin door to find it still locked. She beat on it with her
fists and shouted, 'Let me out. Let me out.'

There was no reply. She listened but could hear nothing
but the pounding of her heart. No sounds of guards talking
to each other or of movement of any sort. She was terrified,
wanted to scream. She banged on the door again, thought of
shouting in Russian but didn't because she knew instinctively
it would be a mistake. Any defence she might offer in Leningrad would be hopelessly compromised if it were known she
could speak Russian.

What about Gallagher? Was he trapped too? What was he
doing? She picked up the dressing-table stool and was about
to bang it against the bulkhead to his cabin when she heard
tapping from the far side. She put her ear to the bulkhead
and listened . . . DY – JUDY – JUDY . . . the tapping spelt
out in Morse code.

She tapped back RRR for 'ROGER' and waited.

The tapped signal came again: KEEP – CALM – HELP
– WILL – COME. The tapping stopped.

Again she tapped RRR.

Darling Ben, she thought. Worrying about me. *Help will
come*. Dear God. How can he know?

She decided she'd bang on the cabin door and shout for
help every few minutes. That couldn't do any harm. Surely

somebody would hear. After all Yenev, Lomov, the chief engineer, Dr Linovsky and other senior officers all had their cabins on that deck and used the passageway, as did the stewards.

She sat on the edge of the bed, frightened and confused, her heart thumping fiercely, her breath coming in uneven gasps. Though death was an occupational hazard in the espionage business, she'd always persuaded herself it was unlikely to come her way; if it did she'd imagined it would be a bullet in the back of the head – not drowning like a trapped rat. She shuddered at the thought, got up from the bed and walked across the tilted floor of the cabin. She stood frowning uncertainly at the door, looked at her watch – 0536. Only five minutes since the collision. It seemed an eternity. From somewhere beneath her came the groans and creaks of fracturing metal and the ominous sound of rushing water.

Much happened in the next few minutes. *Huntress*, *Oska Laertes*, and *Kittiwake* had arrived on the scene and though hidden by fog were standing by within a few hundred metres of the *Antonov*, their foghorns sounding intermittently.

All other shipping had been requested to keep clear and in a rapid exchange of radio and radiophone messages between the rescue vessels and *Antonov* – and Yenev and the senior officer of the Soviet destroyers in *Retivy* – *Huntress*'s offer to take the Russian crew on board had been declined. It had been agreed, however, that they should be transferred to the *Oska Laertes* if and when it became evident that the *Antonov* would sink before the arrival of the *Retivy*. It was left to Yenev to make the final decision.

The lifeboats on the starboard side could not be used because of the list. The two on the port side had been turned out and made ready for lowering but *Antonov*'s heavy list and her stern down trim threatened to make even their use difficult. It had been decided, therefore, that should the Russians abandon ship, *Kittiwake*, small and highly manoeuvrable, would go alongside, take off the crew and transfer them to the Danish ferry steamer.

Ten minutes after the collision there was a power failure. The deck floodlights flickered and died and supply to the wheel-house, chartroom and electronic systems ceased. Yakunin at once switched to the emergency batteries. The chief engineer came panting into the wheelhouse to report that the auxiliary diesel generator had been shut down. 'The flooding has now reached the upper levels of the engineroom on the port side,' he said. 'We have to evacuate all personnel.'

Yenev braced himself against the list, looked through the open door of the wheelhouse down the long slope of the bridge to port where it faded into the fog. Although he could not see the bridge-wing he knew from Lomov's last report that it must be getting closer to the water. 'How long d'you think we have?' he asked the chief engineer.

'No time at all,' shrilled the Commissar from behind him. 'The order to abandon ship should have been given long ago.'

Yenev ignored him.

Zhakaz, looking older and more wizened than usual, blinked. 'Not long, Sergei Yenev. Ten minutes at most.'

Yenev shook his head, tightened his mouth. The Soviet destroyers steaming south at thirty-five knots were still more than an hour away. He turned to Yakunin. 'Pass the order to abandon ship. All hands to muster on the maindeck between numbers three and four holds. Pilot ladders to be hung over the port side amidships. The British patrol boat will come alongside and take off the crew. Lomov is already down there. He will take charge of the disembarkation.'

Having ordered the third officer to sound the alarm bells Yakunin went to the ship's broadcast, powered now by the emergency batteries. The clamour of the bells died away and he passed the order to abandon ship.

'Go and see to your men, Yuri Zhakaz.' Yenev spoke wearily. Zhakaz, who knew him well, having served with him for many years, touched his arm. 'Look after yourself, Captain. Don't leave it too late.'

Yenev nodded understandingly and Zhakaz left the wheelhouse. The Captain called to Trutin who was manning the radiophone at the navigation console. 'Request the patrol boat to come alongside now. Port side amidships. Pilot ladders are in position. Tell them we must abandon ship immediately.'

To Yakunin he said, 'Trutin is to remain with me here. You will take all other bridge personnel to the assembly point.' At that moment Dr Linovsky hurried into the wheelhouse. His face was drawn beneath the dark glasses. 'The self-destruct charges, Captain. Do we set them?'

'No. We've already spoken to Leningrad. Two salvage tugs on station off the Shetlands are on their way. The depth of water here is only twenty-five fathoms. The tugs will take whatever steps are necessary.'

Linovsky hesitated, seemed about to say something, then turned on his heels and left. Yakunin followed, taking with him the third officer, the quartermasters and lookouts.

Yenev saw that Milovych was still in the wheelhouse. 'You, too, Boris Milovych. You must go,' he said brusquely.

'Not yet, Comrade Yenev.' The Commissar's small eyes glinted. 'There's an urgent matter to be dealt with.'

'What is that?'

'The prisoners.' Milovych had lowered his voice so that Trutin at the radiophone on the far side of the console would not hear.

# 25

'The prisoners?' Yenev stared at the Commissar.

'Yes. Gallagher and the woman. What do we do with them?'

'The prisoners?' Yenev passed a hand over his forehead. 'With all this – I had forgotten.'

'I thought so, Comrade Yenev. We cannot release them. They know too much. Once on board the British patrol boat they will talk.'

Yenev turned away, looked through a bridge window into the dark pall of fog, hoping perhaps to find some solution there. 'They are our prisoners, arrested for spying.' He hesitated, seemed lost in thought. 'Get Olga Katutin to drug them. We take them with us as casualties.'

'The Danish ship will want to treat them,' objected Milovych.

'We reject offers of treatment on the grounds that Soviet destroyers – with excellent medical facilities – will shortly take them on board.'

'The ship cannot remain afloat much longer,' said Milovych obstinately. 'Olga Katutin is already at the assembly point . . . it is too late . . .'

He was interrupted by Trutin's voice. 'The British patrol boat is coming alongside, Captain.'

Yenev made for the open door of the wheelhouse to join

Trutin who was leaning over the bridge screen. Milovych called after him. 'The prisoners, Comrade Yenev?'

Without turning his head the Captain shouted back, 'Carry out my instructions.'

Milovych left the wheelhouse in a highly confused state of mind. Terror of drowning and fear of Borodin combined with anger at the Captain's obduracy. The whole thing was crazy. A few minutes earlier he'd had to refuse Lomov's plea to release them. Now the Captain was ordering him to do something which he regarded as dangerously stupid. Was everyone in authority in the ship without any sense of responsibility? There was only one practical way of dealing with the prisoners. It was up to him. He ran into the chartroom. The lights were dim. Battery power going, he thought, and shivered at the vision that conjured up. With trembling fingers he unlocked the small-arms cabinet, took from it a revolver, checked that it was loaded and stuck it into the waistband of his trousers. He took the keys of the prisoners' cabins from the keyboard, a torch from the rack over the chart-table and made his way to Number One Deck. Because of the list he had at times to grab the rail on the high side of the passageway to steady himself. The lights though dim were still on and from below came the fearsome sound of water gushing and of air hissing as it was expelled by the inrush of the sea.

The Commissar was a very frightened man. The ship was sinking fast, the Captain's instructions were absurd in the circumstances, and the idea of drowning appalled him. But he feared even more than death the consequences of Borodin's anger should the prisoners somehow fall into the wrong hands. They were spies, their guilt was beyond doubt. He would, he assured himself as he made his way down the passage, be doing no more than anticipating the decision of the Soviet judge. Borodin would certainly approve. What he was about to do was necessary because of the real danger that Lomov or Trutin, or some other well-intentioned idiot, would at the last moment release them. But for that he'd have left them in their cabins to drown.

It was some minutes after the collision before Gallagher realized how desperate the situation had become. The ship's list, the sound of flooding, of structural failures, and finally Yakunin's 'abandon ship' broadcast, convinced him that little time was left. No one had come to release them. With something akin to panic he had thrown himself against the locked door but it was no use. Next he'd attempted to batter it with a cabin chair but that had soon splintered. He heard Judy shouting and hammering on her door and, realizing the futility of what they were doing, he forced himself to calm down and attempt some constructive thinking.

The *Antonov* had been in collision with another ship; by the feel of it and the fact that the engines had stopped, a severe one. They were in the southern part of the North Sea, busy waters with much shipping. Even if *Antonov* had made no signals for help, the other vessel would surely have reported the collision. Various ships in the vicinity would now be coming to the scene. On the law of averages the majority were more likely to be Scandinavian, German and British than Russian. Yenev and Milovych would know this, would realize that he and Judy could be a dangerous embarrassment. So what would they do? Leave them in their cabins to drown? Very probably.

No sooner had he reached this chilling conclusion than he heard a key being inserted in the lock of the cabin door followed by Milovych's voice. 'We have to abandon ship, Gallagher. You must come with me.' The fact that the Commissar assumed he understood Russian confirmed his belief that their cover had been blown by the discovery of the bug in Yenev's cabin.

Gallagher remained silent, believing that the Commissar's intention might be either to rescue him or kill him. His instinct told him that it would be wisest to assume the worst.

The problem which called for immediate decision was where to hide? The bathroom or the wardrobe? He chose the latter as the less likely to be searched first, slid the door open, crouched in the cupboard and closed the door, leaving a slit through which he could just see the bathroom door. Seconds later he heard the sound of the cabin door opening.

The Commissar reached the door of the pilot's cabin. He would deal with Gallagher first, then the woman. He put the torch in a tunic pocket and inserted the key. As he did so he called out in Russian. 'We have to abandon ship, Gallagher. You must come with me.' His tone was conciliatory; though he couldn't speak English he was now quite sure the American understood Russian.

There was no reply, so he called again. Still no reply. Slowly, gingerly, he opened the door, revolver at the ready. The light was on, the bed clothes disarranged, the bed empty.

Ah. So the American was in the bathroom. That would not help him. Milovych went to the bathroom door, tapped on it. 'Come,' he urged. 'The ship is sinking. You must hurry. There is a British patrol boat waiting to take us off.'

Again there was no reply. What was the American doing? Milovych's heart pounded, his breathing was agitated. As he grasped the handle he heard a faint shuffle behind him and turned, but it was too late. A strong arm encircled his neck and an iron hand clenched the wrist holding the revolver. His cry of terror was cut off by the pressure on his throat.

'Drop it,' commanded Gallagher in Russian. 'Or I kill you.'

The Commissar dropped the revolver. Gallagher threw the Russian heavily against the bulkhead, picked up the weapon, stood over him. 'Get up,' he said hoarsely. 'And if you want to stay alive, open Paddon's door.'

A frightened protest came from Milovych as he dragged himself to his feet, but the revolver barrel pressed firmly into his back ended the protestations and he led the way into the passageway. With shaking hands he unlocked the door of Judy's cabin.

Gallagher said, 'Now open it.' The Commissar did so. The American called out, 'Okay, Judy. It's me,' and they went in, Milovych leading.

Her face was ashen as she looked in astonishment from Milovych to Gallagher. She saw that the American, tall and lean and still in pyjamas, had a revolver in his hand. Milovych's small eyes seemed to her to have grown large with terror.

'My God,' she cried somewhere between tears and laughter. 'Ben – oh Ben – how did you *do* it?'

'Come on,' he said gruffly. 'We have to move fast. This ship won't last much longer.'

Milovych led and Gallagher and Judy followed as they made their way up the steeply-sloping passageway to the bridge-deck.

*Antonov*'s engineroom had no fore and aft bulkhead so the flooding had to some extent corrected the list in what were to be her last minutes afloat.

Rudman, commanding *Kittiwake*, noted this with relief because it made easier his task of taking off the Soviet crew and also reduced the danger to his own ship. There was a slight swell now coming in from the north-west, the aftermath of an Atlantic gale, and a gentle breeze stirred the fog but failed to disperse it.

From the stern of the bulk-carrier came at times the metallic clang of something striking the ship's side. Rudman imagined it was the aftermost lifeboat swinging from its falls. The foremost boat on the port side could just be seen hanging vertically by its stern, the forward fall having somehow broken adrift. From the angle of the maindeck alongside which *Kittiwake* lay, Rudman assumed that *Antonov*'s bows, hidden by fog, were lifting clear of the sea as her stern sank. More important to him at that moment were the men wearing orange life-jackets who were climbing down the pilot ladders in a steady stream, some letting go and jumping the last few feet to the deck. Two of his petty officers and a number of seamen were directing them to various parts of the ship as they arrived. The patrol boat, small and fast, had limited accommodation and most of the rescued Russians had to remain on deck. Rudman was astonished at their numbers. He'd expected about forty in all, but when his first lieutenant reported that there were no more men left on the maindeck of the bulk-carrier, he estimated that close on eighty had already been taken off.

The *Antonov* seemed likely to make her final plunge at any moment and it was with considerable relief that he manoeuvred *Kittiwake* clear, though remaining close enough to the sinking ship to keep it under observation.

The first lieutenant came to the bridge and reported that eighty-one men and five women had been taken on board. Four of the women were stewardesses, the fifth was the ship's doctor. 'Her name is Olga Katutin,' said the first lieutenant. 'She speaks English. Seems very distressed. Says the captain, the ship's commissar and the chief communications officer are still on board.'

'Being noble are they?' said Rudman grimly. 'Well, they'll bloody well have to swim for it. I'm not going alongside again.'

'We'll wait for her to sink, won't we, before transferring her people to the *Oska Laertes*?'

'Yes. *Huntress* has ordered us to stay within visibility distance. Fog seems to be breaking up. We could see *Huntress* and *Oska Laertes* a moment ago, then it closed in again. By the way, are any of the people we've taken off non-Russian?'

'Non-Russian?' The first lieutenant looked surprised.

'Yes. Like French, American, English or whatever.'

'If they are they haven't said so.'

'Then they aren't,' said Rudman abruptly. He couldn't tell the first lieutenant what he knew, what he'd been told at the briefing in *Cyclades*. 'You must not,' Kitson said, 'at any time give the impression – either to your own crew or the Russians – that you know they're on board. If you do, you compromise RN-USN participation in Petticoat and you do your country – and the West in general – a grave disservice. If they come aboard as survivors you'll know what to do – once in our hands we don't part with them – but on no account will you give the Russians or any one else the impression that you have any knowledge of these people. We are not, repeat not, mounting a rescue operation for operatives engaged in clandestine operations. The sole object of Petticoat is to find out what we can about the *Simeonov* class. Is that quite clear?'

'Yes, sir.' He hesitated. 'I don't like it very much.'

'None of us do, my dear chap. But these are the rules of the game. Depart from them at your peril.'

In the radio office Grotskov transmitted his last message on the Soviet naval channel. '*Antonov* is sinking fast,' he said. 'We have abandoned ship. I now close down.'

Leningrad and the destroyer *Retivy* acknowledged and wished him good luck. Grotskov's assistants had, on his orders, left when 'abandon ship' was broadcast. The acute stern-down angle, the gurgle and roar of inrushing water close at hand, the hiss of air venting wherever it could, told him the end was near. Minutes before the Captain had ordered him to leave the ship but he had held on like the single-minded zealot he was. The Captain had told him that Soviet salvage tugs would take care of the ship's confidential books and documents, so he did not have to worry about them. But there was something else he did have to attend to. He went to the cypher-room, opened the steel safe, took out the cassettes which proved Gallagher and Paddon's guilt and put them in a polythene bag. He tied its neck with a plastic-coated twist and put it in his pocket. Taking a life-jacket from the overhead rack, he slung it loosely over his shoulder and with the aid of a torch made for the after end of the bridge-deck. He saw with dismay that the patrol boat had left and was already some distance away, a blurred shape just visible on the fringes of the fog. He believed he was now the only man left on board. The deck where he stood began to vibrate and shake to the accompaniment of subdued rumbles and the explosive sounds of pressure bursts. In sudden panic he ran to the foremost davits on the port side, looked over and saw the lifeboat there hanging vertically from the stern falls, its bow submerged, the swell at times banging it against the ship's side. He made for the aftermost davits. With the ship's stern sunk deep in the water the after lifeboat, which had earlier been turned out and half lowered, was now in the sea alongside, the fall blocks slapping against its thwarts. It was, he judged, about twenty feet below him. He'd heard of men breaking their necks by jumping in life-jackets so he threw his down into the boat. A poor swimmer, he aimed at a point immediately ahead of it and jumped. The surge of the swell against the side chose that moment to thrust the lifeboat forward. His legs just missed its bows but his chin caught the gunwhale and with a sound like the snap of a dry stick his neck broke. Made buoyant by the air trapped in its clothing, his body floated for a few minutes in the space between the lifeboat and the ship's side before slowly sub-merging.

Though the fog had grown less dense and the sky in the south-east lighter with the onset of morning, visibility was still so limited that the small drama of Grotskov's last moments had passed unnoticed. As it happened *Kittiwake* had just lowered her skimmer, Lieutenant Rudman having ordered the coxswain to close the *Antonov* and standby in case those still on board might in the final stages jump. The coxswain had not long to wait for he'd no sooner reached the vicinity of the ship than huge plumes of water leapt from her funnel and the stern began to slide slowly beneath the dark surface of the North Sea.

As the sea reached up to the bridge-deck he saw three figures jump overboard and begin to swim away from the ship. He manoeuvred the skimmer towards them and in no time he and the bowman had them on board. Two men and a woman.

The coxswain said, 'We're Royal Navy. From the *Kitti-*

*wake.*' He pointed to the blurred shape on the edge of the fog. The tall man said, 'I'm a US citizen. This woman is British. We must see your Captain at once.' He spoke with authority, evidently a man used to giving orders. The third man, flaccid and podgy with small eyes like currants in a steam pudding, seemed shaken and confused as he made some sort of protest in a foreign language. The coxswain gave him a blank look, shook his head. 'Sorry, no savvy your lingo.' The coxswain then reported to *Kittiwake* by RT that he had picked up three survivors, an American, an Englishwoman and a Russian.

They watched in silence as the bulk-carrier slid slowly beneath the sea until only her bow remained tilted skyward, reluctant it seemed to make the final plunge; then it too had gone and turbulent water marked the place of its sinking, huge bubbles rising to the surface and bursting, pieces of wreckage shooting up as if propelled from below, and pools of diesel fuel, dark and oleaginous, forming and spreading like expanding carpets, their acrid odour casting an invisible pall over the scene of the disaster. The American looked at his watch. 'Three minutes after six,' he said laconically.

'God, it's cold,' said the woman, her teeth chattering as she pressed water from the long strands of her hair.

'You'll be on board soon, miss. Get a change then,' said the coxswain. He steered his small craft slowly round the desolate scene. When it was evident there were no more survivors he said, 'That's it then,' and opened the throttles of the twin outboards to make the skimmer high-whine its way back to *Kittiwake.*

*Huntress* was still hidden by fog when Rudman reported by radiophone that the Soviet ship had sunk and that he had taken on board two passengers and all her crew but for the captain and the communications officer who had gone down with the ship. He had, he said, marked the site of the sinking with pellet buoys. He added that in accordance with previous instructions he proposed transferring survivors to the Danish ferry steamer *Oska Laertes.*

*Huntress*'s captain at once replied, 'Proceed with transfer of crew survivors, repeat crew survivors, to *Oska Laertes.*'

The Danish ship could not be seen but her captain confirmed by radiophone that he was ready to receive the *Antonov*'s crew. Using radar, *Kittiwake* was soon alongside and the Russians began climbing ladders provided by the *Oska Laertes.*

While this was taking place a wet and bedraggled Milovych went to the patrol boat's bridge with Trutin. Using the steward as interpreter he informed Rudman that as staff captain of *Antonov* he was the senior Russian survivor.

'Good,' said the RN lieutenant. 'I'm glad we've been able to help. Very much regret that your captain and communications officer were lost.'

Trutin translated and Milovych who was blue with cold rattled out a reply in Russian.

'Captain Milovych thanks you for your help and sympathy,' said Trutin. 'But he wishes to know where the American Gallagher and the Englishwoman Paddon are. He cannot find them among the other survivors who were brought on board this ship.'

'Tell him that these people say they were passengers in the *Antonov*, having been rescued after their aeroplane came down in the sea. They have requested permission to remain on board. They wish to reach the United Kingdom as soon as possible.'

As the implications of Trutin's translation sank in, Milovych's face darkened and with excitable gestures he launched into an angry tirade.

The steward looked embarrassed. 'Captain Milovych says you must understand they were not passengers. Our ship did rescue them but they were spies. They were held on board *Antonov* under arrest on the orders of the authorities in Leningrad.'

Rudman put on a show of puzzled surprise. 'Tell Captain Milovych that I have no knowledge of Gallagher and Paddon or what they have done or have not done. This is a British warship. They have requested passage in it and I intend to grant it. They will remain on board.'

Trutin's translation caused the Commissar's small eyes, already bloodshot with fright and anxiety, to protrude alarmingly, the veins on his temples swelled, his cheeks bulged and he gave every indication of an imminent attack of apoplexy. When the steward had finished Milovych burst into an indignant harangue, accompanied by much arm waving.

Trutin shook his head, stared unhappily at Rudman. 'The Commissar says you are bound under international law to return these prisoners to his custody. The Soviet Government will take an extremely serious view if this is not done.'

Rudman went to the bridge window. The last few survivors were already on the pilot ladders. He turned to Trutin. 'Tell your Commissar that his Government is at liberty to take this matter up with the British Government. In the meantime Gallagher and Paddon remain on board my ship. Also inform him that you'll have to make it snappy if you want to join the rest of your crew because I'm about to cast off.'

That was enough for Milovych and Trutin who hurriedly left the bridge, the Commissar still muttering protests. When they had climbed the ladders and were safely on board *Oska Laertes*, Rudman cast off and *Kittiwake* was soon lost to view in the fog.

# 26

While Milovych was protesting about the disappearance of his 'prisoners' they were in the cabin abaft *Kittiwake*'s bridge to which they'd been taken on Rudman's orders when the skimmer arrived alongside. A sub-lieutenant and a petty officer had escorted them, and a lean man with crewcut hair had shown them in and locked the door.

For a moment he and the newcomers looked at each other in puzzled silence. The woman was shivering, her hair hanging in wet strands, her sodden clothing emphasizing the contours of an undeniably attractive body. Sea water still dripped from the man's denim jacket and striped pyjama trousers, and greying hair hung in a wet fringe over his forehead. The faces of both were drawn, their eyes were bloodshot and blood oozed from a cut on the man's temple.

The lean man broke the silence. 'I'm Jack Rossiter. I guess you're Judy Paddon, ma'am. And you'll be Ben Gallagher. Right?'

They shook hands. 'I have to . . .' he paused then, frowning uncertainly. 'I mean – you've had a pretty bad time. You're wet and mighty cold.' He bent down, switched on the cabin heater. 'Take off your wet gear. Rub yourselves down with those.' He pointed to some towels on a rack. From a corner cupboard he took woollen underclothes, socks, tracksuits and Plimsolls. 'Get into these. Probably not the right size, but they'll do.'

Gallagher and Judy looked from the clothing to Rossiter —
a complete stranger — then at each other.

Rossiter said, 'Don't worry about me. Get those things off.
We have to talk while you change.' He smiled reassuringly at
Judy. 'I won't look.' He poured coffee from a Thermos jug,
put the filled mugs into a bunkside rack. 'Drink this when
you're ready.' He looked at his watch. 'We're putting the
*Antonov*'s crew on board a Danish ferry steamer right now.
After that you'll be taken over to *Cyclades*, a British frigate.
I have to leave before then. Maybe we have five minutes
together. Have to talk fast. There's information you must give
right now. Every second counts. You sent that Land Catch
signal. Now tell me — quickly, briefly — why?'

Gallagher had already begun to peel off his shirt, and a
somewhat hesitant Judy was fiddling with the waistband of
her slacks. It must have been the strangest de-briefing any of
them had experienced. In the confined space of a very small
cabin they undressed and rubbed themselves down while
Rossiter got from them all they knew; the bugged conversation
between Yenev and Dr Linovsky particularly interested him,
but there was much else he wanted to know.

The background to these strange proceedings was all noise
and movement: the throaty roar of *Kittiwake*'s diesels, the
harsh vibrations, the rapid movements of the small craft, so
unpredictable and unrhythmic after those of the big ship
they'd just left. Soon there were signs of slowing down, the
hull trembled and the engines were put astern, there was a
lurching and bumping and they assumed they'd gone alongside the Danish ship. A hurried tramp of feet sounded on the
deck outside, muted words of command, the sudden wail of
a siren.

The rubbing down and the change of clothing completed
they sat on the edge of the bunk, the hot mug of coffee in
their hands, their eyes on the US Navy commander whose
questions seemed without end until at last he said, 'Well I
guess that's about all.'

'What's on right now?' Gallagher dabbed with a towel at

the cut on his temple. 'What's the urgency?'

'Don't ask me,' Rossiter threw out his hands defensively. 'Maybe you'll get the story at the final de-briefing.'

'You're kidding,' said Gallagher. 'We never do.'

'That's right. The more you know the more you blow.'

'I'll scream if I hear that again.' Judy's eyes flashed.

Rossiter looked at her in surprise. 'Why?'

'It's so bloody unfair. We do the dirty work. Our cover's been blown so we're more or less out of a job – about as useful as garbage from now on – and yet we're not allowed to know what it's all about – what our feeble efforts have achieved.'

'A hell of a lot,' said Rossiter emphatically. 'You'd rate for Congressional Medals if you weren't clandestine operators.'

'You can stuff them,' said Gallagher briskly, 'and the desk jobs we'll probably be offered. I go for the brass handshake.'

'Very understandable,' soothed Rossiter. 'I guess you're both suffering from shock. It'll look different later.'

'Will it hell!' Gallagher laughed mirthlessly.

The engines were opening up again and they could feel *Kittiwake* beginning to move, listing slightly as she turned to port.

'We must be leaving *Oska Laertes*,' said Rossiter. 'I have to go now. Maybe we'll meet again. I certainly hope so.'

'You going?' Gallagher frowned, as if Rossiter's departure was in some way a let-down.

'Yeh. I have to. So long. Take care.'

He shook hands with Gallagher, turned to Judy. ' 'Bye ma'am. You've done a great job.'

In spite of her nervous and physical exhaustion she managed a sardonic smile. 'Goodbye, Commander. There's always something new. You're the only man who's ever got me to strip two minutes after a first meeting. I must tell Roger Beamish.'

'Who's that?'

'It doesn't really matter.'

Rossiter took her hand and held it rather longer than he

had Gallagher's. 'You're some lady. It's been a privilege to know you.' For a few moments his eyes signalled admiration, and then he'd gone.

Rossiter went to the bridge, had a brief conversation with Rudman and a skimmer was lowered. It was manned by the coxswain and bowman who'd picked up the survivors. Rossiter got in, the bowman shoved off and they screeched across the water to where *Plover* lay close to *Huntress*'s motorboat which was taking soundings over the sunken *Antonov*.

Rossiter boarded *Plover* and went to the bridge. Studdington, the lieutenant in command, introduced him to a small cadaverous man in a wet suit. 'Commander Jim Hayward from the RN Diving School,' he said. 'You'd better go down to my cabin to chat.'

In the privacy of Studdington's cabin Rossiter gave Hayward the essential information obtained from Gallagher and Paddon; he did not, however, mention their names. 'What they told me confirms our belief that the *Simeonovs* have a pretty tight secret,' he told Hayward. 'But beliefs are not enough. MOD and the Pentagon require confirmation. I guess the only way to get that is to see what's down there and photograph it.'

Hayward's eyes were dark slits in a skeletal face. 'You say they saw the Soviet inspection party go down through a door under the foc'sle immediately forward of the coaming to number one hold?'

'That's right. A door they unlocked. Presumably a pretty substantial lock.'

'We'll be able to deal with that.' Hayward's manner was almost offensively abrupt.

Having transferred Rossiter to *Plover*, Rudman increased speed and *Kittiwake* headed for *Cyclades*. The patrol boat's radar showed the frigate to be several miles to the west. Minutes later they reached her and put Gallagher and Paddon on board. *Kittiwake* then turned and took station close astern of the frigate. Rudman's radiophone exchanges with *Huntress* made it clear that both vessels would resume their survey duties as soon as *Huntress* had plotted the position of the sunken ship and placed wreck-buoys for the protection of shipping.

Among the multitude of radio messages cluttering the ether at that time were a number which had to do with the sinking of the Soviet bulk-carrier. For example, *Oska Laertes* was informing those concerned that she had *Antonov*'s survivors on board and was resuming her voyage to Copenhagen; Captain Smolenko, the senior Soviet naval officer in *Retivy*, was thanking *Huntress* and *Kittiwake* for assistance rendered by the Royal Navy, and the captain of *Oska Laertes* for his ship's valuable co-operation. Smolenko added that the Soviet destroyer *Dostoivy*, proceeding in company with *Retivy*, had been detached and was proceeding at thirty knots to rendezvous with the ferry and take over the survivors. It was estimated, said Smolenko's message, that the two ships would meet at approximately 0645 in a position thirty miles to the north-east.

Before long the ether was carrying another message from *Oska Laertes*. This time it was the captain's coded signal to his owners in Copenhagen informing them that Boris Milovych, *Antonov*'s staff captain, had requested political asylum in Denmark having decided to defect to the West.

Soon after six o'clock the dawn breeze which had threatened to disperse the fog fell away and into the clear patches left came curtains of mist, wet and clinging, to reduce visibility once more to less than a hundred metres as *Huntress* moved in towards her motorboat which was still sounding around *Antonov*. Two green wreck-buoys on the survey vessel's foredeck were being made ready for lowering. *Plover* lay stopped close to the pellet-buoys marking *Antonov*'s bows, her skimmer hovering nearby, its coxswain in touch with the mother ship by R/T. Deeper in the fog, now several miles away, the frigate *Cyclades* was moving slowly to the north-east on a course which would take her to a rendezvous with the US Navy's *Belknap* guided-missile frigates. Radio signals between these warships were in a cypher to which it was known the Soviet Navy had a key. The signals indicated that they were carrying out a routine NATO anti-submarine-warfare exercise. The rendezvous to which they were proceeding would place them between the sunken *Antonov* and the approaching Soviet destroyer *Retivy*.

On *Plover*'s small quarterdeck, Commander Hayward in wet suit and fins was briefing his team of underwater swimmers. Compressed air cylinders were already on their backs and last minute adjustments to equipment were being made; weight belts fastened, regulators, underwater cameras and lights, underwater cutting gear and drills and power-packs checked. Each swimmer was equipped with a Wetphone – an underwater voice communications system with microphones built into the mouthpiece of the regulators, and transceivers attached to waistbelts. They would be able to talk to each other underwater and to their mother ship while the dive lasted. All but one of the divers were instructors from the RN Diving School; the exception was Varic, the Czech, an experienced scuba diver who was also a fluent Russian speaker. He had been supplied by US Naval Intelligence.

Rossiter looked at the message sheet a communications' rating had just handed him and whistled. '*Cyclades* reports that *Retivy* will be within fifteen miles in thirty-five minutes,' he told Hayward. 'That's close to visibility distance if this fog clears. Message says the job must be finished and we must have moved off before then. Does that give you enough time?'

'It'll have to, won't it?' Hayward shrugged, turned back to his team. 'Tide's falling. Almost low water now. *Huntress*'s motorboat gives the present depth around *Antonov*'s bow as twenty-two fathoms – say forty metres. That puts the hatch of number one hold approximately twenty-seven metres below the surface. The depth of the hold itself is around twelve metres. So depending on what's in there, Varic and I will have to work down to something like thirty-eight metres.' He spoke to the chief petty officer at his side. 'Diving tables, Chief.'

CPO Jennings handed him a clipboard. Hayward found what he wanted. 'Let's work on thirty-eight metres,' he said. 'Can't be a straight dive. Won't give enough time.' He tapped at a pocket calculator. 'Allowing for two ascent stops for decompression, say five minutes at ten metres and five at five metres, we'll have eighteen minutes down there. Say nine minutes at the thirty metre level and another nine at thirty-eight metres. How we use that time depends on what we find.' He stared at Rossiter. 'The deeper we go the shorter the time scale. That's how it works, mate.'

'How long to force that door?'

'No idea. Two, three minutes, maybe. The longer it takes the less time we'll have to bugger about below.'

Rossiter said, 'You've got to have finished – and we must be clear of the wreck – in thirty-five minutes. You're allowing thirty minutes, plus or minus, for the dive. Aren't you working on a pretty tight margin?'

'Yes, we are,' said Hayward. 'Not my fault.' He looked at the man on his left. 'Roberts, you and Harris will help us force the watertight door. After that you both stay on *Antonov*'s maindeck as our back-up. We'll be in close touch. If we get into trouble help us if you can. Okay?'

Roberts nodded. 'Will do, sir.'

Presumably so that Rossiter would be under no illusions as to the exercise of authority, Hayward spoke to CPO Jennings. 'You'll be in charge up here, Chief. Communications and so forth. Keep a close eye on things. Give us periodic time checks.'

'Aye, aye, sir.'

Jennings lowered three Wetphone transceivers into the water and secured the inboard ends of the cables. 'All set now, sir.'

'I'll give you a signal check from ten fathoms,' said Hayward. He pushed in the mouthpiece of his regulator, pulled down the prismatic mask, set the chronograph of the diving watch on one wrist, checked the depth gauge setting on the other, moved to the side where the guard-rail had been un-shipped, climbed a few steps down the side ladder and tipped over backwards into the sea. For a brief moment his fins showed in a fishlike kick and then he had gone. The rest of the team followed, one at a time, in quick succession. Com-munication checks were completed and the dive began.

Those on deck waited anxiously, looking into the fog and the cold grey surface of the North Sea, unable to see any-thing other than the pictures in their minds. None was more anxious than Rossiter who was listening in to the shipboard end of a Wetphone transceiver. CPO Jennings had another and the third was connected to a tape-recorder the wheels of which were already turning.

The time was 0613.

Kitson was on *Cyclades*'s quarterdeck to greet the track-suited figures clambering up the ladder from *Kittiwake*'s skimmer.

Like Rossiter he'd not met them before and to him they were no more than names – Ben Gallagher and Judy Paddon. She appeared first, her track-suit too large, her hair in a mess and her face without make-up. She looked very tired. But even the lugubrious Kitson had to admit to himself that she was a remarkably attractive woman.

After her came Gallagher looking rather like a decathlon competitor at the end of the longest day – tired, unshaven, dishevelled, dark pouches under his eyes and a bruised temple.

Kitson introduced himself. 'It's good to see you,' he said rather awkwardly. 'You must be very tired.'

'We are,' said Gallagher.

'Come along with me.' Kitson led the way past the heli-copter hangar and in through a watertight door on the port side; then along various stairs and passageways to a cabin in a flat one deck down from the bridge. Members of the ship's company seemed to be everywhere and in the course of their journey they had to undergo the scrutiny of many eyes.

'Number One's cabin,' explained Kitson. 'Yours for the day.' He gestured towards the settee. 'Please sit down.' They did and he took the desk chair.

'I hate doing this,' he said apologetically. 'Because I'm sure you're thinking of hot baths, sleep and that sort of thing.'

'The hot bath will do,' said Judy. 'And something to put on my face. Any women on board?'

'None, I'm afraid.'

'Bloody hell.'

'I beg your pardon.' Kitson looked at her as if she were a dangerous explosive.

'I'll settle for eggs, sausages, bacon, waffles and maple syrup and some real hot coffee,' said Gallagher.

Kitson raised his eyebrows in a polite gesture of surprise. 'As I was saying,' he continued. 'I hate doing this, but I have to ask you as a matter of urgency to tell me exactly what you told Commander Rossiter.'

'Oh no,' protested Judy. 'Not again.'

'For God's sake,' said Gallagher. 'Why?'

Kitson sighed. 'Because Rossiter is somewhere in that fog several miles away and extremely busy. He hasn't time to write it all down, have it encrypted and despatched to me by radio. And it so happens that I have to know now.'

'Why must you?' asked Judy who'd moved off the settee and was standing in front of the first lieutenant's mirror. 'My God! My face. Looks like a disaster area.'

'Don't be unreasonable, Judy,' said Gallagher. 'Captain Kitson's doing his best.'

'Right,' she said, attacking her hair with the first lieutenant's comb. 'But I wish I had something for my face.'

So they told a disconcerted Kitson all they knew. When they'd finished he said, 'I see,' and stared thoughtfully at Judy who was busy with after-shave lotion and talc powder.

Gallagher said, 'I guess this collision – *Antonov*'s sinking – must have fouled up your plans somewhat, Captain?'

Kitson nodded forlornly. 'Most unfortunate. We rather hoped you'd be carried on to Leningrad. Had that happened, and provided of course the bug in Yenev's cabin hadn't been spotted – ' He put up a hand, coughed discreetly. ' – that too was most unfortunate. Well, subject to that you might have learnt a great deal. But of course collisions do occur. Particularly in fog. We'll have to try again with another *Simeonov*.'

Gallagher shrugged, made clicking noises of irritation. 'We did our best. Bugs are liable to be found. Occupational hazard. Sorry if we've let you down. Maybe you and Rossiter should have made that Baron trip. He's a flyer, I understand. You could have been his passenger.'

'Yes,' said Judy, who was being generous with the first lieutenant's *eau de toilette*. 'Marvellous idea. You'd have had Stefan Lomov making passes at you. Or,' she turned and pointed an accusing finger, 'would you have been making them at Natasha Mekhlis?'

'I think,' said Kitson unhappily, 'that you must be suffering from shock.'

Judy turned triumphantly to Gallagher. 'Ben! That's what the other man said. What's his name?'

'Rossiter. Jack Rossiter.'

'Perhaps,' said Kitson, 'you people should see the LMA.'

'What's that?' asked Judy.

'Leading Medical Assistant. The man in charge of the ship's sick-bay. He has some rather good sedatives.'

They managed to laugh and make friends after that and most of the things they wanted followed.

# 27

'Seventeen minutes to go, Jim,' Rossiter prompted. 'How you doing with that door?'

'Still drilling.' Hayward's voice on the Wetphone though blurred was less than enthusiastic.

'Think it'll be much longer?'

'Yes. If I have to talk.'

Rossiter took the hint. Hayward and his team had been down for over four minutes. They hadn't banked on the watertight door giving all that trouble. Two or three minutes they'd had in mind. He took a deep breath, his eyes on the spinning wheels of the recorder, his mind on what lay behind the locked door. Hayward's voice broke in. 'Lock forced. Door open. We're going in.'

Rossiter and CPO Jennings looked at each other with relief, smiled and gazed hopefully over the side as if the hazy grey sea might reveal something of its secrets.

'We've gone three paces forward,' reported Hayward. 'Now another door . . .' Silence then, followed later by, 'Not locked.' A pause. 'We're in some sort of control-room. Looking round. Will get photos.' A longish interval after that.

Rossiter grabbed the handmike. 'You must keep up the commentary, Jim,' he urged. The commentary was vital. There were no cast iron guarantees that the swimmers and cameras would return safe and sound.

'For Christ's sake. It's dark down here. Can't tell you what we see until we've got our lights on it.'

A full minute went by until he spoke again. 'There are two consoles – one starboard, one port. Varic's reading the control markings on the starboard set-up. Hold on. We have to work this out.' Almost another minute before he said, 'Starboard console controls a complex of navigational aids – inertial navigation system, radar scan and data displays, gyro-repeaters, electronic navigator and track plotter, speed dials and . . . wait . . . what's that? Varic's showing me something . . . there's intercom. Phones. Digital call system. Varic says call buttons read *Captain, Wheelhouse, Engineroom, Radio* – What's that . . . *Launching Platform*, Varic says.'

Near to thirty long seconds then before Hayward's voice came again. 'Busy with photos. Now going over to port side console.'

The wheels of the recorder spun silently as Rossiter's mind tussled with the puzzle of the commentary. What was down there? Missile launching and control system? Certainly not anything to do with refrigeration. Hayward and Varic were in the control-room under the foc'sle, forward of number one hold. The answer must lie *in* the hold. But time. Was there time? He looked at his watch, 0619, spoke into the handmike. 'Twelve minutes left, Jim.'

'Yes, we know.' Hayward's voice came through, rough and uncompromising. Later it went on. 'Function of port console not clear. Varic's reading controls. He'll speak direct. Save time.'

Varic's voice now, high-pitched, foreign accented. 'This console is of three parts – right, centre and left sections. The right section has control and displays for sonar, echo-soundings and . . .' A long pause. '. . . there is a panel marked "Analyser" – it has a TV screen . . . digital displays and various gauges . . . also a computer. Wait I look.'

Rossiter waited, watching the seconds tick by, confused pictures in his mind. Varic's voice came through again. 'We already make photos. Now I look at the centre section. There are controls and displays marked with Russian words for . . .'

pause . . . then, 'Yes, *Conveyors* and *Launch Control*. They are sub-divided into port and starboard. Beneath these we see . . .'

The buzzer on the quarterdeck sounded. Rossiter picked up the handset.

It was Studdington. 'Message from *Cyclades*,' he said. 'It reads : Seven minutes left. Do not repeat not permit any time extension. Ends.'

'Okay. Will do.' Rossiter replaced the handset.

Varic was saying, '. . . two sets, one marked *Arming* the other *Release*. Each sub-divided into port and starboard. I see also two sets of controls marked Open and Shut . . . they have pressure gauges, a TV display and other instrumentation. Hold on, we make some photos.'

Rossiter said, 'You have only five minutes left. You must look into number one hold while you still have time.'

There was a delay before Hayward's gravelly voice replied. 'Will do. We're leaving control-room by steel door, port side after bulkhead.'

For Rossiter and Jennings another long minute passed before they heard, 'Descending vertical steel ladder.' There was another pause. 'Twelve steps, about three metres. Now on steel grating . . . it runs athwartships across foremost bulkhead of the hold. We are looking down. About two metres below us there are four rows of . . . some sort of cylinders. Lying horizontally. Casings look like stainless steel. We'll check underneath.' There was a long teasing delay then before he went on. 'Rectangular underneath. They're on what looks like flexible steel tracks of some sort. Conveyors I think. Two rows to port, two to starboard. Fore and aft gangway in centre. Six cylinders in each row. Each unit about . . . say – length, three metres – width, one metre – depth, one and a half metres. Those are very approximate. There are various circular and oval access and inspection plates on the upper sides of the cylinders.' A delay then until he continued. 'The steel tracks lead forward from the after bulkhead and are angled towards the ship's side to port and starboard . . . they seem to feed what look like the inboard ends of torpedo tubes.' Another pause. 'There are two hoists with electric motors on the after bulkhead. The hoists plumb rectangular apertures . . . a bit longer than the cylindrical units. Looks as though the units are hoisted up from a lower hold on to the conveyors.'

Rossiter was thinking: *the inboard end of torpedo tubes.* Hayward knew what torpedoes looked like and he hadn't said that was what they were.

Hayward's voice again. 'There are runs of steel tubing – probably stainless – around the centres of the cylindrical sections. That's . . .'

The quarterdeck phone buzzed again. Studdington's urgent voice. 'Message from *Cyclades*,' he said. 'Reads: Time is up. Recover immediately, repeat immediately. Ends.'

'Okay. Will do.' Rossiter replaced the handset. Hayward's voice was grating like sandpaper in his right ear. 'We are now . . .'

Rossiter broke in, '*Cyclades* has ordered immediate recovery.'

'We are now,' repeated Hayward as if he'd not heard, 'ascending steel ladder and returning to maindeck.'

CPO Jennings's smile of relief froze suddenly. The Wetphone had relayed Varic's urgent call to Hayward. 'I'm stuck. Left leg. Caught in something.'

'Keep absolutely still. Don't tug.' Hayward's voice was calm, unruffled. 'I'm coming up. Got my light on it.' Silence for a few moments, then, 'Looks like a loose power cable. Armoured cable. The bight has somehow got round your leg. Above the knee.'

Joe Roberts's voice. 'Shall I come down?'

'Not yet, Joe. Standby. I'll check first.'

Rossiter and Jennings's faces seemed to age as they looked from each other to their wristwatches. There was little margin for delay. The ascent with its decompression stops had still to come. At least ten minutes for that. More would be needed if the swimmers were down longer.

A minute and a bit dragged by.

'Joe. Bring me the long arm cutters,' Hayward was saying. 'Harris – stay on maindeck at watertight door.'

'Will do,' came Roberts's and Harris's voices.

Hayward was telling Varic to keep dead still. 'Soon free you with cutters, but don't pull. The more you tighten it the tougher the job.'

'Okay,' from Varic.

Yet another minute went by before they heard Roberts, 'I'll drop down outside you, Jim.'

Soon afterwards Hayward's voice again. 'Take the camera Right, pass the cutters.'

For Rossiter and Jennings seconds were beginning to seem like minutes, minutes like hours.

Rossiter shook his head. Jennings nodded, frowning.

'This bloody cable's tough,' Hayward's voice, edgy, troubled. Then Varic's, 'Jesus. It's tight.' A note of alarm now.

Jennings scribbled a message, passed it to Rossiter. *They've not been deeper than thirty-five metres. Adds a couple of minutes to the margin.*

Rossiter read it, smiled thinly. They needed a couple of minutes. Forcing the door had taken four out of the eighteen allowed for the dive. They'd been eight minutes in the control-room. That meant Hayward and Varic had done twelve minutes at the thirty metre level. They'd started up the ladder after five minutes in the hold at thirty-five metres. Another three on the ladder for Varic's foot. What did all that add up to? He lost track. Anyway, that was CPO Jennings's responsibility. His thoughts were interrupted by Hayward's voice. 'Right. That's fixed it. You can move now, Varic. Go on up.'

Hayward again, this time anti-climax. 'Christ. I've dropped the goddam cutters.'

Roberts's voice. 'Want me to get them, Jim?'

'No bloody fear. We're getting out of this. Up you go.'

The next reports by Wetphone indicated that the ascent had begun; Hayward and Varic had left *Antonov*'s maindeck first, followed by Roberts and Harris.

For Rossiter and Jennings it was now a matter of waiting. It was twenty-one minutes since the dive began. Hayward and his team had just reached the ten metre level, the first decompression stop. They'd be there for five minutes then there would ...

'Send down the baskets,' interrupted Hayward's voice. Two lines with steel baskets attached were lowered over *Plover*'s side. Hooked to them were compensating weights, each equivalent to that of an underwater camera.

Soon afterwards Hayward reported. 'Okay. We've exchanged the cameras for compensators. Hoist away.'

Jennings and a seaman hauled up the baskets and took out the cameras. Rossiter stopped the recorder, slipped in a fresh cassette and restarted it. The cameras and the cassette he'd removed were put in a watertight container and passed down to *Plover*'s skimmer. The skimmer raced across the water to *Huntress* where the cameras and cassette were taken to the survey ship's photographic laboratory.

For Rossiter and Jennings the tension of the dive had been replaced by that of waiting; a tension heightened by the steadily clearing fog. The quarterdeck phone sounded. It was Studdington. 'Signal from *Cyclades*. Begins: Have sonar contact with submerged *Romeo* class Soviet submarine bearing one-four-three degrees nine miles *Antonov*. Speed of approach sixteen knots. Echo previously masked. *Retivy* now bearing oh-one-seven degrees distance twenty-three miles. Fog this area clearing. Message ends.'

It wasn't only in *Cyclades*'s area that the fog was clearing. Rossiter could see *Huntress* now, no longer a shadow on the edge of the fogbank but a ship standing out large and clear. And for the first time that morning he could see a merchant ship; a northbound tanker on *Plover*'s starboard side about two miles away. At this rate, he reflected, *Plover*, *Huntress* and her motorboat would before long be seen by one and all. Not that *Huntress* was a problem. She and the motorboat were laying wreck-buoys, rendering a service to all shipping. The problem was *Plover* and the underwater swimmers. If they began bobbing up in sight of ships passing close by the news would spread.

He passed *Cyclades*'s report to Hayward who was characteristically abrupt. 'Too bad. We've still got eight minutes down here. They should have provided a decompression chamber if they wanted us up quicker.' Rossiter couldn't quarrel with that. He began thinking about the *Romeo* class submarine. *Cyclades* would have identified it by its sound signature. Challenged it with IFF, using the NATO code of the day. Surprising the frigates' VLR search sonar hadn't found the *Romeo* sooner. Perhaps it had masked its approach in the wake of a surface ship, or beneath a temperature layer, or it had stopped on the bottom in some sea-bed depression. The submarine was still half an hour away but, if the fog continued clearing, it would be within visibility distance well before that.

He saw that *Huntress* was under way now, moving slowly, turning to starboard. Her foredeck crane had been turned out over the side and from it hung a wreck-buoy. As he watched she moved into position close to the motorboat which had taken station above the *Antonov*'s stern. He looked at his watch once more. A minute to go and the underwater swimmers would ascend to the five metre level. They'd have to spend another five minutes there.

He spoke into the Wetphone. 'Suggest you surface close-to on the port side. *Plover*'s hull will screen you from the *Romeo* if we're within periscope range.'

Hayward agreed.

Jennings said, 'The *Romeo* will probably pick up the swimmers on sonar anyway.'

'Too bad,' said Rossiter. 'They could be seals. Anyway, there's no law against diving in international waters.'

Jennings laughed. 'Or against dropping long arm cutters

marked in Russian "Made in USSR".'

'I thought that was an accident?'

'Dropping them was. Not the "Made in USSR" bit.'

Five minutes later Hayward and Varic surfaced. They were followed closely by Roberts and Harris. Having embarked the swimmers, *Plover* moved away from the wreck and set course for the Scottish coast. The time was 0647 and daylight was taking over.

The fog continued to clear before a light wind from the north-east and from *Huntress*'s bridge visibility in places was up to eight miles.

A number of merchant ships were now in sight, mostly north and south bound traffic, among them a container ship passing less than half a mile to starboard; but it was not until after seven o'clock that the light was strong enough and the fog had lifted sufficiently to reveal the odd assortment of warships approaching the site of *Antonov*'s sinking.

The US Navy's *Belknap* frigates were nearest, coming in from the north-west, the two ships three miles apart on parallel courses.

*Cyclades*, five miles away, could be seen approaching from the west. She was on a course converging with the *Belknaps*. Steaming in from the north-east at high speed, almost six miles away, a white bow wave hissing fanlike under her flared bows, came the *Retivy*, purposeful and formidable. Three miles to the south-west of *Huntress* the *Romeo* class submarine had surfaced and was approaching at fifteen knots. The sighting of these warships, their dispositions, had been no surprise to those on *Huntress*'s bridge who had been watching the state of play on sonar and radar.

Having laid a wreck-buoy to mark the stern of the *Antonov*, the survey ship manoeuvred into position and laid the second buoy about twenty metres ahead of the wreck.

Her task completed she broadcast a warning to shipping that the buoys had been laid. She gave the exact location of the wreck and reported that, at low water, depths over it would be five metres aft (top of radar mast), and seven metres forward (top of foremast). Having rendered that service and hoisted her motorboat she made off in a westerly direction to resume her survey duties with *Kittiwake* whose commanding officer had reported his position by voice radio and announced that he was standing by ready to run the next line of soundings.

As *Huntress* left the scene, the Soviet destroyer *Retivy* arrived. She stopped close to the wreck-buoys and Captain Smolenko spoke by radiophone to the captain of *Huntress*, congratulating him on his prompt and efficient action in marking the wreck and warning shipping. *Huntress*'s captain thanked him and with these courtesies done they parted.

# 28

The survey vessel was thirty-five miles to the west of the sunken *Antonov* when Rossiter arrived on board *Huntress* later that morning. Kitson having been transferred from *Cyclades* by Wasp helicopter was on the quarterdeck to greet him. Rossiter spoke briefly about the dive, told him in outline what had happened.

'Good. Seems to have gone well,' said Kitson.

Rossiter thought of Varic's voice when the Czech was in trouble on the ladder but all he said was, 'How are the photos?'

'Haven't seen them yet.'

'Not ready?'

'They're ready,' said Kitson. 'I've only been here a few minutes. Thought I'd wait for you. Slingsby and Ayott have been on board for about an hour. They're down in the lab now, playing back the cassette and examining the photos. Have you had breakfast?'

'Yes, thanks. I could do with a shave.'

'I suppose so,' said Kitson absent-mindedly. 'Let's go and see what the boffins are up to. By the way – how are Hayward and his people?'

'They seem okay. Varic a bit roughed up, I guess. Tough experience. That little guy Hayward can be an awkward bastard.'

'Oh, really. You found that, did you?'

'Yes. Too goddam surly for me.'

'He's very well thought of, I understand.'

'Yes. I guess so. Knows it too.'

When they got to the laboratory they found Slingsby and Ayott taking turns at a stereoscope. On the table beside it was a stack of photographs.

'What do you people think? Any joy?' Kitson said it hesitantly, as if apologizing for the interruption.

Ayott was at the stereoscope. Slingsby said, 'Yes. Very interesting, but Ayott's the weapons man. I think he'd better give you the detail.'

Ayott, thin, grey-faced, looked up from the stereoscope, wiped watery eyes with a tissue, replaced his spectacles. 'They are m-mines,' he said.

'Mines,' echoed Kitson. 'You mean she's a mine-layer?'

'When she needs to be. Yes.'

'What sort of mines?' Rossiter was looking at one of the photos.

'Sea-bed mines. Not m-moored. They are . . .'

'Magnetic, acoustic, contact – what?' Rossiter seemed to be in a hurry.

Ayott looked at him reproachfully over the rim of his spectacles. 'I was going to deal with that.' He sorted through the photos, found what he wanted. 'Look at this. Those runs of tubing. Over the centre of the cylindrical section.' He indicated them with a ballpoint. 'Probably house sensors for the firing m-mechanism – actuating gear – whatever it may be.'

'You recognize the type? Know what they are?'

Ayott shook his head. 'No. They're entirely new to us. Certainly not a known Soviet mark.'

'How are they detonated?'

'One doesn't know yet. Acoustic or pressure detonated, I imagine. Probably designed for delayed priming. One can do no more at this stage than hazard guesses.'

Rossiter said, 'What's that delayed priming bit?'

'We've assumed they would be laid in an inert state prior

to the commencement of hostilities – say weeks or even months before. When needed they could be primed by satellite – long wave radio transmissions on mixed frequencies. Here and in the United States there are designs for sea-bed m-mines which can be primed or detonated in this way.'

'Horrible world.' Kitson half-closed his eyes.

Ayott put down the photo, shuffled through the others, selected one. 'This,' he pointed again with his pen, 'the rectangular bottom – is interesting. See those six protuberances beneath the carriage – one can just see them in profile. They match the six oval vents along the side of the carriage, probably on both sides of it for that matter. We can only see one side here. They are possibly, and I say no more than possibly, suction excavators. We have designs for the same sort of thing. It enables sea-bed m-mines to bury themselves provided they're laid on a sandy bottom.' Ayott looked at Rossiter with sad eyes. 'US research scientists are somewhat ahead of us with that sort of thing – m-moon and planet probes, you know.'

Kitson nodded, Rossiter said nothing.

Ayott picked up another picture. 'This is the right-hand section of the port console in *Antonov*'s control-room. The closed circuit TV screen, the read-outs and displays and the computer are for sea-bed analysis. We have Varic's commentary on tape if you'd care to hear it.' He pointed to the recorder on the work shelf.

'Not now,' said Kitson. 'I think we're more interested in what you and Slingsby have to say.'

'The sea-bed analyser would give the nature of the bottom, the depth of sand and soil layers. The TV camera and a mechanical scoop or suction extractor are probably housed in a retractable dome in the ship's bottom.' Ayott was sorting through the photos again. 'Ah, yes. Here it is. The port console again. Close-up of the left-hand section of the instrument panel. This is possibly the most significant item.' Once more he pointed with his pen. 'These four small dials – they look rather like ammeters don't they – give Geiger readings.

Measure radio-activity. They are in the console which controls the m-mine-laying operations in number one hold.'

Ayott put the photo in the stereoscope. 'You'll see them — the dials I mean — more clearly now.'

Rossiter and Kitson took turns at the stereoscope.

Rossiter looked up. 'So you're telling us just what, Mr Ayott?'

The Admiralty research scientist blinked. 'Size, design, instrumentation, control, operational requirement, all seem to point in the same direction. Necessarily one has to engage in a good deal of speculation — the information now available must be researched in far greater depth — but I may say that Slingsby and I are so far substantially in agreement. Are we not, Gordon?'

'And what is that, if one may ask?' Kitson's tone was very formal and polite.

'Nuclear m-mines.' In the silence which followed Ayott appeared embarrassed, as if he'd told a dirty story which hadn't gone down well.

Later that day in the privacy of the Captain's cabin, Kitson and Rossiter, armed with pink gins, discussed the morning's events.

'I think,' said Kitson modestly, 'that Petticoat really went rather well.'

'I guess I'd have been happier if the *Simeonovs* were missile firing ships. They'd be a lot less dangerous equipped that way than as nuclear mine-layers.' Rossiter sipped his gin. 'Jesus! Can you imagine it. Nuclear mines outside — maybe *inside* — the West's principal ports? Laid before the balloon goes up.'

'Remember the discussion at our first Petticoat meeting?' Kitson held up a finger as if demanding attention. 'When Maltby talked about the problem of a *Simeonov* lying in harbour, able to destroy not only the port but the city around it.'

'Yeh. I said the blackmail angle in that situation was some-

226

thing that had got the Pentagon worried. That was on the assumption they were fitted for missile launching.'

'And Freddie Lewis was flippant about the ship having to destroy itself if it destroyed the harbour.'

'That's right.' Rossiter rattled the ice in his glass, looked at the sideboard.

'With nuclear mines that wouldn't be necessary, would it?'

'You're dead right.' The American gestured with his empty glass towards the gin bottle on the silver salver. 'Guess we could use some more of that.'

Kitson went to the sideboard, shook a few drops of Angostura into the empty glasses, twiddled them expertly, added gin, water and ice and passed a glass to the American.

Rossiter tasted the mixture. 'Great. I needed this. Can you imagine,' he repeated, 'nuclear mines – say, twenty-five kiloton warheads – going off in the Hudson. Make the Bikini Atoll look like a vicar's tea party.'

Kitson sipped his gin in the discerning manner of a connoisseur. 'A point occurs to me – wish I'd asked Ayott – if one detects the presence of a nuclear mine, and assuming it's booby-trapped, how does one neutralize it?'

'That's quite a question.' Rossiter flourished his glass in affirmation. 'Yessir. That's really something.'

'A clever idea, isn't it,' went on Kitson. 'Laying from the bows – well below the waterline. The operation invisible to observers by day or night.'

'Right. I guess they could be laid by a ship at anchor waiting for a berth outside a congested port – or when underway.'

'On the Aghulas Bank, the Grand Banks, the Jarvis Straits, the Malacca Straits, the Panama and Suez Canals.' Kitson ran a finger round the rim of his glass. 'There's no end to the list. All the "choke" points. Leave them there until they're needed. Then prime by satellite. That's a rather terrifying new concept.'

'You realize,' said Rossiter, 'that laying nuclear mines is a flagrant breach of the Sea-Bed Arms Control Agreement.'

Kitson regarded him with sorrowful, disenchanted eyes. 'My dear chap, the whole history of armaments is littered with breached agreements.'

'Yeh. I guess you're right. Know what? I think our statesmen, scientists, defence chiefs – the whole goddam lot – have lost their way in the nuclear jungle.' He drained his glass, held it out to Kitson. 'So what the hell. Let's have another drink.'

# 29

The man with the crocodile briefcase and a copy of the *Financial Times* had evidently decided he could do better elsewhere; with his departure they had the first-class compartment to themselves.

'About time,' said Gallagher. 'Haven't been alone with you for days.'

'No. We haven't, have we?' Judy gave him a curious sideways look that became a smile.

*Cyclades* had landed them in Hull that evening in time for the night train to London.

Gallagher yawned. 'It's been a long day.'

She yawned in sympathy. 'Sorry. Terribly long, hasn't it. Except for an hour in Number One's cabin I haven't slept since four o'clock this morning.'

'That's right. When the fog came down. Some morning. We were jumping for it a couple of hours after that.'

'Ugh. That water. Freezing.' She shivered at the recollection, pulled the borrowed duffle coat tighter.

'Can't say I noticed. Too busy swimming.'

'Awful being locked in that cabin after the collision.'

'Yeh. I'll say.'

She looked at him quizzically over the turned-up coat collar. 'I don't think Captain Kitson was very pleased with us, was he?'

'Not really. Nothing succeeds like success – and I guess we

weren't successful.'

'Not our fault,' she protested vigorously. 'We were given the bugs. Told to use them. They knew the risks.'

'Too bad. We boobed. They'll have to try again – but not with us. Let's talk of something else.' Outside the windows the lights of a farmhouse flashed by; then darkness again, relieved only by the reflected lights of the train racing through the night beside them.

'And now?' She regarded him with the calm expression he'd grown to know so well. 'What's the future?'

'De-briefing in London, then some leave.'

'After that?'

'Get out, I guess.'

'What's that mean?'

'Cover blown. No more clandestine operations. Desk job not my line. So it's out for Ben Gallagher. And you?'

'Same I suppose. I shan't be sorry. I yearn for the quiet life. After the de-briefing I'm going back to my real world – to rest.'

'Where's that?'

'Dervaig – on Mull. In the Western Isles. Know it?'

He shook his head. 'No.'

'Like to come with me?' She watched him keenly. 'I'd love to show it to you.'

'The Western Isles in November?'

She frowned, looked out of the window.

'What's wrong, Judy?'

'Nothing. It's so beautiful there. I thought you might like it.'

'There's an island – a small island – in the Dodecanese. A few olive groves, some fishermen, a handful of houses, odd windmills and a taverna. No tourists. Belongs to a friend. Blue water, white beaches, plenty of sun.'

'In November?'

'Yeh. In November. I want to lie on those beaches under that sun.'

'Lucky you.'

'Not just me.' He took her wrist, pulled her towards him. She put on a show of resistance but anyway he was too strong. 'I want you to come too, Judy. I've got used to having you around. There's a lot of things we have to discuss . . . like . . .'

She turned to him and he saw good humour in her eyes. 'Like what?'

'Future employment. Maybe other things.'

There was a rat-a-tat on the glass door and they separated hurriedly as the ticket-examiner slid it open.

'Evening,' he said. 'Tickets.'

It must have been the Plimsolls, the legs of the track-suits showing below the duffle coats. 'Some sort of athletic meeting was it, then?' He smiled genially.

'You could call it that,' said Gallagher.

'Win anything?'

'Yes – a trip to the Dodecanese,' said Judy.

The desk phone rang. O'Dowd picked it up. 'Who is it?'

'McGann here. I'd like you to come down, Commander.'

'Is that essential?'

'I'm afraid so. Won't take long. I'll send a car. Matter of minutes.'

'Can you tell me what it's about?'

'I'd rather do that when you're with me.'

'Okay. But I'll have to come right back. There's a lot going on here at the moment.'

'You'll not be detained,' said the Assistant Commissioner with customary abruptness.

McGann was on the phone when O'Dowd was shown into the office. The Assistant Commissioner nodded a greeting, pointed to a chair. Soon afterwards he put the phone down. 'Good morning, Commander. This way please.'

Not a man to waste words or time, reflected O'Dowd.

The lift took them down two floors after which he followed McGann's stocky figure along several passages and up a short flight of stairs to a door guarded by a plainclothes man. The door was opened and a waft of antiseptic air hit them.

McGann switched on the light, shut the door. On one of several stainless steel tables under a cluster of arc lights lay the body of a man, fully clothed.

'Recognize him?' McGann stared at the American.

O'Dowd stood over the body, looked closely at the blue-jowled face, the glazed eyes, the large moustache. 'Yes. It's him all right. What happened?'

'His cab was found in Epping Forest this morning. Off the road. He was in the driving seat. Shot in the back of the head.'

'The KGB you think?'

McGann's mouth tightened. 'Dead men don't talk.'

'Seem to have heard that before. Know his name?'

'Brewster's the name on the driving licence. Harry James Brewster. Stepney address. But there's nobody there. Neighbours say his wife's in the North. He's been photographed and fingerprinted and the forensic people have been busy.' McGann switched off the light and they went back into the passage. The plainclothes man shut and locked the door.

'All right, sir?' he asked.

'Yes, Simmons. Let them know.'

Number 57 was a drab Victorian-terraced house in a little-used cul-de-sac off the Fulham Road, its brickwork impregnated with decades of grime, the paintwork tired and peeling.

Twenty yards or so up the road a taxi stopped at the kerb. A man with a burn-scarred face stepped out into the wet and blustery night. He paid the fare and the taxi pulled away. He walked along the pavement to the gate of number 57, went up the steps and knocked on the door with the handle of his umbrella. A light came on in the porch and he knew he was being watched through a spy-hole. There was the sound of bolts being drawn and the door creaked slowly open. It was closed behind him by an unshaven man wearing a collarless shirt and faded cardigan. He bolted the door with the slow deliberation of someone who didn't like to be hurried and switched off the portico light. 'Mr Lassinger's waiting for you. Come this way.' He spoke with a cigarette in his mouth.

Gryzan followed him up a staircase and along a short passage to an austerely furnished living-room.

'Your visitor, sir,' his guide announced.

At the far end of the room a tall man was warming his hands in front of a gas fire; without turning he said, 'Thank you, Fred. You can carry on now.' When the unshaven man had gone Lassinger said, 'Good to see you, Jan.'

'Good to see you, Bob.'

They sat down for a few minutes, exchanged the small talk of men who know each other well but see each other seldom. A plump woman wearing a greasy apron over a frock several sizes too small brought coffee. When she'd left the room Lassinger said, 'You've done well, Jan. Maltby's very pleased – so are we. Petticoat's given us what we wanted.'

Gryzan hunched his shoulders in a deprecatory gesture. 'I don't know all of Petticoat. Never will do, but if I helped that's great. What's happening about Khazarov?'

'Still being held. Doubt if he can be brought to trial. Diplomatic immunity. The Brits will probably make good use of him as exchange material. At least they'll get him out of the country. That's worthwhile. He's been a goddam nuisance.'

'How did Borodin get wise to Gallagher and the Bort, Garde Optics connection?'

'We laid on a feed-in in Leningrad.'

'Who's idea?'

'Maltby's,' said Lassinger. 'After the first Petticoat meeting he put it to us. Thought the Petticoat committee mightn't wear it. Believed Rathouse wasn't sufficiently ruthless. Maltby was afraid the Russians would put Gallagher and Paddon ashore at the first opportunity. Land them in the Cape Verdes before they could do anything useful.'

Gryzan looked at the coffee pot. 'Any more of that?'

'Sure. Can do.' Lassinger poured the coffee.

'O'Dowd's abduction. Who thought that up?'

'Maltby again.'

'How come? More inspiration?'

'No. Conscience this time. When you told us of Borodin's message to Khazarov we realized the project had blown – that Borodin knew the ditching was deliberate and that the operation had RN/USN support . . .' He stopped, poured himself more coffee. 'We passed the news to Maltby. He was upset – felt responsible. He knew of course that Gallagher and Paddon were for the chop. He didn't – still doesn't – know about you. But he realized we had someone well placed in the KGB here. So he suggested Borodin should be told that O'Dowd's abduction was feasible. He reckoned that if it was properly staged we could catch KGB agents red-handed in a kidnap situation. That would offset any Soviet protests about a joint RN/USN operation to get spies on board *Antonov*. We got you to put the abduction project to Khazarov – I guess you know the rest.'

Gryzan ran a tentative finger over the burn scars on his face. 'Did you and Maltby reckon on getting Khazarov?'

'No. That was a bonus. A really beautiful one.'

Gryzan replaced his cup on its saucer. 'Wouldn't mind another.'

Lassinger filled the cups. He knew how Gryzan liked it; black with no sugar.

'Thanks,' said Gryzan.

Lassinger went to the gas fire, held his hands in front of it. 'Maltby's a devious character but he has a genius for seeing several moves ahead of most people. Entirely without scruples, I'd say.'

'Without scruples?' Gryzan's eyebrows lifted. 'I thought he'd had an attack of conscience about Gallagher and Paddon?'

'It was nothing to do with Gallagher and Paddon. He believed the feed-in had somehow blown a liaison operation which involved not only CIA-SIS but RN-USN. That was what he felt bad about.'

'Do we know how the operation was blown?'

'No, not really. They think it may have been the discovery of a bug in Yenev's cabin. Personally I doubt that. Must

234

have been something more positive. God knows what.'

The discussion drifted on to personal matters, enquiries about families and mutual friends. Bob Lassinger was not only Gryzan's CIA case officer but his friend; their relationship was a good one and they both enjoyed the few occasions on which they were able to be together. It was some time later that Gryzan looked at his watch. 'It's close on eleven,' he said. 'I have to get back to my place before going on to Grosvenor Square.'

'What time's your duty?'

'Midnight.' Gryzan sighed. 'And boy, is it boring.'

'It won't be long now. You're to be transferred.'

They left number 57 separately, Gryzan by way of the front door opened for him by the unshaven man in the collarless shirt. Ten minutes later Lassinger left by the back door which the plump woman locked behind him. The night which greeted them was dark and cheerless, wetter and more windy if anything than when they'd arrived.